MURDER THROUGH
THE LOOKING GLASS

by Andrew Garve

"There's no better author of the suspense story than Andrew Garve. He's the master of the tingling spine."
—*Columbus Citizen*

"Mr. Garve...writes with a first-hand knowledge of the Russian correspondent's life ... [with a] sardonic liveliness of view."
—*New York Herald Tribune Book Review*

MURDER THROUGH THE LOOKING GLASS

by Andrew Garve

PERENNIAL LIBRARY
Harper & Row, Publishers
New York, Hagerstown, San Francisco, London

This story was published in England under the title of *Murder in Moscow*.

A hardcover edition of this book was originally published by Harper & Row, Publishers.

First PERENNIAL LIBRARY edition published 1978

ISBN: 0-06-080449-1

78 79 80 81 82 10 9 8 7 6 5 4 3 2 1

MURDER THROUGH
THE LOOKING GLASS

I

THERE'S SOMETHING about the very thought of Moscow that makes my skin prickle. It's very little to do with politics; it's a personal and professional thing. All the frustration and bitterness and fascination of the years I spent in that city during the war—and, indeed, earlier—come rushing back at me, as overwhelming as a tidal bore. So that when my editor asked me, at the beginning of 1951, if I would be willing to return there for a short time and collect material on some of the changes that had taken place, I was temporarily knocked off balance. In the end, of course, curiosity won—that, and a sentimental urge to revisit the source of so many vivid and poignant memories. I said I'd go.

The main hurdle to be taken was the visa. Since the war the U.S.S.R. had been particularly sticky about letting in people who knew the country, unless they were likely to prove useful spokesmen in the outside world afterward. Even then, the mesh was fine. However, the Russians are incalculable people, and to my surprise my permit came through in less than a month. I took my old sheepskin *shuba* out of the trunk which it practically filled, and reminiscently caressed its stiff folds. Moth balls rattled to the floor as I drew from one of the pockets the caracal hat with the ear flaps which had been singed on an underground stove near Stalingrad when the temperature outside had been thirty-seven below. I couldn't help feeling excited.

By the middle of February I was away. I flew first to Berlin, where there was a little office business to transact with Barnes,

1

our resident correspondent. By the time that was finished, a wave of blizzards had begun to sweep across Eastern Europe and the met. forecasts were hopeless. I soon got tired of making abortive trips to the airport and decided to go on by train. This was the signal for Barnes to throw a tremendous party "in my memory"—he seemed to think that war was inevitable and that the balloon was likely to go up at any moment. Those of the party who were capable of it came to see me on to the train, where I settled down in a *wagon-lit* of ancient vintage to sleep off the effects of Barnes's hospitality.

The train got stuck in a drift for five hours somewhere west of Poznán, but otherwise the first part of the journey was uneventful. The carriage was warm, the food in the dining car was passable, and I had plenty to read. There was a mere handful of passengers to be examined at the Oder frontier and the Poles didn't seem very interested in my luggage. We made good progress after that, with no more drift. At about eleven on the following morning we rumbled into Warsaw—and that was where the fun began.

Even before the train stopped it was apparent that something out of the ordinary was afoot. A brass band was playing "Auld Lang Syne" very loudly and inaccurately, and a substantial part of Warsaw's population, including regiments of children, seemed to have been marshaled on to the bleak, windswept platform. They stood in orderly files behind a screen of security police, stamping their feet to keep warm, and holding aloft red banners inscribed with such slogans as "The Peoples' Democracies Strive for Peace" and "Ban the Atom Bomb!" At the point where the sleeping car had come to a halt, a space had been cleared. In this privileged arena stood a nonchalant group of about half-a-dozen Red Army officers, squat short-necked figures in heavy gray overcoats. A little removed from them, a much larger group of civilian and military Poles conversed with eight people whose bizarre winter clothes and outlandish collection of hats stamped them unmistakably as foreigners. There was a good deal of noisy laughter and back-slapping, and from this air of exaggerated bonhomie I judged that an important delegation was being seen off to Moscow. It was only when I went to the carriage door and heard the booming tones of the delegation's leader that I realized what I'd run into. Once heard, that rich, round voice was unforgettable. This must be the Rev. Andrew Mullett's "peace" delegation from England—one of the most publicized of the many "representative" delegations that were beating up support for Russia's international policies at that time.

I went back to my compartment rather gloomily, wiped the steamed-up window, and settled down to watch the show. I'd never met Mullett personally, unless you can call covering one of his big postwar meetings an encounter, but I knew plenty about him by reputation. Everybody did—he'd taken good care of that. He'd started off, to the best of my recollection, as an elementary school teacher somewhere in southeast London, and he'd had a spell as a lay preacher before becoming a minister of one of the Free Churches. I suppose he'd always been fond of the sound of his own voice, particularly in places where people couldn't answer back. It had struck me at that meeting in the Albert Hall that his manner had perfectly combined the didacticism of the pedagogue with the professional unctuousness of the divine. His interest in Russia dated back to the late twenties. He had got the idea then that the Soviet Union was the one country in the world where the Sermon on the Mount was being translated into practice, and he'd plugged that line ever since and made a lot of other people believe it too.

I didn't know who the other delegates were, and anyway, out there on the platform in their concealing fur and sheepskin, they were practically indistinguishable from each other. Two of the eight looked as though they might have been women and one of the women, who was wearing a bright imitation leopard skin coat, looked as though she might have partaken too freely of Polish hospitality. Unless that jig she was doing was to keep her toes warm!

After a while there was a tactful toot from the engine, and the Red Army officers boarded the train. There was a great deal of handshaking on the platform, and porters hurriedly finished stowing luggage under the supervision of a little Pole with a red rosette in the lapel of his overcoat. Someone planted a microphone in front of Mullett and he delivered a last-minute message in English to his uncomprehending but enthusiastic audience. As soon as he'd finished, the band struck up "Auld Lang Syne" once more in a different key and Mullett began to shepherd his flock into the coach. I heard the little Pole apologizing because there wasn't a separate compartment for each delegate—the result, I gathered, of the Red Army's unexpected incursion. Mullett said it didn't matter in the least and that he'd arrange everything, and for the next few minutes he fussed up and down the corridor as though he were allocating seats in the Kingdom of Heaven. Presently the engine gave another toot, there was a burst of cheering from the platform, the woman in the leopard skin shrieked, "Good-by, tovarisch," from the door, the little Pole stood back with a rather weary smile, and we drew slowly out of the station to a crescendo of brass.

There was a good deal of coming and going in the corridor as the delegates sorted themselves out. My compartment was at the extreme end of the coach so I wasn't well placed to see who was who, but from time to time I caught some choice fragments of conversation.

"It's intolerable that I should be expected to sleep with that odious woman," an affected female voice complained. "I can't think why they had to bring her. Listen to her now!"

There was a pause for listening. The "odious woman" was crooning to herself in the drawn-out, maudlin accents of the comfortably intoxicated. A man with a musical baritone voice.

laughed tolerantly. "It *is* trying for you," he agreed. "She's not a bad soul at heart, though."

"I think she's quite insufferable. She's loud and vulgar and ignorant." The Kensington tones had become distinctly chilly.

"You're sisters under the skin, don't forget," the man teased.

"Nonsense!"

There was another pause, and then Mullett's voice boomed along the carriage. "If you like to bring your Russian grammar now, Cressey, we can resume our studies."

The "sisters-under-the-skin" man muttered, "Pompous ass!" For a peace-loving delegation, I reflected, they seemed to be getting off to a fine start.

There was a last, agonized wail from the singer, and then all was quiet. The voices faded away along the corridor. I turned to the window and for a while sat watching the battered suburbs of Warsaw sliding past. "One of the loveliest cities in Europe," I'd been told before my first visit there. I remembered how I'd stood on one of the Vistula bridges—it must have been around 1930, when I was en route for Russia for the first time—and thought how right the verdict had been. Well, the place hadn't much beauty now.

I picked up a book. Presently someone sauntered past my door, came back to take a second look, and stopped with an exclamation of surprise. "Surely it's George Verney?" It was the man I'd heard talking in the corridor.

For a moment I couldn't place him. He was a tall, wide-shouldered fellow in his early thirties, very good-looking in a dramatic way, with curling black hair, dark intense eyes, and a sensuous, mobile mouth. I knew that I'd seen him before, and I groped in my memory for time and place.

"Islwyn Thomas," he said, helping me out. "Don't you remember—the bad boy of the Military Mission?"

I did remember, then. I don't suppose I'd spoken to him more than a couple of times, but I clearly recalled the incident which had got him sent home in disgrace from Moscow. He'd been a passionate Welsh nationalist—the sort of man who'd have gloried in pinching a Coronation Stone if there'd been a Welsh one to pinch. One day he'd got very tight on Welsh eloquence and Russian vodka and had socked a brigadier who, he said, had insulted his country. He had given trouble before, I fancy, and that was considered the last straw.

"What happened?" I asked. "Were you court-martialed?"

"Yes, I most certainly was. I told the court that I didn't recognize its jurisdiction—it was an English court, of course—but they gave me three months and reduced me to the ranks. It was only the kind of justice I expected."

I hardly knew what to say. "What are you doing with this outfit? Are you hoping that Wales will be liberated by the Soviet Union?"

"Perhaps. Wales certainly won't remain an English satellite much longer."

"You can't be serious!"

"I was never more serious in my life."

That turned out to be the truth. Thomas was as bitter about the remote conquest of Wales as a Dublin leader writer about the iniquities of Cromwell. With a flash in his eyes he began declaiming about the Welsh national struggle, working himself up into a white heat by a process of spontaneous combustion, and sounding more and more Welsh as his periods lengthened and rolled. He was more than a romantic, he was a fanatical Anglophobe, and I was staggered that anyone could become so verbally violent with so little provocation. With his impetuous temperament I could almost visualize him starting a sort of Welsh "underground" in the hills. "The fact is," he said, "that Soviet Russia is the only country that cares for the rights of small nations. . . ."

It was too preposterous. I certainly wasn't going to get involved in an argument with him. He must have seen my hand groping for my book, for the torrent suddenly ceased. He gave a rather embarrassed laugh, and changed the subject.

"Anyway, Verney," he said, "what are *you* doing these days? Are you still with the *Record?*"

I told him I was.

His black eyebrows arched. "And the Russians have given you a visa? I thought all the correspondents who were in Moscow during the war were out of favor."

"Only those who wrote books about it when they got away. I didn't write a book."

He chuckled, throwing his head back. He was given to rather theatrical gestures. "Did you want to go back, or is this just a job?"

"A bit of both. I must say I'm looking forward to seeing Moscow again. I don't suppose it's changed a lot in six years, but some of the old things were pretty good . . . Lepeshinskaya at the Bolshoi; and *boeuf Stroganov* at the Aragvi, with a bottle of Mukuzani!"

"You sound quite nostalgic."

"You can call it that. I always liked the people, you know. It's the tragedy of this century that we haven't been able to get together with them in a civilized way."

"No wonder they gave you a visa!"

"For liking the Russian people? There's no visa appeal in that. It can work the other way if you like them too much." I took out my pipe and settled down more comfortably in the corner. "Tell me about this delegation of yours—who's on it? Anyone I'd know from the old days?"

"I doubt it. Several of them were in Moscow during the war, but before your time, I think. You came in forty-three, didn't you? Let's see, now—there's Mullett, of course."

"The pompous ass? Yes, I know about him."

Thomas shot me a quick glance, and then grinned. "So he is. I can't stand that overbearing manner. Well, then there's Robson Bolting, the Labour M.P. for Longside—have you met him?"

"Not in the flesh," I said. "I know him by reputation, of course."

Robson Bolting, indeed, was almost as much-publicized a figure as Mullett himself. I was a little vague about his personal background, but I had an idea that he'd been attached to the Moscow Embassy in some quite minor capacity during the early part of the war. In any case, about that time he'd caught the pro-Russian fever, and in the General Election of 1945 when people had believed that "left could speak to left" his attitude had helped to carry him into Parliament for what had always been regarded as a safe Tory seat. Since then he had become outstanding as the leader of a dangerous little group of "fellow travelers." Personally, I found his approach nauseating. He'd go out of his way to admit that Russia was by no means always right, yet on all practical issues he'd advocate the policies she favored. He'd agree that the Russians had been "difficult," but he'd somehow manage to leave the impression that the postwar breach had been our fault. He'd publicly regret Communist intolerance behind the Iron Curtain, but that wouldn't prevent him putting his name to telegrams of salutation and friendship on appropriate occasions. He'd hotly deny that he was a Communist, but he'd never mind appearing on the same platform as one. His attitude to the United States was the same as his attitude to Russia, but in reverse. He'd acknowledge that we owed something to America, praising with faint damns, but if an opportunity came to blacken her, he'd rush in with joy. He was either very clever or very naïve, and I didn't believe he was naïve. If, as seemed clear, the Russians were setting great store by Mullett's delegation, Bolting was an obvious choice.

"Well, then there's Schofield," Thomas went on. "You know, the professor of Economics. He's rather a cold fish. He was in Moscow, too, early in the war—on some financial mission. Quite brilliant, I believe."

I nodded. Schofield was not much more than a name to me,

but he was a big name. He was one of the most incisive of the intellectuals who had gone over to the Russian side. There had been a movement, I remembered, to have him sacked from his university or deprived of his chair or something, but it hadn't come to anything. I tried to recall some of the books he'd written—mainly reinterpretations of Marx, I rather thought, and textbooks with innocent-sounding titles like *Value, Price and Profit* that were absolute dynamite if you could under-stand them.

"Then there's Miss Manning," Thomas said. "Perdita Manning, you know—the sculptress."

I didn't know. "Is she any good?"

"Oh, I think so." He looked a bit self-conscious. "I believe she's a leading exponent of Socialist realism. Very down on the Greeks." He had the grace to laugh. "Not that I know much about it. They think a lot of her in Russia, though, I can tell you that. They're giving some special reception for her."

"Let's hope I'll qualify for an invitation," I said. "Well, who else?"

"There's a fellow called Richard Tranter—an official of one of the big peace societies, I forget which. He's a pleasant chap, rather quiet—got a gammy leg. Then there's Cressey—he's a factory worker, a protégé of Mullett's. And, of course, Mrs. Clarke."

"The dancing girl?"

He looked startled, and then broke into a loud laugh. His sense of humor seemed to be normal enough except when he was talking about Wales. "Oh, you saw her on the platform? Yes, she's the representative of some Co-operative Women's League in South London—always talking about 'the Co-op point of view'! Perdita can't stand her, but they get left to-gether a good deal as they're the only two women. The real trouble with Mrs. Clarke is that she's not used to all this drink and it goes to her head. She's sleeping off the effects now. I daren't think what she'll be like in Moscow."

I grinned. "If you ever have to carry her through the revolving doors at the Astoria, I trust I'll be there. That's where you'll all be staying, I suppose?"

"I imagine so. It's not exactly a gay hotel, but I'm quite looking forward to getting back there. Last time I was there . . ."

His reminiscences were cut short by the appearance of Miss Manning. "Oh, here you are, Islwyn." She pronounced his name *"Izzle-win,"* obviously in order to tease him. She gave me a rather condescending glance, and Thomas introduced us. She was very striking. She had sleek, beautifully dressed dark hair, deep blue eyes under long dark lashes, and pale, aquiline features. She was of medium height, but slender, and the expensively tailored, close-fitting costume she was wearing made her look taller than she was.

She sat down and looked lazily across at me. "What paper do you write for?" she asked.

I told her the *Record.*

"Really? How can you bear it?" She had an infuriating drawl. Her eyes traveled round the compartment and she gave an exclamation of mild annoyance. "You don't mean to say you've got this place all to yourself?"

I smiled. "Naturally, I'm a capitalist pariah."

I could see that she was mentally working out possible permutations and combinations and not getting anywhere, except back with Mrs. Clarke.

"I suppose," she said, "you're going to write a lot of nonsense about Russia?"

"I don't know what I'm going to write, yet."

"That's unusual—most correspondents make up their minds before they've even seen the place."

"I've been there before," I said. "Have you?"

"This is my fifth visit," she said loftily.

I nodded. "Those prewar conducted tours were such good value, weren't they? Leningrad and Moscow, a few days in the

Crimea or the Caucasus, a trip down the Volga . . . 'Will you give me now, please, your sightseeing coupons!' Delightful!"

"It may surprise you to learn, Mr. Verney, that I've made quite a study of the country and that I'd very much like to work there."

"You'd have to lower your standards a bit," I said. It wasn't the first time I'd heard that sort of thing from a fashionable woman.

"That simply shows how little you know. As a matter of fact, people with creative imagination make an excellent living in Russia. Not that that's so important—what matters is that they can feel some sense of purpose there, too. It's the only country in the world where the artist knows exactly where he's going."

"*I* knew one who went to a forced labor camp."

"Nonsense!" she said, without heat. Her air of conscious superiority was hard to take. Thomas was gazing at her in evident admiration. I could easily have lost my temper, but the luncheon bell saved me. Perdita got up, very gracefully. "How *tedious* all this eating is!" She gave me a disdainful nod. "Coming, Izzle-win?" He went after her happily, like a puppy called to heel.

I lingered for a while. I didn't much fancy having to listen to the eight of them going into an ecstatic huddle over Russia in the dining car. In the end, however, hunger called—I was too recently out of England to share Perdita's view that eating was a bore.

A couple of compartments along, I almost collided with an emerging Mrs. Clarke. She was a plump, large-framed woman, with a neck and chin that formed one *massif* of flesh. Her face was flushed, and she seemed to be having a little difficulty with her breathing.

"Was that the lunch bell, dear?" she asked, and then she noticed that I was a stranger. "Oh, excuse me," she said, pushing a fuzz of dark, dyed hair behind her ear, "I didn't know . . . "

I smiled. "Yes, it was the lunch bell."

"I don't think I want any lunch. Something I had for breakfast hasn't agreed with me. If you're going in there, I wonder if you'd mind telling some friends of mine that I'm feeling a bit poorly?"

"You mean Mr. Mullett and company? Yes, I'll tell them."

"That's very kind of you, I'm sure." Mrs. Clarke looked at me with new interest. "Are you joining the delegation?"

"No, I'm a newspaperman."

"Oh, one of *them!*" I feared I was to be plunged back into pariahdom. "Well, mind you write the truth, that's all. The working class has come into its own in Russia, and don't you forget it. There's no 'nobs' there; it's fair does for everybody. You put that in your paper, young man, and you won't go far wrong."

"I'll remember," I said gravely. I would have passed on, but there was barely room to squeeze by. "How are you enjoying the trip, Mrs. Clarke?"

"It's lovely," she said, "but I can't say I'll be sorry when we get there. Tiring, that's what it is. On your feet the whole time—it's worse than canvassing. But they're all such *nice* people. Give you a real welcome, they do, and no class distinctions. Look at these flowers they give Miss Manning and me—makes you feel like a princess."

"Beautiful," I said. "I've just had the pleasure of meeting Miss Manning."

Mrs. Clarke's face lit up. "Now there's a real nice girl for you," she said. "Got money, you know, but she doesn't boast about it. We go around everywhere together—you wouldn't find that happening in England, would you? But she believes in the working class. A bit stiff she was, at first, but I soon put her at her ease. 'Call me Ethel,' I said, 'we might as well start the way we're going on.' Now we're just like sisters. We have fine old times together, going to meetings and parties and theaters."

For the first time I felt a certain regard for Perdita. At least she'd taken the trouble to conceal her real feelings from her companion.

"She's clever, too," Mrs. Clarke went on. "She does these statues and things. Real people, like Madame Tussaud's, only in marble. Course, I've only seen photos—she's brought lots of photos with her. Clever—you'd never believe! They're going to give her a sort of sworry when we get to Moscow, and she's going to do a statue of Comrade Stalin's head if he's got time. Mind you, he's a very busy man, we know that, but he wouldn't have to stop working, would he? Good luck to her, I say. Oh, well, I mustn't keep you from your dinner. Don't forget to tell 'em, will you—I'm all right, you know, but just off me food."

I said I wouldn't forget, and walked through to the dining car. I was still being segregated—the attendant showed me to a place on the opposite side of the gangway from the delegation and a couple of tables away. The Red Army officers were also on their own.

Thomas nodded to me, and when he could get a word in he introduced me to Mullett across the gap.

"Ah," said Mullett affably, "a gentleman of the press, eh? Well, we shall all have to mind our p's and q's now. What paper, Mr. Verney?"

"The Record," I said, feeling slightly aggressive.

"Ah—the Record." He gave a sigh of well-mannered disappointment. "I can't say it's a paper I see very often myself. A little—er—sensational, perhaps. However . . ." In turn, he introduced me to the other delegates.

I said: "Oh, Mrs. Clarke asked me to tell you that she wouldn't be in to lunch. She isn't feeling very well."

"Dear me," said Mullett. "I hope the celebrations haven't been too much for her."

Robson Bolting looked across at Perdita. "Mightn't it be as well, perhaps, to see if she needs anything?"

"All she needs is a rest," said Perdita. "She'll be much better left alone."

He nodded. "I dare say you're right."

"After all," she added, with a touch of malice, "it isn't as though she's one of your constituents."

Bolting's eyes twinkled, but he made no reply, and Islwyn Thomas jealously engaged Perdita's attention again.

I finished my soup and sat back to study the delegates. Mullett himself, a big tall man in his late fifties, had seemed to have a certain dignity and power on the platform, but at close quarters it was no longer apparent. He had a large, obstinate forehead with receding red hair. His eyes were small and closely set, and a trick of peering up just under the top rims of his heavy glasses gave him an oddly suspicious expression. He had a little button mouth and a double chin. Altogether, his features looked too small for the size of his face. His hands were white and fat, and as they clove the air in illustration of some point he was making—he was always, it seemed, making a point—pale freckles showed on the backs, and tufts of red hair glistened below each knuckle. His Fleet Street nickname of "Red" Mullett was evidently due quite as much to his physical as to his political characteristics.

On his right, looking slightly subdued, was his protégé and pupil in the Russian language, Joe Cressey, a stocky, solid figure in a patently new dark blue suit. Cressey's pink face was as smooth and shiny as a schoolboy's, and his black hair was plastered down as though he were just off to a party. A long, heavy chin gave him a somewhat ponderous appearance, and his reactions seemed slow.

Robson Bolting was at the second table, with the Professor and Tranter. If I'd known nothing about him I'd have put him down as a successful buinessman rather than a Labour politician of extreme views. He was about forty-five, with a well-fed, well-dressed appearance and an air of self-confidence and strength. His thick brown hair was swept back from a broad forehead, and he wore glasses with heavy tortoise-shell rims. Though I abhorred his politics, I decided that on the whole I rather liked his face, which was intelligent and not without humor. By contrast, Professor Schofield had a lean and hungry look. He was a man nearer Mullett's age, I guessed; tall, with graying hair and thin sardonic lips. His clothes hung on him and his side pockets bulged. Tranter, who was quite unknown to me, might have been anything between forty and sixty. A head of beautiful white hair gave him a rather Quakerish appearance and his face had the earnest look of a man devoted to Causes.

Bolting and the Professor seemed to be getting on pretty well together, and their conversation covered a wide field. Tranter made very little contribution himself, but appeared interested and rather impressed by the range of their talk. The other table was still dominated by Mullett, who was telling a long story about how he had been hurriedly evacuated from Moscow to Kuibyshev in 1941. I could see Perdita and Islwyn Thomas becoming increasingly restive under his ceaseless monologue. When the arrival of coffee temporarily silenced him, Thomas plunged abruptly into a new topic.

"The snow should be in wonderful condition after this fall," he said. "How about trying to get some skiing, Perdita?"

She gave him a pitying smile. "I can't think of anything I should loathe more." She didn't look as though outdoor sports were much in her line.

Thomas turned to the other table. "You'll come, Bolting, won't you?"

Bolting shook his head. "Sorry, Islwyn, count me out. Last time I skied in Moscow I fractured my skull. It'll be a long time before I try it again."

"What a misfortune!" said Mullett. "Very bad luck. However, I'm sure you had the best possible treatment. That's one thing you can always count on in the Soviet Union, Cressey—good medical treatment. I remember . . ."

"We'll have to make up a party somehow," Thomas persisted. "What about you, Cressey? Shake your liver up a bit."

Cressey glanced at Mullett. "Well, I'd like to try, Mr. Thomas, if it wouldn't inconvenience anybody."

Mullett looked owlish. "I think we should remember," he said, "that we're a serious delegation, and that we have a heavy program in front of us. There's no reason why we shouldn't take a little recreation, of course, but our hosts have gone to considerable expense to bring us out here and we must be careful not to fritter away our time. As a matter of fact, this may be a suitable moment to discuss our timetable. I had a message from Madame Mirnova just before we left Warsaw, suggesting that if the delegation had any special desires . . ." He stopped suddenly, and seemed to remember my presence. "I hope we're not disturbing you, Mr. Verney? Of course, this isn't of any professional interest to you. . . ."

"I'm off duty," I said shortly.

"Ah—quite so." He screwed up his eyes at me and turned back to the others. "Well, now, as we shall have only a fortnight I think we shall probably have to divide up in order to cover as much ground as possible. I imagine that you, Professor, will wish to meet some fellow economists and possibly spend some time at the State Planning Commission. Mr. Thomas has expressed a wish to devote himself mainly to the minorities question. Cressey will certainly need to talk to fellow workers in the factories and trade unions. Mrs. Clarke will no doubt be interested in—er—let us say nurseries and housing. Mr. Tranter will be making a special report on the attitude of the Russian man-in-the-street toward peace—perhaps the most vital aspect of our work. I myself shall hope for an opportunity to see something of the religious life of the community."

Professor Schofield gave his thin-lipped smile. "I don't suppose anyone will wish to deprive you of it, Mullett."

"Now what about you, Miss Manning?" Mullett went on, ostentatiously ignoring the Professor. "Is there anything special you have in mind, or will you just cover the general field of culture?"

"I think I'll leave my plans until we get there," drawled Perdita. "I'm rather hoping to be able to do a portrait bust of Stalin." She spoke in a matter-of-fact tone, as though she were contemplating taking a ride on the Metro.

Mullett's fat neck went red. "I see. I wasn't aware of that. You don't think, perhaps, that such a request would be stretching hospitality rather far? We don't want to abuse our friends' kindness by making impossible demands."

"I see no harm in asking," said Perdita icily.

"Well, of course, it's entirely up to you." Mullett was obviously very angry, and trying hard to control himself. "I would have thought, though, that if you concentrate on such a very specialized—and, if I may say so, *personal* aim—you'll hardly have time for anything else. After all, we are a delegation and we have responsibilities toward one another."

Perdita gave him a look that would have slain a more sensitive man. "It's no more a specialized interest than visiting idiotic churches," she said. "That *is* a waste of time."

Mullett had recovered himself. "You seem to forget, Miss Manning," he said with great dignity, "how the Soviet Union has been maligned in this matter. It's of the greatest importance that the world should know how free the Russian people are to worship in their own way. Cressey here probably thinks that religion is persecuted, eh, Cressey? Well, you'll see that nothing could be further from the truth."

Schofield took his pipe from his mouth. "At the same time, Mullett, I think Miss Manning has a point. If we're short of time, first things should come first. You yourself attach great importance to these superstitious survivals but I doubt if the working man in England is any more interested in ikons than he is in busts of Stalin. It's the bread-and-butter business that he wants to know about—how far economic planning is offering security and better standards."

"Now, Schofield," said Mullett indulgently, "you and I know that we differ on these matters, but because you happen to be an expert in your own—shall I say, rather limited—field, you musn't underestimate the value of the spiritual side. Faith, you know, can move mountains."

"I'd like to see that demonstrated," said the Professor.

I suspected that he was merely baiting Mullett, but if so he got no satisfaction, for Mullett merely said, "Well, I don't think we ought to hold up these good people any longer," meaning the waiters, and they all got up and straggled out of the dining car. I sat for a while over a cigarette, thinking about them. Though they were "fellow travelers," one and all, they seemed to be traveling Moscow-ward for very different reasons, and I imagined that their individual reasons might be fascinating if one could get to the bottom of them. Mullett, of course, was a fairly clear case. He was a woolly wishful-thinker who happened to be inordinately vain as well, and the combination had led him to espouse an outrageous cause that kept him well in the limelight. Bolting's motives must be very different. He might deceive others, but he was, I felt again, much too astute to deceive himself. Possibly he was the hardheaded, ambitious type of left-wing M.P. who saw "fellow-traveling" as a steppingstone to notoriety, nuisance value, and ultimate advancement. His timing wasn't very good, perhaps, but plenty of people in the Labour Movement had started that way and finished up very respectably in the Cabinet.

The Professor, again, was another type. He seemed, as Thomas had said, a cold-blooded sort of fish, and I could believe that his interest in the Soviet Union was as detached as that of the vivisectionist in what was on the slab. Thomas himself was, politically, just a retarded adolescent, and in any

Communist revolution would be certain of achieving the martyrdom he was inviting. No doubt he'd been included in the delegation on the old Communist principle of mobilizing every variety of malcontent.

As for Perdita, she was a typical drawing-room Red. She had about as much in common with the proletariat as I had with Mullett. Something, I felt, must have gone badly wrong with her life to bring her into this company—some deep personal dissatisfaction or grievance. Perhaps she had an inflated ego, and having failed to get what she considered proper recognition of her talents at home, had embraced Marxism in return for flattery and homage. In any case, for a person with an inferiority complex the chance of setting up as an authority on a subject where there could be few informed critics must have been attractive.

Tranter had me guessing a little. Tentatively I put him down as one of those high-principled, head-in-air idealists who work in blinkers and never suspect that some of those who go along with them and shout for peace are grinding axes for anything but pacific ends. Mrs. Clarke, I thought, was typical of thousands of Labour housewives who attend meetings and organize whist drives and move resolutions and serve on committees. With a hearty and perhaps overgenerous nature like hers, it was natural that she should be attracted by what she thought was "fair does" for the underprivileged, and as she was such an outspoken member of her class her value to the Russians was obvious. The same thing went for Cressey. He also seemed representative of a type—the straightforward, down-to-earth working man, whose report on his visit would carry weight. The delegation had undoubtedly been chosen with great skill.

Presently I strolled back to the sleeping car. Mullett had somehow managed to pin down one of the Red Army officers in a corner of the corridor and appeared to be giving him a lecture on the Soviet Union, in quite execrable Russian.

Thomas was in the Professor's compartment and they were discussing the "great man" theory of history. I gathered that
what Wales needed was a Lenin, and I wondered if Thomas
could possibly have cast himself for the role. Perdita had taken
advantage of his preoccupation to assume a decorative pose in
Bolting's compartment, and was obviously trying to flirt with
him. He had laid aside a copy of the *New Statesmen and
Nation* and was regarding her with an interested but slightly
cynical smile. I hadn't a doubt that he was fully capable of
keeping his end up.

As I walked toward my own compartment, Joe Cressey
came shambling along the corridor. He gave me a rather shy
smile as he pressed himself against the partition to let me pass,
and I stopped.

"How's the Russian going?" I asked him.

His face clouded. "I'm afraid it's going to be too much for
me," he said. "It's the letters being upside down and back-to-
front that worries me. Mr. Tranter thinks it's a waste of time
to bother with the alphabet—he says he's going to learn a few
simple words and manage with them. But Mr. Mullett says if
a thing's worth doing it's worth doing properly." He seemed
really worried.

"Fom what I've just been hearing of Mr. Mullett's Russian," I said, "I doubt if he's qualified to teach you. I shouldn't
take him too seriously."

Cressey looked surprised.

"The way most people learn, of course," I added, "is to
wait until they get to Moscow and then find a nice girl friend.
It rarely fails."

"Oh, I don't think Mrs. Cressey would approve of that," he
said dubiously. "She didn't really like the idea of me coming
at all."

"Why did you?"

He scratched his long chin. "Well, you see, I was chosen, so
I had to. It was this way. I'm in a firm that makes electric light

fittings, and Mr. Mullett, he knows our chairman. They're both Methodists, or something like that. I don't know all the ins-and-outs, but I think what happened is they got into a bit of an argument about Russia, friendly-like, and Mr. Mullett said why didn't our chairman let one of the chaps from the factory go out with his delegation and see for himself what it was like. So Mr. Grove—that's our chairman, he's a very progressive man—he called a meeting and he said there was a free trip going, sort of holiday-with-pay, and what about electing somebody they could all trust to give a fair report. And blowed if they didn't elect me! I'm a mechanic, really, and I don't understand all these things they talk about. Come to that," he added morosely, "I don't know that I want to."

I laughed. "Quite a responsibility, eh?"

"It is. That's what worries me."

"I don't see why it should," I said. "I'd sooner take your view than—well, Mrs. Clarke's, for instance."

He brightened. "P'r'aps so. But the others, they all know so much. At least, Mr. Tranter's all right—he hasn't been to Russia before—but the others seem to know everything about the place. I don't know why they bother to come. Mind you, I've nothing against them—they're all very nice to me. Especially Mr. Bolting—he doesn't keep on at me the way some of them do."

I felt sorry for him. Mullett, I considered, had worked a pretty dirty trick. He'd brought this chap out, and the whole lot of them would proselytize him for a fortnight, and of course the Russians would make a tremendous fuss of him and almost choke him with hospitality, and he'd be practically bound to get a favorable impression, and even if he didn't he wouldn't have a chance to get his point of view over when it came to preparing a joint report. He'd be under greater pressure than the odd man on a jury. And when the trip was over, of course, the joint verdict would be quoted as his, and one more honest man would have been made a Communist tool.

I said, "What do you think of Mr. Mullett?"

Cressey said disgustedly, "Between you and me, I think he's an old fool." Then he added, as if slightly ashamed of himself, "What I mean is, I sometimes wonder if these people that are paid to talk so much ever stop to think."

I moved on to my own compartment feeling greatly cheered. Evidently Mr. Cressey wasn't nearly as slow-witted as he looked. They might, after all, have to impanel another jury.

We reached the Polish-Russian frontier late that afternoon and the delegates became very excited, as though they could already hear the trumpets sounding for them on the other side. The station was unfamiliar to me—the border had been moved far to the west, of course, compared with the prewar line—but the reception technique hadn't changed. The usual bannered arches had been rigged up over the railway line with "Workers of the World, Unite!" slogans in a variety of languages, and there was a sort of tawdry gaiety about the *décor* of the station. We crossed the now-covered platform in the gathering dusk, watched by a dozen stolid, silent peasants and a group of ragged, peaky-looking children. The delegates escaped all customs formalities and I think some of their reflected glory must have fallen on me, for my own bags were given only a perfunctory examination. We passed through a comfortable waiting room with a carpet and soft chairs and a picture of an avuncular Stalin embracing a small girl, and on into a quite presentable restaurant. Here, the usual segregation followed. Mullett's crowd had been officially greeted by some local bigwig—probably the district Mayor—and his retinue, and were now escorted to a magnificently spread table near the window for what in any other country would have been called a banquet. There were hors d'œuvres of every description, cold meats and game, ice puddings and fruits and chocolates, with vodka and two or three different wines and liqueurs to induce a comradely flow of talk. In the center of the table was a sheaf of little flags—the Union Jack, the Soviet Hammer and Sickle,

and a Cross of St. David specially for Thomas. On occasions
such as this, the Russians were thorough. They had stream-
lined their instinctive hospitality to make it an instrument of
policy, and if circumstances required it they could lay on a
spread like this at a few hours' notice in the remotest part of
the Union. If necessary they simply flew the whole thing to the
spot, waiters, toothpicks and all.

I was accommodated at a small table near by, and I must
say I also had nothing to complain of. I ordered some *zakuski*
and a couple of hundred grams of Moscow vodka, and effaced
myself.

The banquet followed a well-established pattern. The proceedings were opened by the Mayor, or whoever it was, who
welcomed the delegation in a short speech. Mullett replied in
a slightly longer one. Then they fell to. On the left of each
guest sat a Russian host, smiling, friendly and courteous, ready
to meet all wants, to engage in appropriate conversation, and
to ply the visitor with liquor. The Russians toasted the delegation, collectively and individually, and the delegation toasted
the Russians, collectively and individually. Then they drank
to Anglo-Soviet co-operation, and peace, and confusion to the
imperialist aggressors, and as they got less inhibited Islwyn
Thomas toasted Stalin in passionate Welsh ("Oh, *Izzle*-win,
how dramatic of you!" said Perdita as he sat down), and
Perdita, to be different, toasted Mao Tse-tung, and the Mayor
gallantly toasted lady sculptors and one in particular and
kissed Perdita's fingertips amid applause, and it became quite
a party. I almost forgot we were at a railway station. Mullett,
I noticed, drank nothing but mineral water, but then he was
a man who didn't need alcohol to loosen his tongue. Cressey
seemed to be holding his own surprisingly well with a hard-
drinking neighbor who evidently wanted to have to carry him
onto the train, and my respect for him rose. Mrs. Clarke, however she might try, was being seduced again into intemperance.

The noise and laughter grew so loud that I missed a lot of

the conversation, but it seemed that even at a party Mullett couldn't refrain from doing his stuff. I heard him telling Cressey across the table that the food position in Russia was very good now, and that it had only been bad during the war because of the great efforts the Russian had made on behalf of their allies, and that though Cressey would probably see queues at Moscow food shops that was merely because the Russians were such sociable people and liked getting together.

The only fly in the amber was that just as the champagne corks were popping there were scrabbling noises at the uncurtained window and three little white faces with noses flattened against the glass peered in at the festive board like the kids in Maeterlinck's *Blue Bird*. The Mayor ignored the children at first, but as their excited chatter gradually drew the attention of the delegates, he became restive and told a waiter to shoo them away. As the door opened, they scuttled off.

"Children will be children," said Mullett tolerantly.

I caught Cressey's eye, and jerked my head toward the window. "It's merely that they're interested," I said. "They don't like rich food." Mullett gave me a very dirty look, but he didn't say anything.

About an hour later everybody returned to the train with varying degrees of assistance, and promptly went to bed. Next morning I found most of the delegates very cool—I think Mullett must have had a word with them about me. It was clear that they were getting ready to slough me off directly we reached Moscow, which suited me very well.

After breakfast I sat at my window and watched the rolling countryside that runs in a picturesque belt thirty or forty miles west of Moscow. Perdita, in the corridor, was talking rather pretentiously to Islwyn about the "shape" of the snow-laden silver birches, which were in fact very lovely. I was beginning to feel stirred myself now as old memories came crowding back to me. We press correspondents had covered this ground pretty thoroughly after the German retreat, grinding over corduroy.

roads in decrepit lorries, picking our way through the in-credible litter of old battlefields, sleeping in peasant huts, checking up on atrocities, interviewing terrified prisoners in the dead of night. Every place name in the last hundred miles had had its sharp wartime association—Vyazma, Gzhatsk, Mozhaisk. No doubt things had changed a lot since then, but there were plenty of permanent things to make me nostalgic— the delicious whiff of wood smoke in the crisp air when we were checked at a station, the smell of the tobacco substitute, *makhorka,* the squat peasants with their dangling ear flaps and old felt boots and heavy wooden sleighs, the colored churches, and the log cabins with their carved window frames. I sank into a long reverie.

When I again began to take notice, we were running through the outer suburbs of the capital and Mullett was starting his fussing all over again. I wouldn't have been a member of his delegation for all the rubles in Russia.

The scene at the terminus was very similar to the one in Warsaw, except that everything was on a far grander scale. There was a larger brass band, and a more vociferous demon-stration, and a much more impressive reception committee. The Russians were evidently setting great store by this delega-tion. As the train came to rest, I noticed several familiar faces in the assembled crowd—Alexander Kropin, the writer; a poet named Suvalov, a man from the Soviet Foreign Office who had once been a censor, and several high officials from VOKS, the All-Russian Society for Cultural Relations with Foreign Countries. One of them was Mirnova, a plump, at-tractive woman with high cheekbones and a heart-shaped face who always wore an expression of great candor and simplicity although in fact she was one of the toughest Party members in Moscow. I recognized one of her assistants, too, a pretty girl named Tanya, one of a pair of English-speaking twins who had been very popular with the correspondents during the war. She looked more sophisticated and her clothes were better, but she still wore her fair hair in a fringe with a page-boy bob.

I kept well in the background and allowed the delegation plenty of time to get ahead. Islwyn Thomas gave me a casual nod of farewell as he turned to help Perdita down to the platform; Cressey came and shook hands. There was a lot of excitement below me as introductions were effected, and news cameras flashed, and the inevitable microphone was stuck in front of Mullett. At last they all moved off to an accompaniment of cheers and music. As the noise died away I managed to find a porter and I made my own way out of the station. I'd timed it very nicely. As I emerged, Tranter was just easing his stiff leg into the back of one of five luxurious limousines, and a moment later the convoy moved off.

II

AS I'D expected, there was no sign of a taxi anywhere about, so I went back into the station and telephoned a friend of mine who was staying at the Astoria—an American correspondent named Jefferson L. Clayton whom I'd got to know pretty well during a trip to Washington and who was just about coming to the end of a three months' assignment in Moscow. I thought it probable that a car would be part of Jeff's office equipment, and it was. When I phoned he was on the point of going to see his Ambassador, but he promised to send the car right on to pick me up. "Gosh!" he cried. "Am I glad to hear your voice!" I told him I could hardly wait to hear his news and rang off, feeling pleasantly exhilarated. Jeff's company was always a tonic, because everything he did and said was positive. I hung around for a while, and about twenty minutes later a surprisingly lush car rolled into the station and a smiling young chauffeur wrapped me up in rugs.

From what I could see as we sped down the Tverskaya, the city hadn't changed a lot in six years—not outwardly, at least. By contrast with the dazzling snow on the rooftops, everything looked drab and dilapidated, and more in need of paint than ever. Here and there along the route there were new buildings of a superficial impressiveness, but the vista was mainly of flaking walls and crumbling cement and cheerless courtyards stacked with timber and littered with accumulated rubbish. The streets were as noisy as ever, with tram bells ringing and car horns hooting incessantly. A distorted voice on the open-air loud-speaker system was exhorting citizens to contribute to the

latest voluntary state loan. The ancient single-decker trams
which clattered over the worn tracks were packed so full
within and without that a sardine would have felt jostled.
Gangs of women with padded jackets and shawled heads were
brushing and chipping away at the snow and ice in the ceaseless winter struggle to keep the streets clear for traffic. On the
uneven pavements, bulky figures carrying brief cases and parcels and string bags were shuffling expertly along in their high
felt boots, silent, dogged and pinch-faced in the keen frost.
Paper flowers on sale at a corner kiosk seemed to mock the
distant spring. The green towers and golden domes of the in-
comparable Kremlin provided a fantastic background to the
dour winter scene.

The cold was just beginning to numb my fingers and toes as
I pushed through the double set of revolving doors into the
Astoria Hotel, taking a wedge of icy air with me into the warm
vestibule. Inside, everything was as familiar as though I had
left the place only yesterday—the threadbare red carpet, the
huge glass chandeliers with their inadequate quota of bulbs,
the great gilded mirrors, even the green-shaded lamp on the
receptionist's table. Everywhere there was the same air of
faded ornateness and slow decay. Shapeless figures who had
crept into the building to get warm hung furtively around the
door as they had always done. The porter who took my luggage was the same porter I had known in the old days—an
ageless, obsequious gray-head named Ivan. The Astoria was
probably the only place in Moscow where the servants still
bent low and touched their caps.

There was no difficulty about getting a room, for I'd sent a
wire to Jeff telling him I was on my way and he'd taken care
of everything. In exchange for my passport I was given the key
of room 434 on the fourth floor—Jeff's was 436—and I went
up in the big, shaky lift, feeling absurdly excited. Nothing
seemed to have changed except the faces of the manageresses
who sat at strategic points on each floor, watching and noting.

There was quite a commotion on the fourth floor, and it
soon became apparent that the whole delegation was being
accommodated along the corridor where I was to be housed.
Luggage was still being taken into the rooms. Cressey and
Tranter were ambling around in a rather bemused fashion and
Islwyn Thomas, who had evidently managed to get his old
room again, was going into reminiscent raptures in a loud,
excited voice. As I turned the key in 434, Mullett himself
came out of 435 and passed me with a stiff little nod. I almost
felt like asking for a transfer!

I dumped my stuff and had a look at my quarters. The
room was a fairly standard type for the Astoria—high, light
and spacious, with a curtained-off bed annex opening in turn
into a private bathroom. The furniture was an odd mixture—
Louis Quinze chairs and couch, a huge divan with a mirror at
the back, a cheap deal wardrobe, a heavy mahogany table and
a brass-knobbed bedstead. I pulled the bed away from the wall
and wondered if there were any bugs. For two years during the
war I had waged a running fight with them in this hotel, and
had left just as victory seemed in sight. But perhaps things
were different now. There was one marked improvement since
the war days—the radiators were hot and the room was comfortably warm. In a month when the thermometer outside
could fall as low as minus thirty centigrade, there was nothing
more important than that. The tall French windows—double,
like all windows in Russia—had been sealed along all the
cracks with broad strips of brown paper to keep out the cold
air. This, again, was the general practice between October and
April. If you wanted ventilation you could open a tiny door at
the top of the window, called a *fortachka,* and then the temperature became arctic in a few minutes. Most people kept it
firmly shut.

Outside the French windows there was a railed-in concrete
balcony with an inch or so of frozen snow on it. In the summer
it would have been a pleasant place to sit, for it looked out on

the broad expanse of Teatralni Square with the Bolshoi
Theater massive in the background and in front a formal
garden with small trees. The only drawback about this side of
the hotel was that trolleybus routes intersected just below, and
there was usually a lot of noise. The rooms at the end of the
corridor, round the corner, were better—they looked out over
a quiet side street. I was reminded, however, as I gazed down
upon the square, that they weren't nearly so much fun because
you missed half the amusing things that went on. Just below
me, for instance, a pedestrian was taking a short cut diagonally
across the open space, which was in flagrant defiance of regu-
lations. A militiaman on the corner removed a cigarette from
his mouth and blew his whistle angrily, but the offender took
no notice. The whistle was blown again—a series of long
blasts. The man looked round but continued doggedly on his
way. The militiaman shouted, and began to follow him in a
rather halfhearted manner. The man quickened his pace, and
the militiaman shrugged and broke off the pursuit, turning to
harangue some children about Socialist discipline in a loud,
grumbling voice. It was so characteristic of Moscow.

I'd just about finished unpacking when Jeff breezed in, with
a whoop of delight and a crushing handshake. Jeff looks like
the bobby-soxer's dream come true. He's tall and strongly built,
with crinkly brown hair and a blunt nose in a round, rather
puckered face. No one would call him handsome, but he has
a great deal of charm. He's been practically all over the world,
and he knows his job through and through. He likes getting his
facts straight, and saying what he thinks, and drinking anything with alcohol in it, and pretty girls. He hates censors, and
"handouts," and humbugs, and stuffed shirts, and being on his
own. He usually appears rather cynical, and as far as his job's
concerned he's seen plenty to make him, but he's got a strong
sentimental streak as well and he can get quite emotional.
We've been friends for a long time, in the hail-and-farewell
fashion of foreign correspondents. He once threatened to

knock my block off—or whatever the equivalent American expression is—at a party in London when we were both tight and he said that W. D. Wills on the cigarette packet was a better guy than H. O. Wills on the same packet, and I said he wasn't! That's the only time we've had what I'd call a major difference of opinion.

Before we got down to an exchange of news he insisted on a drink to celebrate. He marched me off to his room and with the precision of a *maestro* he smacked the bottom of a vodka bottle. The cardboard stopper flew off. He poured out two lethal doses and produced some crackers. "Here's to civilization," he said. "May we live to see it!" We threw our heads back, tossed down the colorless spirit, and made the sort of faces you have to make over vodka.

"Well, you old son of a gun," he beamed, "how's Paradise Regained?"

"You know," I said, "it's a funny thing—I always hanker to get back to Russia, and when I've been here a couple of hours I can't for the life of me think why."

"Nuts! You know you're crazy about it."

"I suppose most people feel something for places they've spent a long time in," I said. "I know men with a passion for Clacton-on-Sea. By the way, thanks for fixing my room."

"Think nothing of it, old boy." The "old boy" was very much in quotes. "Though I reckon it's just as well I did—a bunch of your fellow countrymen have just moved in. The corridor's stiff with 'em."

"I know. Mullett's Circus. I traveled with them from Warsaw."

If I'd told him I'd just escaped from Dachau he couldn't have looked more concerned. "You poor s.o.b.! A thing like that would take years off me. That guy Mullett gets right under my skin."

"Why, do you know him?"

"I'll say I do. I wrote a profile of him when I came through

London last year, and did he make a fuss! I believe he thought
he could get me fired. He talked of libel and God knows what,
but it didn't come to anything, of course. What a prize jerk!"

"You know he has the room next door—435?"

"You don't say! We'll have to organize a pincer movement." He poured out two more shots of vodka.

I said, "How's work been, Jeff?"

He gave me a dirty look. "You know damn well how it's
been."

I had to laugh. I'd seen him in London just before he'd left
to take up this assignment, and like all good newspapermen
he'd been sure that he could do what everyone else had failed
to do. He'd had no political illusions, of course, and neither
had his paper, but with no personal experience of Moscow
he'd simply been unable to believe that working conditions
could be quite as bad as they were reputed to be. "Don't give
me that gloom stuff," he'd said. "You guys just don't know
the right approach. I'll soon have Vishinsky eating out of my
hand."

Now he broke into a rueful smile. "You were dead right, of
course," he said. "They like to have one or two of us kicking
around, but they hate our guts, and the way they behave is
out of this world. We can't go anywhere, we can't see anything
except what's too public to hide, and we can't talk to anyone.
I've put a lot of lines out but there hasn't been a nibble. The
ordinary Russians are too scared to speak to us. Every request
has to be funneled through the Press Department, and *their*
job is plain obstruction. I've been waiting six weeks for VOKS
to fix me a visit to a kindergarten. Practically every day I go
and bang on Ganilov's table—he's the head of the Press Department now—but he only blinks at me through his thick
glasses and says I must be patient. Patient!—can you beat it?
It's bloody well hopeless. I'm not sorry I came—it's been a
fascinating experience—but as far as the job's concerned I
sure won't be sorry to leave."

I nodded sympathetically. It hadn't taken him long to get the situation sized up. "When are you going, Jeff?"

"That depends on how soon they can squeeze me into a plane, I guess. I applied for my exit permit yesterday."

"Pity! Never mind, we'll have fun while we can. By the way, how's the censorship these days?"

He snorted. "Practically impenetrable. As far as the censor's concerned this country is perfect and he passes nothing but friendly propaganda, if any. You can't even say that the *corps de ballet* was a shade off color today! The only pieces I've succeeded in getting through were heavily ironical, and that's always risky."

"How right you are!—and that goes for both ends. I'll never forget an ironical piece I filed toward the end of the war, about some spontaneous demonstrations by freedom-loving Persians in favor of Russia taking over their oil. It got away from here all right, but some damn-fool sub at home put up a heading 'Persian Oil: The Truth at Last!' It taught me a lesson. No, the only thing to do is to collect what material you can and use it later."

"Sure—in a couple of paragraphs. You're lucky, of course—you can talk the lingo. I guess that must help a little, if you can find anyone to talk it to. The only words I've picked up aren't any use except in bed. If I want to ask any questions I have to have my secretary go along with me, and directly people realize I'm a foreigner they shy away as though I were radioactive."

"Who is your secretary, Jeff?"

"I call her Zina—she's got some unpronounceable name. She's quite a character. I think she'd be a good secretary if there was anything for her to do except get in the groceries and collect the 'handouts.' As it is, I guess the only real work she does is to keep tabs on me for the M.V.D."

The M.V.D. were the security police. "Those fellows are

always changing their name," I said. "In my time they were the N.K.V.D. We used to call them the four-letter boys."

"That's still okay with me," said Jeff. "Any four you like!"

I asked him what other newspapermen were in Moscow.

"Well," he said, "there are the agencies, of course. They're pretty well cut down to skeleton staffs, and there's darned little for them to send. They don't live in the hotel—they've still got their apartments. There's actually only one other guy with a room in the hotel; he's British, name of Potts. He's a curious bird. He's supposed to have an assignment from one of your magazines, but he spends all his time doing his own private mass observation. I think he's collecting material for an 'Inquire Within.' There's John Waterhouse, of course, but he's in a class by himself. And that's about all, except for the Communists and fellow travelers."

"Quite a social whirl you must have."

"I'll say! There are some weeks when we actually see a new face."

"What about the embassies?"

"Oh, they're cut to the bone, too—some of the smaller legations have closed down altogether. It's partly expense, of course, but I expect a lot of people are getting out while the going's good, and I don't blame them. I wouldn't fancy spending the Third World War as the prisoner of these ginks. . . ." He lit a Lucky and blew smoke savagely across the room. "No, it's been about the loneliest assignment I can remember."

"You must have found a girl friend . . . ?" I began.

"Ah, sure I've got a girl friend, but—hell, you know how it is here. I like picking my own dames, but if you were to choose one out of the crowd here, supposing you could get near one, it'd be like signing her death warrant. And if you don't, you have to take what the system offers. My kid's not too bad, I suppose, and maybe she quite likes me as well as my nylons, but it's bad enough to be spied on during the day without feeling that someone's making mental notes about you while you're in bed."

I nodded. "Who is she, Jeff? Do I know her, I wonder?"

"You might. Name of Tanya—one of the VOKS crowd. She works for that smooth operator Mirnova."

"Oh, Tatiana Mikhailovna! Of course I know her. As a matter of fact she was at the station today, meeting the delegation."

"She would be. She's been attached to them as interpreter."

"She's attractive."

"Oh, she's attractive, all right. She knows her stuff, too." He caught my eye and gave a wry smile. "Okay, bud, don't say it—I know she's had practice."

"Is she living in the hotel?"

"Sure. She's in 433, the room on the other side of yours."

"Why don't you swop with me—then you'll be right next to her."

"I can walk that far," he said.

"Tanya used to have a twin sister—Kira Mikhailovna. Is she still around?"

"Yes, she's around. She works at Sovkino—she's one of the hostesses when they show their lousy propaganda pictures to foreigners. She's a pleasant kid, too—she looks in here from time to time."

"You don't get them mixed up?"

He laughed. "They use different nail polish."

There was a knock on the door, and he called out, *"Da!"* All the doors were on spring locks, but he'd left his catch fastened back. A waiter came in with a bottle of pink champagne and a bottle of cognac. He glanced across at me as he put his tray down, and then stared as though he couldn't believe his eyes.

"Nikolai!" I said. "How are you?" I got up and he came over and shook hands, beaming with pleasure. "I'm glad to see you again, Nikolai. Well, well, so you're still going strong?"

"The same," he said. "I have no complaints. And you, *Gospodeen* Verney? I never thought you'd come back."

"I couldn't keep away, Nikolai."

"Hey, what's going on?" said Jeff. "I didn't know you two had a beautiful friendship. I'd better get another glass."

"Good idea," I said. I turned to Nikolai. "Well, it certainly is nice to see your face again." He was looking much more frail than when I'd seen him last—by now he was well on in his sixties, I supposed—but he had the same look of patient sweetness that I remembered. He'd been a servant in a big household in Moscow and his master's family had been broken up during the Revolution, by death and flight and one thing or another. Nikolai had had to fit himself into the new setup, and because of his background it had been difficult for him, especially as he'd been fond of the people he'd served. He couldn't accustom himself to the regime and wanted no part of it, but he'd had a small son on whom all his hopes were set and for the boy's sake more than for his own safety he'd loyally accepted it. He'd told me all this back in the war, and a lot of other things as well—stories of the old Russia that filled in big gaps in my understanding and were as fascinating as *War and Peace*.

I explained some of this to Jeff while he poured out a third drink. He looked quite disgusted at the thought that he'd been unaware of this rich mine of human interest just under his nose. "See what I mean—that's what comes of not knowing the language. Anyway, here's to us." We all drank each other's health.

"What about Boris?" I asked Nikolai—a little diffidently, because in Russia so many unpleasant things could happen to a man in six years, over and above the normal hazards. But it was all right—Nikolai's son was doing well as a doctor in a Moscow hospital, there were three grandchildren, and everything was wonderful. Nikolai's dreams had come true. "There are many things," he said, "that I do not like today, but I must admit that in the old times Boris could not have studied medicine. I am glad that he was able to. However bad the world, a doctor can always serve humanity. That is the best thing of all." He smiled and set down his glass. *"Merci, Gospodeen* Clayton! *Dosvedanie, Gospodeen* Verney!" He inclined his head with grave courtesy and went out with his tray.

"Well, what do you know!" said Jeff. "I always thought he was a nice guy, and Tanya dotes on him, but I never knew he had all that in him."

There were fresh footsteps outside and a moment later John Waterhouse appeared, with a man whom I hadn't seen before. "Come right in," Jeff called out. "Wipe your feet!"

"Champagne, eh?" said Waterhouse. "I hoped we'd be in time for the celebration. Hello, George, how are you? It's good to see you again." We shook hands warmly. "This is Edward Potts—George Verney."

Waterhouse hadn't changed much, except that he was a little grayer. He was a rather dapper man of sixty or so who always wore bow ties. An unashamed poseur, he always contrived—among his colleagues, at least—to give the impression that he was keeping the white man's flag flying in a country of savages. He wasn't exceptionally tall, but he affected a slight stoop. He had bright, satirical eyes, and could be extremely charming when it suited him. He'd been a newspaperman in Moscow as long as anyone could remember; he had a comfortable flat somewhere behind the Kremlin, and a servant, and acquaintances in town that he'd known at the time of the Revolution. How he lived was something of a mystery, for though he was still an accredited correspondent he hadn't sent much news out for years. I had heard that he wrote novels under a pseudonym. There was almost nothing that he didn't know about Russia, and he was completely cynical about the regime, but he'd somehow managed to rub along without mortally offending the authorities and, incalculable as ever, they hadn't bothered to throw him out. Perhaps they regarded

him as privileged, like the old court jesters. I'd asked him once
why he stayed on when there was so little to do, and he'd said
blandly, "Art for art's sake, dear boy," and then shot me a
bright, amused glance. I think it was just that he'd got used to
the place—he even traveled on the trams!—and that he
hadn't any interests anywhere else. It was his intention, so he
said, to have his ashes scattered on top of Lenin's mausoleum.

Potts was an anemic-looking individual, tall and thin and
pale, with sparse hair and glasses and an earnest, donnish
manner, and he wore black boots, the largest I'd ever seen. He
didn't look like a newspaperman and he didn't shake hands
like one.

I couldn't help thinking back to the days of departed glory,
when there had been twenty or thirty correspondents in Moscow, representing the world's greatest newspapers. Now, apart
from the agencies, there were just the four of us, and one of
us was soon going, and one of us was Potts!

Jeff charged the glasses and asked Potts how his mass observation was going.

"Well, you know, it's most interesting," said Potts in a reedy
voice. "I've been outside the hotel today, studying winter
clothing habits." He fumbled for a notebook. "I found that
forty-five per cent of the men wore felt boots and fifty-five per
cent other kinds of boots. The women were different. Sixty-
eight per cent of them wore felt boots. The breakdown into age
groups may be revealing." He gave a dry little cough. "Then
forty-eight per cent of the women wore shawls, and fifty-two
per cent hats and berets. Seventy-eight per cent of the men
wore fur hats, and twenty-two per cent wore caps."

"That sure is a scoop," said Jeff. He looked at Potts with
wonder, as though at a strange animal, but there was no
malice in his tone.

"It's the sort of thing that people like to know about," said
Potts. "Somebody has to do the field work, after all. There are
little gems of information that I keep picking up. For instance,

about half the people in this city sleep in their day under-clothes—did you know that, Clayton?"

"I know that half the women sleep in their brassières," said Jeff with a grin, "if they get the chance."

"He hasn't got around to the other half," I said.

"A fair sample is sufficient," Potts said with complete seriousness. "I've found out something else that may surprise you. Double beds are almost unknown in Russia. There's no room for them because of the overcrowding."

"That's right," I said, "they won't fit in the passages." I looked at him curiously. The material he was collecting might be so much lumber, but his initiative was admirable. "Of course, you know what'll happen to you—one of these days you'll be picked up and charged with espionage. Housing conditions fall under the heading of economic secrets and you can get ten years for extracting that sort of information from Soviet citizens. So can they for giving it."

"Really?" Potts looked worried. "That seems rather absurd."

"Everything's absurd," said Waterhouse. "Which reminds me, how are the mice, Mr. Potts?"

"Very bad indeed," said Potts. "I estimate that they've increased by fifty per cent in the past week."

"I thought the hotel people lent you a trap," said Jeff.

"They did, but they took it away again. They said there was a man on the third floor who also had mice, and that as I'd caught two and he hadn't caught any, it was only fair he should have a turn. So now I've applied for the hotel cat."

"What do you mean, *applied?*"

"Just what I say. I had to make a written application to the hotel manager in triplicate, and I got a reply on hotel notepaper saying that the application would be sympathetically considered and that if it were approved I'd be issued a permit." He shook his head in perplexity. "They are extraordinary people."

We hooted with laughter, as much at his expression as at his story. Presently Jeff said, "You know the delegation's here, do you, John?"

Waterhouse gave him a slightly pained look, as though the suggestion that a piece of news might have escaped him were bad form. Not only did he know of the delegation's arrival, but it turned out that he knew several of the members quite well. He'd met Schofield in 1942 at the time of the supply mission, and Bolting when he'd been an accounts clerk at the Embassy, and he'd actually traveled to Kuibyshev with Mullett in the great evacuation.

"*Not* a very nice man," said Waterhouse regretfully. "Dangerous, too. He set a lot of people on the wrong road back in the thirties. There's a young fellow at the Radio Center who took Mullett's advice and came out here to work and has regretted it ever since. Can't get back now, of course—and I imagine he's far from being the only one who was led astray. By the way, you know we're going to be invited to accompany the delegation on its rounds?"

"Invited?" said Jeff. "I didn't know they had a word for that."

"They have when they want something, dear boy. They want this delegation to go over with a bang—you can see that by the build-up they've given it in their own press and radio. Now they want us to toddle round and pick up the pearls of wisdom that fall from their lips."

"Yeah? They've got a hope! I can just see my chief's face if I cabled five hundred well-chosen words on a peace-loving visit to a *kolhoz*."

"An emotional view, Mr. Clayton. We don't have to file stories. We shall get some excellent meals."

"Sure, and have to listen to a lot of hooey," said Jeff disgustedly. "What about you, George? Are you going to tail along?"

"I think I might," I said. "I feel as though I've read the first chapter of a serial story, and I'd rather like to know what happens next. There's a friendly type called Cressey I want to keep an eye on for one thing—and the unfriendly ones intrigue me. I don't see that we can lose anything. You might even get a chance to speak to a Russian."

"You think so?" Jeff put down his glass. "Bud," he said, "you've got me really excited."

III

NEXT MORNING, after breakfast, I tried to draw up some sort of a plan of work. I had no expectation that the Press Department would give me any assistance, but the usual motions had to be gone through, if only for the record. Besides, you could never be *absolutely* certain. Russia's relations with Britain at that moment were perhaps just one shade less bitter than her relations with the United States, and the Soviet Foreign Office was quite capable of marking the difference by a modest show of favoritism. Soviet officialdom could be incredibly small-minded at times. I hadn't forgotten how, during the war, the assumed postponement of the Second Front had coincided with a sharp curtailment of theater tickets and other small concessions to correspondents.

Anyhow, just on the off-chance I drew up a careful list of requirements. I wanted to see someone at two or three of the ministries; to be given some figures about housing, wages, prices, and taxation; and to visit a number of institutions. It was routine stuff—the sort of thing that every incoming newspaperman asked for. I also made a private note of things I intended to do, irrespective of official sanction. I was pretty sure I could still move around in shops and markets, parks and places of entertainment, without being spotted as a foreigner, and you could learn quite a bit from casual conversations. I also had one or two old addresses that I thought I might telephone later on. It seemed unlikely that I should succeed in renewing past contacts, but again the attempt had to be made.

Having prepared the ground for what in any Western country could have been a fruitful tour of duty, I went off to pay my respects to the Ambassador. He gave me a glass of excellent sherry and I gave him a description of the delegation, which seemed to cause him some wry amusement. Then I went on to see the head of the Soviet Press Department and collect my press card.

I'd taken the precaution of ringing up beforehand and making a firm appointment, but there were wearisome formalities to be gone through before I could even enter the Foreign Office building. It was necessary to call at a neighboring "security" building and get a temporary pass from a shaven-headed, steely-eyed man who worked behind a grille, and there was a queue of about twenty intimidated Russians already lined up there, patiently waiting on the bureaucrat's pleasure. Bracing myself, I marched to the head of the queue, apologized to the man who stood there, and rapped sharply on the grille, which had a board across it. "Shaven-head" whipped the board away, stared at me much as the workhouse master must have looked at Oliver Twist, and told me curtly to fall in line. When he put the board back I rapped on it again, and some extremely nerve-racking exchanges followed. In the end, after claiming a close personal acquaintance with the whole of the Politburo and losing my temper in a highly undignified fashion, I got the pass. It was a routine I'd always hated, but it was unavoidable unless you were prepared to stand about for half a day, as the Russians were.

When I was finally shown up to the Press Department, Ganilov kept me waiting for nearly three quarters of an hour. That was routine, too—one of the thousand and one small things calculated to induce in any normal newspaperman a sense of intolerable exasperation. I sat down in the familiar press room, now peopled only with the spirits of the past, and wondered how I'd ever managed to endure two years of it. What a fund of good will toward Russia, I reflected, had drained away over the years in that unsympathetic annex.

Ganilov came out at last, and extended a clammy hand. He was a big, ungainly man of forty or so, with a mop of black hair, hunched shoulders and peering eyes distorted by thick lenses, so that you couldn't see his expression or have the least idea what he was thinking. He led the way into his well-appointed room, indicated one of two leather chairs, and offered me a cardboard-tipped cigarette. He asked me in excellent English if I'd had a good trip, said that he was glad I'd decided to pay another visit to the Soviet Union, and indicated that he'd be pleased to place all the usual facilities at my disposal.

He was completely deadpan, and so was I. I produced the list I'd prepared and he put the paper close to his eyes, his pink lips moving as he read, and then he sat for a while nibbling his finger ends.

"It's a little difficult just now," he said. "You see, everyone is very busy. The Ministry of Agriculture is preparing for the spring sowing, the Housing Commission has just launched a new program. . . . Yes, it will be difficult. However, I will certainly do what is possible. Meanwhile . . ." he reached for a typed sheet, "you are invited to accompany Mr. Mullett and his delegation on their visits. As you will see, they propose to cover a great deal of ground. For the foreign press, this is a unique opportunity."

I glanced at the paper. The program was certainly an extensive one. None of the items in the itinerary was particularly original, but the delegates were going to see more in a fortnight than a correspondent could normally hope to see in a year.

"Unfortunately," I said, "Mr. Mullett and his activities are not very popular in England."

Ganilov indicated that he understood the difficulty. "However," he said, "facts are facts whatever the composition of a particular delegation. I am sure you will find much to interest you—and much to write about."

I smiled. I felt we understood each other perfectly.

The next few days were among the busiest I've ever spent in the Soviet Union. On the first evening, I attended a great "peace" rally at the Bolshoi Theater. The delegates were all up on the stage with the Party "big shots," and the auditorium was packed with hand-picked representatives from various Soviet bodies. The organizers had managed to create the atmosphere of a great occasion. A massed band played stirring British and Soviet tunes—not omitting "Men of Harlech!"— and the air was hot with the floodlights of cinema cameras. Press photographers kept bobbing up toward the speakers and it was clear that the features of the delegates were going to become very familiar to the Russian public. On this occasion, it was Tranter who was given most of the limelight. He limped to the microphone with a sort of shy smile on his face and seemed quite overcome by what is known in the Soviet press as "stormy applause." His line turned out to be sweet reasonableness and brotherly love. All the peoples of the world, he said, craved for peace, and so there was no earthly reason why we shouldn't have it. All that was necessary was that we should try to see each other's point of view and be ready to compromise and not let our statesmen drag us into adventures. The audience vociferously cheered the sentiment that they should restrain their statesmen! I thought of all the hard work that Tranter must have put in on behalf of his peace society back in England, and felt almost sorry for him. Far better if he'd devoted his philanthropic energies to something practical, like homes for the aged.

The other speeches were a little briefer, but there were a great many of them, both Russian and English. Perdita's few barbed words had a good reception. Islwyn, impassioned and dramatic in the spotlight, appeared to have forgotten that peace was the object of the meeting and gave a remarkable exhibition of verbal paranoia. Mrs. Clarke was confident and strident and I quickly revised my earlier view of a possibly overgenerous nature. On the platform she was a termagant, and her shrill, vulgar voice set my teeth on edge. Bolting, on the contrary, was controlled and persuasive. Whereas the others had all needed the services of a translator, he spoke, to my surprise, in almost perfect Russian and got an extra cheer for it. He looked most distinguished in his well-cut clothes and snowy linen and I wondered how he managed it on an M.P.'s salary. The Professor wasn't called upon, and neither was Cressey.

It was Mullett who, in spite of his cloth, struck the harshest note of the evening. He had the Communist claptrap off by heart, and spat out phrases like "imperialist warmongers" with real venom. There must have been a lot of rancor in his soul, and I suppose the applause he got was balm. When all the talking was over, resolutions were put and carried with the customary unanimity and the delegation, having earned its supper, was taken off to a banquet at the Moscow Soviet. I went back to the hotel and tried, without much success, to interest Jeff in the proceedings. He said he had to draw the line somewhere and he drew it at Communist "peace" meetings.

The next day was a busy one for all of us. First thing in the morning we accompanied Mrs. Clarke and Perdita and a strong VOKS contingent to a new housing estate. Mrs. Clarke asked an enormous number of questions and took copious notes for the report she would be making to her Co-op women. Perdita hung back rather superciliously and preferred to talk to Mirnova. Halfway through the morning we linked up with Cressey and Tranter and toured a chocolate factory. Jeff had by now become converted to the view that these visits were worth while, for when the delegates were carrying on their interviews with the help of Tanya and Mirnova, we managed to have some useful chats with isolated Russians who in the

ordinary way wouldn't have dared to open their mouths to foreigners.

On the Tuesday we were all taken out in limousines to a
collective farm on the Mozhaisk *chaussée*. It was a sunny day
with only about ten degrees of frost, and walking around in the
sparkling snow was most enjoyable. Mullett was very hearty,
and in the course of the morning drank seven glasses of warm
milk to show good will. Then, at about four in the afternoon,
we were invited to one of those enormous Russian meals where
the unwary eat steadily for an hour and are just sitting back
with a sigh of repletion when the main course is brought in.
Some of the delegates were beginning to have a slightly congested look, but they could still break into argument at the
least provocation. At our end of the table a warm discussion
developed about a case, reported in that day's *Komsomolskaya
Pravda,* of a boy—a member of the Young Communists—who
had won public acclaim by denouncing his father as a "social
fascist." Thomas was all for it—"the cause must come first"
was his view—and so was Perdita. Schofield made some re-
marks which suggested that he thought moral considerations
almost irrelevant against the general background of the cosmic
plan. Mullett hummed and hawed, but was inclined to agree
that it was impossible to have too much "Socialist vigilance"
in a revolutionary period. Mrs. Clarke also favored what she
called "vigilance," but for children to spy on parents was
apparently not in the Co-op tradition and she didn't hold with
it. Bolting looked as though he didn't care much either way.
He seemed to find the whole delegation mildly entertaining.

After the meal, we were joined by a group of spruce young
collective farmers, male and female, including a boy with a
balalaika. By now we were all very mellow. There was a lot
of singing, and then the indefatigable Russians cleared a space
for dancing and we really let ourselves go. There was one
extremely handsome girl—a dark Don Cossack—who danced
some of her native folk dances with enormous zest. She was

later monopolized by Bolting, and from what I could see as
the air grew thicker and the fumes headier, he was making fast
progress with her. He was a man, evidently, who enjoyed the
good things of life.

The bonhomie of that evening didn't last. Relations between
the two women in the party were becoming increasingly
strained, and by the third day Waterhouse, who was now
almost as intrigued by the human side of the delegation as I
was myself, was prepared to lay odds on an early and violent
breach. The atmosphere was particularly threatening on the
Wednesday, when Perdita had to spend the morning with Mrs.
Clarke going over a nursery and the afternoon interviewing a
Heroine-Mother who had won a medal for producing ten
children. The climax came in the evening at the ballet. The
women, as usual, were sitting together and Mrs. Clarke—
who had put on a staggering violet frock for the occasion—was
in one of her most voluble moods. In the second entr'acte she
started to tell Perdita about her daughter Ruby who had won
a prize for jiving at some South London *palais* and had always
thought it would be nice to be a ballet dancer, until Perdita
suddenly cried, "Oh, for heaven's sake!" and stalked out of
the theater.

This open rupture had repercussions the next day. Still out
of temper, Perdita vented her annoyance on Islwyn, who
became very sulky. She didn't make things any better by ostentatiously switching her attentions to Bolting. By this time she
was barely on speaking terms with Mullett and Mrs. Clarke
had become very cantankerous, so one way and another there
was quite an atmosphere. Also, Cressey was being difficult.
After lunch at a Chlidren's Home on the Thursday, Mullett
began talking about how successful the "peace" rally had been
and what a fine report of the Russian spirit they'd be able to
give when they got home. Cressey, when pressed to agree, said
that of course the spirit *had* been fine, but there was something
he couldn't quite understand. Mullett, eager as ever to help

him over any little difficulty, probed deeper, and Cressey said
rather diffidently that he'd happened to hear a broadcast by
Mr. Attlee just before leaving England and what he couldn't
understand was how the Western countries could be warmongers when they practically hadn't got anything to fight
with and the Russians could be peace-loving when they'd got
170 divisions and about 25,000 tanks. He raised the matter in
such a modest way, as though he realized it was only his own
stupidity at fault, that everyone tried hard to be patient with
him, but he certainly cast an ideological cloud over the latter
part of that luncheon. Perdita, who had formerly referred to
Cressey in her patronizing way as "that sweet little man," now
looked at him as though he were a viper in the delegation
bosom.

The high spot of the week was the reception given by
VOKS in honor of Perdita. It was on the Saturday, and the
press attended in full strength, for the buffet meals provided by
VOKS were famous. It was held in a fine old house with high
carved ceilings and Empire columns, and there were probably
a couple of hundred people there, comprising the artistic and
intellectual elite of Moscow. Perdita, despite her accumulating
resentments, was in her most regal mood and looked terrific in
midnight-blue velvet, cut with devastating slinkiness. The
photographs which she had brought with her to Russia had
been carefully framed and hung on the walls, and for the first
half hour we all strolled round and made the admiring noises
which are expected on such occasions. There were several
Russian sculptors present, and the air became thick with
technicalities.

When everyone had said everything that could possibly *be*
said about the somewhat exiguous collection, we all moved
into another room where chairs had been set out in rows as for
a·meeting. The president of VOKS, a man called Vassiliev,
opened the proceedings with a brief but fulsome eulogy of
Perdita and then she was called upon to give a talk about "her

Art," which Mirnova translated with great virtuosity paragraph by paragraph. It all sounded most erudite. I caught phrases like "the rhetorical magnificence of the baroque," "the ardent yet naïve simplicity of archaic art," and "the pursuit of realistic verisimilitude." Perdita was very cool and sure of herself, and she was obviously reveling in the limelight. She must have managed to avoid all the ideological pitfalls, for the lecture was received with prolonged and enthusiastic applause and she sat down with a flush of pleasure. She was followed by a tedious old man named Rabinovitch, introduced as one of the Soviet Union's most famous sculptors, who said a lot more nice things about her. I noticed that Mirnova cut him a little in translation.

Finally we adjourned to the banqueting room for what VOKS called a *"chai."* The word means "tea," but to VOKS it meant a spread that Nero himself could hardly have rivaled. There was, as Waterhouse put it, "everything but a vomitorium." Perdita was carried off by Mirnova to grace a special table where the elite of the elite were gathered for worship, and the rest of us had our wants attended to by a bevy of young and charming hostesses. Mrs. Clarke, still in her violet frock, was waited upon by a rather pansy young man. A blonde attached herself to Islwyn Thomas and Jeff's Tanya was soon deep in conversation with Cressey. Jeff himself was still exploiting his unusual opportunities, and had buttonholed a Russian who spoke a few words of English.

I was helping myself to a plate of hors d'œuvres when Waterhouse edged toward me through the crowd, his eyes sparkling with mischief. "Well, George," he said, spiking about half a pound of smoked salmon, "what did you think of it?"

"I'm not cultured," I said. "As entertainment, I thought it went on too long."

He laughed. "Well, I do happen to know something about it, and you can take it from me, dear boy—that woman's fourth-rate. Fifth-rate! This stuff of hers . . ." he waved a derisory hand at the exhibition, ". . . it's pitiful." He poured out some vodka. "As for this preposterous notion that Russia leads in culture—pah! Art?—Soviet Russia hasn't produced any art, not for years. Remember what Shaw wrote in *Back to Methuselah?* 'Art has never been great except when it has been providing an iconography for a living religion.' That's the trouble here—there's no living religion. There hasn't been since the early days of the Revolution. These people have ritual and dogma but they don't feel anything inside any more. Their communism is just a husk."

He looked up at me sardonically and then round at the cultured throng whose claims he had dismissed. There was a clatter of plates and a rising buzz of conversation and above it all boomed a monologue from Mullett.

"By the way," Waterhouse went on, "did you know that la Manning has asked if she can model Stalin?"

"I knew she was going to."

"Well, she has. There's a rather nice story going about. It seems that Mirnova consulted Mullett on the subject, because she didn't want to hurt the lady's feelings, and according to the story Mullett said—you know that clubfooted humor of his—'I don't think we need take Miss Manning's desire to confer immortality on Mr. Stalin too seriously.' The Russians are tickled to death—my secretary heard them talking about it at the Press Department. What's more, it appears that the lady's heard about it, too, and she's furious."

"So that's why she's not on speaking terms with him!"

"I imagine so." Waterhouse balanced his vodka glass on his plate, preparatory to moving off. "Now who, I wonder, would appreciate that little story?" He gazed round the room again as though choosing a suitable recipient for his conversation, and his eye rested for a moment on Tranter. "It's odd, you know—I can't help feeling I've seen that fellow before somewhere, but for the life of me I can't remember where. . . . Ah, well, excuse me." He wandered off, and soon I saw him bending toward one of the agency men.

A waiter swept past me with a loaded tray, and an eddy of humanity carried me to the side of Joe Cressey, who was with Tanya and Tranter. At the same time, Bolting converged on the group.

"Oh, yes, the factory was all right," Cressey was saying, apparently in reply to a question from Tanya, "but what surprises me is the way ordinary everyday things don't get seen to here. You don't seem to be what I'd call thorough. Only this morning I was looking out of my window and three times I saw one of those trolley arms jerk off the wire at the same place. There must be some little thing wrong, but nobody seems to bother. Now why's that?"

"I was watching exactly the same thing last Sunday," said Potts, who had crept up on us silently. "In three hours it happened twenty-two times."

Bolting gave him much the same sort of look that Jeff had done. "Quite a vigil, Mr. Potts!"

"Actually I was reading, but the flashes made me look up. I estimated that only seventy-three per cent of the buses got through without trouble. It was really quite an amusing sight."

Tranter said mildly, "I dare say you'd find just as much to amuse you at home, Mr. Potts, if you kept your eyes open there as well." It was the first time I'd been really close to Tranter, and I turned to have a good look at him. He had seemed so quiet and undistinguished at first sight, and until now I'd never noticed how extraordinarily cold his blue eyes were. There was no mildness there! I began to wonder if I'd been mistaken in the man.

"At least, Mr. Cressey," said Tanya, smiling prettily, "you must admit that our trolleybus girls are very efficient at scrambling onto the roofs of the buses to fix things." She was looking directly at him as she spoke, and I had the impression, not for the first time, that she was deliberately trying to cultivate him. Perhaps she was intended to be part of the Soviet embrace. She looked very dashing in a little black suit with gilt frogging. Jeff's nylons couldn't have been shown off to better advantage, and her exquisite small shoes were far too frivolous to have been bought in Moscow. I thought again how very attractive she was, with her high cheekbones, lovely complexion and dancing blue eyes. She might be all the things Jeff knew she was, but I felt pretty sure he'd miss her.

Bolting intercepted her smile. "Would you think me an enemy of the people," he asked, "if I told you of a funny incident I once saw in that square?" His usually melodious voice was a trifle husky, as though he were just starting a cold.

Tanya said, "Not you, Mr. Bolting," with a reproachful glance at Potts.

"Well, it was one summer during the war. I was sitting out on my balcony, and just across the road was a trolleybus stop. A man had been watering the streets with a hose from a hydrant, and he'd left the hose leaning against something and still sluicing out water while he went off somewhere. It was very hot, and all the buses had their windows down, and one of them pulled up at the stop with its first window right in the line of fire. The passengers yelled, of course, and the driver realized that something was wrong and moved forward. But he did it very slowly, so that the hose played the whole way along the bus. All the passengers were soaked, and they were all yelling like mad. It was quite one of the funniest things I've seen."

"In the summer, at least, it wouldn't hurt them," said Tanya, smiling in spite of herself. "They would soon dry." She sighed. "If only it were summer now! Mr. Cressey, why did you have to come in the winter—that was a mistake. Russia is so beautiful in the summer—the wide fields and the flowers and the big rivers."

"It can be lovely in winter, too," I said. "Hundreds of miles of virgin steppes, with the smooth snow lying in wind ridges, blue in the shadow, yellow in the sun. Wonderful!"

"I agree, Mr. Verney, but I still prefer the summer. The Caucasus in the summer is heavenly. Last year I was there for six whole weeks."

"That's a long holiday," remarked Cressey.

"It was at a rest home for workers. You know our workers have wonderful holidays, all quite free." Tanya didn't explain the selection system. "It was near Mount Elbruz, and on one expedition I climbed four thousand meters, right up into a glacier. It was a mass climb in celebration of the founding of the autonomous republic—very exciting, with ice picks and ropes. A special postage stamp was struck in honor of the event."

"Talking of postage stamps," said Tranter, "I'm reminded that I promised a nephew to take some back with me. I mustn't forget."

"I will go with you to the post office myself," Tanya said, "and I will choose you a beautiful selection. You, too, Mr. Cressey—you must take some of our stamps back with you. They are very artistic."

"They're not much good from the collector's point of view," said Cressey. "You've printed too many of them."

Bolting laughed. "Joe," he said, "I sometimes think you deliberately set out to be difficult. Now why don't you accept Miss Tanya's offer nicely—you can always learn something fresh, you know."

"Well, you see . . ." began Cressey, but before he could begin to explain Jeff burst upon us with apologies, and took Tanya's arm. "Honey," he said, "would you come and translate something for me? There's a guy here who's trying to tell me about some meteorite that fell last year. . . ."

Tanya said, "Will you excuse me?" and followed Jeff through the crowd, taking Cressey along with her. The others began to circulate—all except Bolting. As I turned to the table to refill my glass he picked up a bottle of wine and examined the label. "Tsinandali 1933," he said. "An excellent wine—very sound indeed. Will you join me, Mr. Verney?"

"With pleasure. Are you a connoisseur?"

"Only in a very minor way." He filled my glass and then his own and looked at me oddly. "So in spite of your political prejudices, Mr. Verney, I gather you like this country. Shall we drink to eternal Russia?"

I smiled. "I'll be happy to join you in that."

We drank, savoring the wine, which was indeed not at all bad. Bolting, who was evidently in an expansive mood, said, "I was born here, you know."

"Is that so? Then that accounts for your fluent Russian at the meeting the other night. I wondered how you'd managed to get such a perfect accent."

"Yes, I was born in Baku, actually. English parents—my father was an oil engineer. I left Russia when I was ten, but I went to school in Baku for a bit."

"Not a very salubrious spot."

"No, oil towns never are. It was handy for the Crimea and the Caucasus, though, and I developed a liking for the country that I've never lost. Did you ever happen to take a long sleigh ride over those steppes you were talking about?"

"That's something I missed, I'm afraid."

"It's a wonderful way of getting about. Bumpy over the ridges, but when you get a smooth stretch it's like floating on a cloud."

He smiled—his charm was quite disconcerting. Of course, if he'd been born in Russia that might easily account for his current fellow traveling, though he wasn't a man I'd have suspected of sentiment. There was one thing about Bolting—he didn't obtrude his political views on every possible occasion, as Mullett did.

Presently Schofield joined us. He looked, for once, less like a cold fish than a fish out of water. "Regrettable institutions, these parties," he said, with a nod to me. "Don't you think so, Bolting? Noise is a poor substitute for conversation."

"Have a glass of Tsinandali, Professor, and drown the noise."

"No, thank you, I've already eaten and drunk to excess. Our hosts are very attentive." With a little cough, he added, "A delightful young lady has just been telling me how a Russian named—er—Popov, I think—invented electricity." He gave me a sidelong glance, and Bolting grinned. Their attitude baffled me.

"Professor," I said, "I don't want to start a long discussion but could you tell me in a few words what it is about the Soviet Union that has attracted you to its side. I'm really intrigued to know."

"Certainly, Mr. Verney. Gravitational pull. Marxism is a huge and growing force—whether one likes it or not is quite irrelevant. Personally I take a poor view of creation, but I accept it. It is foolish to resist the irresistible."

I laughed, and so did Bolting. "Talking of the irresistible, Schofield," he said, "there's a very clever woman I should like you to meet. . . ."

I moved on thoughtfully through the crowd. The party was certainly warming up now. Champagne had arrived with the ice cream and was flowing freely. A burst of laughter came from a corner table where Tanya, Jeff, Potts, Thomas and Cressey were sitting with a group of Russians. At another table, Mrs. Clarke was wedged happily between Mullett and a Russian colonel, all her resentments forgotten. She seemed to have lost whatever awe she might once have felt for the reverend gentleman, and was archly trying to make him take a large glass of champagne.

"A pleasant party, Mr. Verney," said a voice at my ear. It was Tranter again, his usually pale face quite pink and his white hair falling in a damp lock over one ear.

"It certainly is," I acknowledged. "In fact, one way and another it's been quite a week."

"A memorable week. I must confess it's been a great delight to me to find how extremely friendly everyone has been. In existing circumstances, one could have forgiven them for showing a certain—well—mistrust . . ."

He was hopeless, of course. He hadn't even begun to understand.

"That big meeting we had," he went on, "it was so heartening. I'm a little surprised that it wasn't reported more fully in the British press. I cannot believe that we shall ever find ourselves at war with such cordial people."

"It would be a tragic thing," I said, "for everyone."

"It astounds me that there are those who can contemplate it. Have you ever seen battle, Mr. Verney?"

"Only as a war correspondent."

"Ah, yes, of course. At least you know what it means. I've had my share of it. This leg . . ." he patted his stiff thigh, ". . . was the result of a wound I got on the Somme in the first war. I was just eighteen. When I came out of the army I resolved that I would devote the rest of my life to the struggle for peace. A long, hard, disappointing struggle it's been, I'm afraid."

I had to agree. "Is the society you represent completely pacifist?" I asked him.

"Oh, by no means. I happen to be a pacifist myself, but my committee is not. Nor, of course, are the Russians—one has to admit that. At the same time, I feel there is a will to peace in this country—they have suffered so much, it's inconceivable that they'd want to fight again. Ah, well, we must go on trying. . . ."

He moved on. I helped myself to a glass of champagne from a passing waiter and glanced around to see if I could spot a friendly blonde. There seemed to be a spare one near the elite's table, and I moved over. Perdita, incredibly, was still holding forth. They hadn't even got off the original subject, and she was making some preposterous statements. "In England," I heard her drawl, "there's practically no interest in culture, of course—just a huge unsatisfied demand for entertainment."

Mirnova was watching her with that misleadingly innocent expression of hers. "I was thinking, Miss Manning, that you should make a broadcast about Soviet culture."

"I should love to," said Perdita, "but I thought you'd arranged that Mr. Mullett should broadcast for the delegation."

"That is true. Mr. Mullett will be broadcasting tomorrow, but in Russian, for *our* people. It would be nice if you could talk next week in our program for England. You can say exactly what you like, of course."

"I feel honored," said Perdita.

"Then I shall ask the Radio Center to arrange it with you."

There was a sudden hush in the room as the president of VOKS clapped his hands for attention. "And now," said Mirnova, "I think that Madame Lamarkina is going to sing for us."

IV

JEFF GAVE a small party of his own on the Sunday evening —life was like that in Moscow—and as I had nothing whatever to do I dropped in early. It had been a day of rest for the delegation and by all appearances most of them were still resting, for there was an air of somnolence about the warm, dimly lit corridor. How long it would last was another matter, for Nikolai seemed to be very busy attending to orders for bottles of this and that. I think he was finding the delegation a full-time job.

Zina, Jeff's secretary, let me in. I'd got used to her by now, but I confess I'd had a bit of a shock on first seeing her. She was very plump and very blonde and positively bursting with Russian vitality. Beside Zina, everyone else seemed just a little less than life-size, and just a bit pallid. Although she wasn't by any means young she loved wearing bright colors and extremely short silk frocks—she had very pretty ankles—and she simply adored parties.

Jeff called a greeting from the bathroom and suggested I should mix the cocktails. There were the ingredients for a good one, for he'd been accumulating pink champagne and cognac over the past week and Tanya had wheedled a lump of ice out of Nikolai. I sliced some lemon peel and stirred the concoction gently in a big glass bowl. Zina, who—as Jeff had said—was as much a housekeeper as a secretary, was preparing a buffet supper of immense complexity, and I had to break off for a moment to open one of those tins which are so easy to deal with if the key isn't lost, and such a devil if it is. There was also a good deal of clearing up to be done; for a man who hadn't filed anything longer than a service message in a month Jeff managed to give his room an astonishingly busy appearance, and his office junk was lying everywhere. By the time he emerged we'd made the place presentable and were ready to get down to the serious business of the evening.

He looked, I thought, slightly peeved, and I asked him what was the trouble.

"Oh, Tanya's got stuck with some work for the delegation," he said. "Typing some bloody nonsense for Mullett. How I hate that guy!"

"You mean she won't be coming?" I said. It was unthinkable that in Moscow anyone should put work before a party.

"Maybe later on, she says. I guess I'll be able to prize her away. Anyway, let's sample this poison of yours." He poured three glasses and we drank.

"Wow!" he said. "Not bad—not bad at all! Ah, here's someone else we can try it on."

It was Waterhouse, and he also had his secretary with him. Her name was Vera, and she was the complete opposite of Zina. She was slender and dark-featured, and she had the most gloomy countenance I've ever seen—so excessively gloomy that Jeff said she always made him feel cheerful by contrast. She seemed to personify all the cold and hardship and suffering of Mother Russia, but her moroseness was partly redeemed by a subtle sense of humor and a rare, slow smile.

Waterhouse proved to be in great form. He was a man whose whole being could be warmed for hours by the recollection of a single felicitous remark, and he was still savoring one of Perdita's. Apparently he'd been telling Joe Cressey that morning about a particularly unpleasant bit of graft that some house manager in the Arbat had been involved in, and Perdita, who was listening, had rebuked him. "You only see the dead fish floating on the pond," she had said. "You never look below into the crystal beauty of the Soviet pool."

We agreed that it was choice, and the secretaries appreciated it as much as we did. They were odd creatures. You'd have thought that they would have resented the criticisms they so often heard of their Soviet way of life, but they never seemed to mind. After their long association with correspondents, I think they'd become as politically neutral as microphones.

A couple of American agency chaps came next, trailing a small cloud of pneumatic blondes. One of the men, named Wheeler, said as he shut the door behind him, "Looks like Mrs. Clarke's been hitting the bottle again."

"She can't blame the Russians today," I said.

"I guess she's taken to secret drinking. We just passed her in the corridor—she's practically ricocheting from wall to wall."

At that moment Potts arrived and completed the party. He'd been doing some of his mass observation—"Potts' Poll," Jeff called it—on the second floor, and as usual he was full of information on all sorts of recondite topics.

"By the way, there's something special happening down there tonight," he said. "I think it must be a meeting of some sort—I just saw Goldstein arrive." Goldstein was a big shot in the Party's Propaganda Section.

Waterhouse gave him a twinkling glance. "A smart newspaperman would have interviewed him, Mr. Potts."

"I hardly think that would have been possible," said Potts seriously. "My corridor seems to be full of those M.V.D. men. I wonder why they all wear black cloth caps?"

Jeff thrust a glass into his hand. "Here, get a hold of this, will you, and for Pete's sake let's not talk about the Party or the M.V.D. or the delegation. This may be my last Sunday evening here and I want to have happy memories. Cheers, all of you!"

That was the beginning of a pretty good evening. Zina's buffet supper went down very well and after supper, inevitably, we sang. Zina had the most vibrant soprano voice I've ever heard and she gave us several unaccompanied solos without a trace of inhibition. Then we had a female chorus, which was really something, and afterward Vera, who could only dirge, dirged a convict song about shackled figures trudging through the snow that made Jeff weep with laughter. When we'd all just about sung ourselves hoarse the ever-competent Zina produced an old portable gramophone and we danced. By this time we'd all had a fair amount to drink and the blondes were giggly and everyone was having a very carefree time. Jeff took a few turns with one of the girls and then he broke off and said, "Say, do you folks mind if I take a little drink in to Tanya? Poor kid, it's a darned shame, missing all this."

We told him to go ahead, and he filled a glass rather too full and walked rather too carefully to the door with it, losing not more than half on the way.

"I suspect," said Waterhouse, "that that is the last we shall see of Mr. Clayton for some time."

Vera had gone to sleep, and Potts said his feet ached and he'd like to wind the gramophone, so there were just four couples and we went on dancing. It was shortly after nine o'clock, while a record was being changed, that Waterhouse suddenly cocked an ear and said, "Listen—isn't that Mullett broadcasting?"

There did seem to be a familiar sound coming from the direction of the street. I opened the *fortachka* a little—we needed air, anyway—and sure enough it was Mullett, being relayed from the public loud speakers on the corner of the square. He wasn't doing too well, either—his Russian, as usual, was wretched and he kept stumbling over his script. His subject matter was nauseating.

"Do we *have* to listen to that guy?" asked Wheeler. "I thought this was a day of rest."

I shut the *fortachka*, trapping a block of air that must have been at least twenty below. I could still hear Mullett droning away and now that my attention was caught I found it difficult to disregard him. Zina took over the gramophone and put on a famous guerrilla song about the beauties of fog which wasn't much better than Mullett. There was a bit of an argument and the record got broken. Soon we were dancing again.

Presently Jeff came back, looking a little the worse for wear. "I can't drag her away," he said. His speech was slurred and he was evidently feeling sorry for himself. "Typewriter's redhot—won't stop for a second—never saw such baloney." He seized a blonde. "Baby, let's dance."

It was a quick fox trot, and we let ourselves go. The girls knew some of the words and sang them. Vera had woken up and was dirging the tune about half a bar behind. Every now and again there were uncontrollable collisions and much loud laughter. We were all pretty buzzed. When the record ended I could just hear Mullett moving into his peroration.

Suddenly there was a loud hammering on the door and an agitated cry. I was nearest, so I opened it. Nikolai was standing there, wringing his hands and almost incoherent with distress. "*Gospodeen* Verney," he gasped, "please come—oh, it's terrible, *terrible*. . . ." His old face was as white as his apron.

"What is it—what's happened?"

"*Gospodeen* Mullett—he's had an accident, a shocking accident. In his room. Oh, *bozhe moi*, I think he's dead."

V

I KNEW there must be some mistake, but that wasn't the moment to argue. Mullett's door was open and I rushed in, with Jeff at my heels and the others crowding behind.

Well, it was Mullett all right! I thought at first that I must be having hallucinations, but there was no mistake. He was lying crumpled up near the table, and on the carpet beside his head there was a huge patch of blood. I bent over him and saw that he was quite dead. Strewn beside him were the shattered fragments of a mineral-water bottle. A wallet protruded from his inner breast pocket as though it had been hastily stuffed back, and papers were strewn beside him.

"My God," I said, "he's been bashed with a bottle. He's been murdered!" At that moment, the radio voice outside suddenly stopped. It was uncanny.

"That broadcast must have been a recording," said Jeff. He was looking rather white, and the shock had sobered him completely. "Well, bud—we've got a story at last!"

There was a brief moment of quiet after that. The girls had rushed out of the room, Waterhouse had gone off to get the manager, and Potts to knock up a doctor who lived on his floor. The agency fellows were questioning Nikolai in the corridor and momentarily Jeff and I were left alone. Jeff gazed around and suddenly said, "What's that on the floor? Quick, grab it!" I pounced. It was a sealed envelope, unstamped, and it was addressed in Russian typing to "Miss Perdita Manning, Astoria Hotel." I showed it to Jeff and, on impulse, slipped it into my pocket. He nodded approval.

Then everything started to happen at once. People were appearing from all directions, and in a few moments pandemonium had broken loose. A chambermaid looked in and went out screaming, and Schofield shot across the corridor from his room opposite, and Tanya burst in wanting to know what on earth was happening and took one look at Mullett's head and collapsed in a faint. The floor manageress arrived, and Waterhouse with the manager, and presently the doctor turned up, and Islwyn and Bolting, and hordes of Russians. Perdita came in, said, "Oh my God, how horrible!" and went out looking as though she were going to be sick. The babel was unspeakable, both inside and outside the room. In the middle of all the confusion a man arrived from the Radio Center with, of all things, a package for Mullett.

I took advantage of the temporary chaos to have a look round the room and try to fix the scene in my mind. The room itself was practically a replica of mine, except that everything was the other way round. There was a tray on the floor by the door—Nikolai's tray—with a full bottle of mineral water on it. There was a screwed-up hand towel lying near the body, and when I looked in the bathroom I saw that Mullett's hand towel was missing. I glanced automatically at the balcony windows, but of course like everyone else's they were sealed. There were no clues that I could see, unless you counted a soaking wet, two-day-old copy of *Pravda* and an empty tin with a trace of water at the bottom which I unearthed from the wastepaper basket and put back there. Apart from a framed picture of Stalin that hung slightly askew on the wall and looked as though it might have been jerked out of place there were no indications of a struggle. I'd have liked to go over the room with a fine comb but in a few minutes a couple of militiamen arrived and after some noisy argument we were all drummed out into the corridor. The door was closed on Mullett and whatever secrets his room held, and one of the militiamen mounted guard over it. The other instructed us not to leave but made no attempt to question anybody. Higher authority was evidently being invoked.

The newspapermen were trying to get as much information as they could while the opportunity lasted. Nikolai had already told his story. He had, it seemed, been crossing the fourth floor landing soon after nine o'clock on his way to the kitchen when Mullett had stepped from the lift and called to him to bring a fresh bottle of mineral water to his room. Nikolai had collected the mineral water and some vodka for two other rooms and had taken it along the corridor. Mullett's door had been ajar. He'd knocked, and as he'd received no reply he'd gone in, intending to leave the new bottle and take away the old one. He'd seen Mullett lying on the floor soaked in blood, and had come straight along to tell us. He was asked if he'd seen anyone else in the corridor at the time and he said he didn't think so, but he was evidently badly shaken and not in the best condition to remember.

It was almost impossible to get anything like a clear picture of events because of all the chatter and confusion, but the floor manageress, who had been sitting at her desk near the lift, made an interesting contribution. It was actually to the manager she was talking, but we hovered on the edge of the conversation and they were both too knocked off balance to bother about us. It seemed that Mullett had stopped to collect his key from her in the usual way and that as he'd turned to leave, Mrs. Clarke had appeared on the landing in a rather noisy state. Mullett had rebuked her for her behavior and Mrs. Clarke had been extremely abusive in reply. She'd followed him and continued to abuse him as he went off to his room.

I looked around for Mrs. Clarke, but she was one of the delegates who hadn't put in an appearance. It seemed worth while to find out what had happened to her, so I slipped along to her room to see if she was there. She was, but she evidently wasn't in a condition to come to the door. All the reply I got was a slurred "Lemme alone, can't you?" I called through the door and told her there'd been an accident, but even that didn't register. Finally I gave it up and returned to the throng in the corridor.

The man from the Radio Center was still clutching his package and looking as though he didn't know what to do about it. I stopped to talk to him, thinking that perhaps he could clear up the mystery of the Mullett broadcast. He turned out not to be a Russian, except by adoption—he was actually, judging by his slight cockney accent, a Londoner.

"Oh, yes," he said, in a quick, rather ingratiating voice, "I can tell you about Mr. Mullett. You see, he came along about seven to rehearse his talk, but his Russian was so bad that we didn't dare let him go on the air 'live.' He was meant to, but Mr. Kolarov wouldn't risk it. It was a good thing he didn't, too, because we had to make three recordings before we got a passable one." He gave an agitated glance in the direction of the crowd. "It's a terrible thing about Mr. Mullett, isn't it?"

I agreed that it was.

He tapped the package. "I brought this record for him—his talk, you know. Mr. Kolarov thought he'd like it, so I was sent after him. I'm really the assistant announcer. I suppose the only thing is to take it back when the police'll let me." He shot another quick glance to right and left and licked his lips.

I thanked him for his information and passed on. Jeff was back in the corridor, busily trying to piece things together, but he hadn't been able to find out much. Apparently none of the delegates had seen or heard anything that threw any light on the murder. Perdita, Bolting, Thomas and Schofield had been in their rooms all the evening. Cressey, who had turned up in the middle of all the confusion, had been taking a solitary walk round the Kremlin walls. Of Tranter there was still no sign, and nobody seemed to have any idea where he was.

In about fifteen minutes higher authority began to arrive, and thereafter kept on arriving in a steady stream. First came a bunch of obvious plain-clothes men whom I took to be the equivalent of our C.I.D. I'd have given a lot to watch them at work, but they disappeared into Mullett's room with cameras and little attaché cases and an Iron Curtain closed down behind them. Meanwhile, high officials were arriving in droves, all very grave and anxious—the president of VOKS and Mirnova to soothe and shepherd the delegation, and several chaps from the Soviet Foreign Office, and the head of the Sovinformburo, and others whom none of us knew and who were probably big-shot security officers from the M.V.D. After a while a stocky little man with a bald head and shrewd gray eyes and an air of authority started to sort us out and ask questions. He did it in the smoothest way, and seemed most anxious not to offend. The questioning took a long time, but as far as I could see nothing of any value emerged. What he mainly wanted to know, of course, was whether anyone had seen anyone go into or out of Mullett's room at the material time, but no one had. Nikolai repeated his story, but couldn't add to it. The floor manageress mentioned Mrs. Clarke, and was discreetly taken aside. Jeff was asked if Mullett's door had been ajar when he'd taken the drink to Tanya and when he'd returned from her room, and he said he couldn't be sure but he didn't think so. The man from the Radio Center explained his business on the fourth floor and left his package with the police. A lot of Russians were questioned, a shade more brusquely, but to no effect, and that was about all. The hotel residents were asked to return to their rooms, and the VOKS people went along to Bolting's room with the delegates to talk over the terrible occurrence. Gradually the hotel quieted down.

I typed out a cable for my paper and rang for my messenger to take it across to the censor. There was little one could say at this stage, and in any case the Russians would almost certainly hold up our stories until they'd had a chance to investigate the crime. When the cable was out of the way I walked past Mullett's guarded door and went in to talk to Jeff.

In the next hour or so we discussed the murder from every angle. The time of it, fortunately, could be narrowed to a very short period. Mullett hadn't come in until well after nine— about ten past nine, Nikolai had told the police, and the floor manageress had confirmed that—and his body had been found just before 9:25, when the broadcast had stopped. Fifteen minutes. But it must have taken a little time for Mullett to walk along the corridor and get rid of Mrs. Clarke, and for the murderer to approach; and a little more time at the end for the murderer to get clear. Say ten minutes. Whoever had followed Mullett in, or been admitted by him, had evidently acted with speed and decision.

The fact that the wallet and its contents had obviously been tampered with suggested theft as a motive—but theft of what? Neither of us could believe that Mullett had been killed on a sudden impulse for the money he was carrying—he was most unlikely to have had much, and anyway the Astoria was an improbable setting for that sort of robbery. You could expect to have your linen filched but not your head cracked. Dark alleys were the place for small-time "hit-and-grab."

If, on the other hand, the motive had been theft of something more important than money—something that we didn't know about but the murderer did—then at once there was a snag. Theft of that sort spelled premeditation. Yet a blow with a bottle that happened to be lying around suggested sudden anger or fear, rather than premeditation. It was a dangerous weapon for the user, even if a towel *had* been wrapped round the neck of the bottle, for the murderer could easily have been badly cut and that would have given his identity away. It didn't even strike us as a very efficient weapon. People had often been hit with bottles and recovered.

Of course, all that disarray of wallet and papers might have been a blind—theft might not have been the motive at all. The murderer might have stepped in and had a quarrel with Mullett, and that would have accounted for the unpremeditated appearance of the killing. All the same, it seemed hardly possible that a fortuitous quarrel could have blown up and been so violently settled in so short a space of time.

There were other puzzling things—loads of them. We both found it quite impossible to imagine the circumstances in which a murderer could have been let in by Mullett and could somehow have managed to get through into his bedroom and bathroom and collect the bottle from his bed table and wrap it in a towel and strike a blow with it, all without apparent objection or resistance from his intended victim. It didn't make sense—not even if he'd been well-known to Mullett and trusted by him.

It was odd, too, that the murderer had left the door open behind him. If he'd shut it, surely he'd have had more time for a clean getaway?

If the motive hadn't been theft at all, but something more personal, the choice of suspects seemed narrow. It was, of course, just conceivable that Mullett might have made some enemy during one of his earlier visits to Russia, and that this was the pay-off, but it was rather more conceivable that one of the delegates had done it. Several of them had had the opportunity. Mrs. Clarke, certainly. Schofield, certainly. There was no corroboration that Bolting and Thomas and Perdita had been in their rooms, as they had said. Cressey was in the clear if he'd really been walking round the Kremlin, but Tranter's story was still to be heard.

Mrs. Clarke, of course, was the most obvious suspect. She'd not merely been around—she'd been intoxicated, and she'd been heard squabbling with Mullett, and she'd been seen to follow him. It was possible that she had pursued him into his room and continued the quarrel. But nobody seemed to have heard her in the corridor and it was equally possible that she had gone straight to her own room. Besides, neither of us could seriously believe that, even in her cups, she would have gone to the length of hitting Mullett with a bottle. She had succumbed to Russian hospitality, but she was essentially a repectable woman, not a slum brawler. It was one of those things that physically could *just* have happened, but that simply didn't carry any conviction.

What about the others? I thought back over the long journey I'd made with the delegation, and all the little animosities that had revealed themselves, then and since. No one had really liked Mullett, of course. Bolting had been fairly neutral, but Schofield had been contemptuous, Joe Cressey had resented him, and Perdita—yes, Perdita had loathed him. Hurt vanity—that could lead to a lot of trouble. But Perdita with a bottle . . . ? Thomas hadn't been able to stomach him, either, and Thomas was a hothead—but not that hot, surely?

We were still considering the position of each delegate in turn when the bald, stocky little man who had questioned us knocked at the door.

"*Gospodeen* Verney?" he said, as Jeff opened up.

"*I'm* Verney," I called. "What is it?"

"Could you oblige me, perhaps, by lending me the key of your room and permitting me to enter?"

I was a little surprised. "Of course," I said, getting up and handing him the key. "What's the idea, though?"

"It is a question of what can be heard through the walls of *Gospodeen* Mullett's room," he explained. "We could make the tests here, but we do not wish to disturb you and as your room is empty . . ."

I shrugged. "That's all right with me. Do what you like." He thanked me politely and departed.

Jeff grinned. "I imagine you're high up on the list of suspects! Gee, I'd like to know what they're up to. Why didn't we ask that guy if they've found any clues yet?" Suddenly he gave an exclamation. "Say, we're a couple of boneheads. . . . What about that note you picked up?"

In all the excitement it had completely slipped my mind. Now I produced it and we had another look at the envelope.

"Let's steam it open," said Jeff.

That took a little time—it was an operation that neither of us was used to and it had to be done carefully. When we did finally extract the contents, they proved to be very disappointing. I think we'd both been hoping for some heart throb, though the official-looking typing should have told us. The note was simply a message from the Radio Center asking if the following Thursday at 8 p.m. would be a suitable time for Perdita to do a ten-minute broadcast to England on Soviet culture.

"So that's all it is," said Jeff disgustedly. "Hell! Well, I suppose we'd better seal it up again and shove it under her door."

"Half a minute," I said. "We still don't know how it got into Mullett's room."

"Isn't that pretty obvious? He happened to be over at the Radio Center so they asked him to bring it back with him, and he was careless and dropped it on the floor."

"That could be it, I suppose." I didn't feel so sure—somehow, I couldn't see them doing it. This was official business, and from their point of view important business. Russian bureaucrats didn't take chances, and Mullett was hardly a messenger boy. "I'd have thought one of their own people would have brought it. They could easily have given it to that chap they sent along with the recording. . . ."

Jeff's interest suddenly revived. "Holy smoke, I believe you've got something there. Maybe he *did* bring it—maybe he did the job. Don't you remember Waterhouse telling us the other day about some guy at the Radio Center who knew Mullett? This could be the guy. Didn't he have a grudge of some sort?"

"Easy, Jeff!" I protested. "This fellow didn't arrive until after the body was found. I saw him join the crowd."

"Maybe you did," said Jeff, "but you didn't see him come into the hotel. He may have been around for quite a time before you noticed him. I agree it's a long shot, but I'd sure like to hear what he has to say."

"That shouldn't be too difficult." I went to the phone and looked up the Radio Center number. I'd remembered now that the man's behavior *had* been a bit odd.

There was the usual bother with the exchange, but the connection was made at last and I asked for the English Talks Section. An American voice answered me—a woman's voice.

"This is George Verney of the London *Record*," I told her. "I was talking a little while ago to a man from your outfit who brought a recording to the Astoria Hotel for Mr. Mullett. Can you tell me if he's around?—I don't know his name."

"Hold the line," said the voice. There was a slight commotion at the other end, and then a man's voice said quickly, "This is Arthur Gain speaking, Mr. Verney. Did you want me?"

I recognized the cockney accent and the faintly sycophantic tone. "Yes," I said. "I wondered if by any chance you'd lost a letter."

There was a long silence—so long that I began to think he must have left the receiver. But he was there all right. "As a matter of fact, I have," he said, much more slowly. I could almost hear him thinking. "It's—it's a bit awkward. Have you got it?"

I shot Jeff a swift glance. "Yes, I've got it."

"Oh." I thought I detected a note of relief in the monosyllable. "I suppose . . . I suppose you couldn't send it along to the right quarter for me, could you?"

Considering everything, I thought the request pretty cool. "Certainly not until I've seen you," I told him. "It was found in a rather peculiar place."

There was another pregnant silence. "All right," he said at last, "I'll come round to you. I can't come tonight, though—I'm on duty. I'll come tomorrow morning at ten o'clock, Mr. Verney, if that suits you."

"That's okay."

"You won't . . . ?" he began hesitantly, and then stopped. He was in a spot, of course, with people in the room listening.

"I won't tell anyone about it till then, if that's what you're trying to say." I hung up.

Jeff got to his feet and stretched. "It looks like this case is going to be a short one," he said. "I guess I'll go to bed."

VI

GAIN TURNED up the following morning on the stroke of ten. The acute nervousness which he showed as he slipped into my room was not unconnected, I felt, with the watchful interest of the plain-clothes man posted outside Mullett's door. The fact that he had come at all was a sign of his desperation. He was slightly out of breath and very pale, as though he hadn't had much sleep.

"Better take your coat off," I said. "We may be here for some time." I studied him with a good deal more interest than on the previous evening. He was a man of about forty, thin and hollow-cheeked, with unkempt hair and dark, restless eyes and a sullen, downward-drooping mouth. Not, on close inspection, by any means a prepossessing character.

I went to the phone and told Jeff our visitor had arrived. Gain stiffened with fright. "You said you wouldn't tell anyone, Mr. Verney."

"Clayton was here last night when I phoned you," I told him shortly. "He heard everything."

I turned away, not wanting to look at the man. He seemed a pitiful, nerveless creature, and I wasn't feeling very happy about the interview. I had no *locus standi* in the matter except that I had happened to pick up the letter, and little more than an academic interest in who had killed the egregious Mullett. Getting a story was one thing, but personally hounding a creature like Gain was quite another. I was almost sorry we hadn't let the letter lie, and felt glad when Jeff came in to share the burden.

He gave Gain one quick look, said "Hi," and dropped into a chair. "Okay, George, shoot!"

I produced the letter, which by now was carefully sealed up again, and showed it to Gain. He looked at it with undisguised relief. "Yes, that's it," he said. "Where did you find it, Mr. Verney?"

"Don't you know?"

His eyes flicked from me to Jeff and back again. "Was it in Mr. Mullett's room?"

"It was."

"I thought I must have dropped it there," he said. "Gosh, I'm glad it was you that found it. When the phone rang at the office last night, I made sure it must be the police. If they'd spotted it, it would have been all up with me."

I couldn't understand him at all. In the circumstances, his manner struck me as being confidential to the point of naïveté. "Mr. Gain," I said, "you gave the impression last night, to the police and to us, that you arrived on the scene after Mr. Mullett's body had been found. You may think it's no business of ours, but we would be interested to know just how and when the letter got into Mullett's room."

"Of course I'll tell you," he said with an ingratiating smile that was worse than the scared look. "You're English—I can trust you. I've nothing to hide, Mr. Verney, not from you, or from Mr. Clayton. I know what you're thinking—you're thinking it was me that killed Mr. Mullett. I didn't, though— you're quite wrong."

"How did the letter get there?" asked Jeff.

"I'll tell you—from the beginning. You see, just after Mr. Mullett left our place the record was brought in wrapped up and ready for him, and as I hadn't to announce for a bit Mr. Kolarov asked me to slip over here with it and to bring the letter for Miss Manning at the same time. I got here just after Mr. Mullett, and I asked at the desk downstairs for the numbers of the rooms, and then I came up here and knocked at his door."

"See anyone else about?" Jeff inquired.

Gain hesitated. "No, the corridor was empty. The room wasn't, though. I heard voices inside—people talking. Two people, I think. I couldn't hear very well, but they were English voices, I can tell you that. Probably Mr. Mullett and whoever did him in. Anyway, I knocked twice but it didn't seem as though they wanted to be disturbed, because no one answered the door."

"Were they quarreling?"

"I—I couldn't say, really. I suppose they must have been." Jeff snorted.

I said, "So what did you do?"

"Well, I thought I might as well deliver the letter to Miss Manning and come back to Mr. Mullett afterward, so I went along to her room. I'd been told to deliver it personally, so I knocked, but she wasn't in."

"You mean she didn't answer," Jeff said.

Gain looked puzzled. "She wasn't there, Mr. Clayton. I'm sure she wasn't. I knocked twice."

"You couldn't have knocked hard enough," I said. "I think you're lying. Miss Manning says she was in her room all the evening."

Gain cringed. "I swear I'm telling you the truth, Mr. Verney. I did go there, and I knocked very hard, and I listened, too. It's very quiet there, round the corner at the end of the corridor, but there wasn't a sound."

Jeff said, "It wouldn't have been a woman's voice you heard in Mullett's room, would it?"

"It might have been, Mr. Clayton. I couldn't be sure, though."

I looked hard at him. He was a slippery, evasive customer, if ever there was one. "Well, go on," I said, "finish your story. What did you do next?"

"I came back to Mr. Mullett's room," Gain said, with gathering fluency, "and this time his door was open a little and there didn't seem to be anyone about. I knocked, and when I still didn't get any answer I put my head inside and there was Mr. Mullett lying on the floor with blood all over him. I went right in and saw that he was dead. I was too ruddy scared to tell anyone and I felt like dashing out of the hotel but I couldn't leave just like that because I'd got the package to deliver. I rushed out of the room and went along to the cloakroom to think out what to do. After I'd been there a few minutes I suddenly noticed that the letter was missing— I'd tucked it under the string of the package, and it must have dropped out. I got in a real panic, then, because I thought I might have dropped it in Mr. Mullett's room and that would show I'd been there. I was in such a sweat I couldn't face going back to look for it, not right away. I—I just didn't know what to do. Anyway, in the end I did see I'd simply got to risk it and I was just going to leave the cloakroom when I heard an awful shemozzle along the corridor, and I knew that the body had been discovered. After that, I simply couldn't think at all—I was just dithering, Mr. Verney, and that's a fact. I joined in with the crowd and looked around for the letter, but I couldn't see it anywhere, and I felt sure the police would get hold of it. And that's all—you know the rest." He mopped his forehead with a grubby handkerchief and looked anxiously at us in turn.

Jeff stirred. "I don't get it, Mr. Gain. It's a slick story, but what did you have to be so scared about? You find an open door and a corpse—okay, that's unpleasant, but why panic about it?"

"I thought they might think I'd done it as I was there."

"Because you'd known Mullett back in England and had a grudge against him?"

The scared look crept back into Gain's face. "It wasn't just that, Mr. Clayton. You see, there'd been a bit of trouble at the

Radio Center that evening. I'd—I'd said something to Mr. Mullett that he didn't quite like and he'd complained to Mr. Kolarov. I thought they might find out about that and think that I'd tried to get my own back on Mr. Mullett."

I nodded. "How did you come to know Mullett in the first place?"

"He taught at the school I went to when I was a kid," said Gain sullenly. "In Deptford."

"And then what? When did he suggest you should come out here?"

"It was in 1931," he said, running a thin hand through his untamed hair. "During the depression. I was a young chap, a fitter actually, but I couldn't get a job anywhere. You remember what it was like, Mr. Verney—two million unemployed and nothing but the ruddy dole. I got interested in Russia, like a lot of others, and went to meetings, and one day I heard Mr. Mullett talking about the place and it sounded pretty good, so as I'd known him when I was a kid I went up to him afterward and asked him what sort of chances there were in the Soviet Union for a young fellow like me. Well, he said there was a fine life for everybody here, particularly for chaps with a trade—he made it sound lovely. So, to cut a long story short, I came out here to work and everyone was so decent I decided to give up my British passport and become a Soviet citizen. That was about a month after I got here."

"I see. And yesterday evening, when you saw Mullett again, I suppose you told him it hadn't panned out so well, eh?"

For a moment Gain's eyes glittered, and I thought he was going to let himself go. At some time or other he must have been a man of fair spirit, to take a chance in a new country and burn his boats behind him. Then he glanced toward the door, and the sullen expression came back into his face. "I wouldn't say that, Mr. Verney—that it hadn't panned out, I mean. Things could be worse. It was just that—well, last night I was a bit fed up with everything, being pushed around and so on, and when Mr. Mullett started saying what a lucky chap I was to have had twenty years in Russia I told him *I* wasn't on a delegation, just quietly like, and he took offense. But actually things aren't too bad—I wouldn't like you to think I was complaining."

For a moment I felt profoundly sorry for him. He was too scared to say what was in his mind, but I had a pretty good idea what he thought. I'd seen his type too often. He'd come out in the vigor of youth and the flush of high enthusiasm, full of big ideas about the new Utopia, and by the time he'd found out how wrong he'd been, it was too late to do anything about it. He'd become what almost all these expatriates became once they'd lost the protection of a foreign passport—a sort of half human, not Soviet and not foreign, not accepted and not rejected, politically just a "poor white." He'd become disillusioned, frustrated and neurotic, and—I suspected—tortured by the thought of what he'd thrown away. He'd become a creature, and the only thing that surprised me was that he'd said anything to Mullett at all. Usually they were too thoroughly intimidated to raise a squeak, and the bitterness just festered.

Such a history commanded sympathy, but it also put Gain high up in the list of suspects. He might well have hated Mullett. He might have followed Mullett up to his room, nursing accumulated grievances, and delivered the record and struck the blow, and dropped the letter in his flight. Motive and opportunity were both good. If the Soviet police had found that letter he wouldn't have had a chance. All the same, I was inclined to believe his story, or at least to give it a run. Looking at him, I couldn't believe that he would have had the guts to hit Mullett. He was too conditioned to subservience. A single bitter retort under provocation—yes, that was possible, but not murder. I certainly had no desire to hand over either him or the letter to the Soviet police.

I was about to say something of the sort to Jeff when the

door flew open and Zina burst in unceremoniously. She had a typed sheet of paper in her hand and she looked ready to explode.

"Mr. Clayton," she said, "they've just sent this round from the Press Department. I simply can't believe it."

We all gathered round. Zina translated for Jeff's benefit and I looked over her shoulder and Gain peered round Jeff's shoulder. What I read left me gasping.

"As is known," the announcement ran, "Mr. Andrew Mullett, who has been leading a peace delegation to the Soviet Union, was found dead last evening in his room at the Astoria Hotel. As a result of swift and efficient police action, it has been established that Mr. Mullett was murdered by a waiter at the hotel, Nikolai Nikolaevitch Skaliga, who attempted to cover up a political motive by trying to make it appear that the object of the murder was theft. This secret White Guard and enemy of the Soviet people has now confessed that he committed this abominable crime at the instigation of Anglo-American agents seeking to disrupt peace and unleash a new war. The vile conspiracy is being unmasked with the utmost zeal."

For a moment I was too thunderstruck to speak. It was so utterly, incredibly, ludicrously monstrous! The idea that Nikolai, the mild, gentle, senescent Nikolai, would have hit Mullett on the head with a bottle was just a grotesquerie. Never, in a long experience of Soviet announcements, had I known a more fantastic allegation.

It was Gain who spoke first. "Well," he said, "that seems to let me out."

I swung round on him in a fury. "You damned fool! You don't believe this tripe?"

He shrugged, and it was apparent that he was quite ready to believe anything which removed suspicion from himself. "He's been arrested—he's confessed."

"Confessed!" My fingers itched to strike him. "You little swine, have you never heard of the M.V.D.?" I regretted having wasted even a moment's sympathy on him. "And anyway, if that's your attitude you've got quite a bit more explaining to do."

He took a step back. "I don't see what," he said, and swallowed. "I've told you everything."

"You told us that when you knocked at Mullett's door the first time, you heard English voices inside, and that one of them was probably the murderer. Remember? Well, whoever was with Mullett then, it certainly couldn't have been Nikolai, because he doesn't speak a word of English. It seems to me, Mr. Gain, that you are going to be the leading witness in Nikolai's defense! You can work out for yourself how long it'll be after that before the police decide you were a participant in this precious conspiracy."

The blood slowly drained from his face, and his eyes glittered in caverns of shadow. He stood stock still, his active, twisted mind groping for a plausible explanation. Finally, he found one.

"As a matter of fact," he said, watching us, "what I told you about hearing someone inside the room when I first went there wasn't true. I made it up because I was afraid you suspected *me*. The truth is that I didn't hear anything when I knocked."

"You rat!" muttered Jeff.

"What about Miss Manning?" I said. "*Did* you go to her room, or was that a lie, too?"

"It was true—I did go. Honestly, Mr. Verney."

"And she wasn't there?"

"No, she wasn't. There wasn't a sound. I wouldn't tell you a lie, not now, really I wouldn't."

I went and opened the door for him. He gathered up his things. "What about the letter?" he whined.

"What about it?"

"If it isn't delivered, I'll get into trouble."

"I'm sorry for you," I said. "As sorry for you as you are for Nikolai."

He made one last effort. "You won't let the police know—please, Mr. Verney."

"Get out," I said.

VII

"I GUESS we need a little fresh air," said Jeff, and opened the *fortachka*. "Okay, Zina, thanks for the good tidings!" He gave her shoulder a friendly slap of dismissal and she went out looking unusually subdued.

I sat down, feeling pretty sick. The thought of those thugs carting off old Nikolai in the middle of the night and getting to work on him in one of their underground cells just about turned my stomach.

"If he was a sensible guy," said Jeff, seeming to read my thoughts, "he'd tell them what they wanted to hear without arguing. Maybe he's not come to much harm—not yet."

I wasn't reassured. "They don't like things to be that easy," I said. "They like to beat it out of you."

I picked up the announcement and read it through again with mounting indignation. It wasn't merely the contents but the tone of it that made me see red—the laconic way in which it stated outrageous improbabilities as though they were established facts—the contemptuous "take it-or-leave-it" attitude, as though it had been prepared by cynics for morons.

Finally I threw it aside in disgust. "The damned effrontery of these people! Why, they don't even take the trouble to make it *sound* likely."

"They don't have to," said Jeff, "while they've got the four-letter boys to persuade doubters."

"But this is for the outside world as well—they expect *us* to swallow it. It's probably been put out on the radio already. Why, the thing's an insult to the human intelligence. Who do they think we are?" I paced up and down, hardly able to control myself. "God, I wish there was something we could do about it."

Jeff gave a wry smile. "I guess there's nothing short of war, chum."

I flung myself back into a chair. "It's such a bloody shame to pick on Nikolai. Why, you wouldn't find a gentler old boy if you searched for a year. 'Instigating a new war . . . !' What claptrap they talk!"

"The whole thing's screwy, if you ask me," said Jeff. "What do you suppose is in their minds? What's the idea?"

"God only knows. I suppose they're sore at having Mullett bumped off on their territory and they've pulled in the first handy person as a scapegoat."

"But why all this baloney about a conspiracy? Theft would have sounded a darned sight more likely."

I shrugged. "I suppose they found out that Nikolai was tied up with the old regime and they couldn't resist the temptation to make political capital out of the case. I don't know—perhaps I've got it all wrong, but I can't think of any other explanation."

Jeff got up. "Well, I guess I'll go down to the Press Department and see if they've got anything to add. Are you going to file?"

"Not now," I said. "If I wrote what I'm thinking I'd be given forty-eight hours to leave. Besides, what's the use?—you know they won't pass a line."

"Okay, bud—see you later."

I lit my pipe and wandered over to the window. I don't think I'd ever felt more depressed. It was the sense of helplessness that was so hard to take—the knowledge that an unspeakable injustice was being done and that there was absolutely nothing that we or anyone else could do for Nikolai. He'd "had it"—and if I knew the ways of the Russians, it wouldn't be long before his son Boris and Boris's family were roped in too. Even if we'd been in a position to produce irrefutable evidence that some other person had done the murder, it wouldn't have made any difference. Nobody would listen now, because nobody wanted to listen. For reasons of their own, they'd decided that Nikolai was the man, and Nikolai it would have to be. Unless they needed a public confession from him to bolster up charges against other people, or decided to stage one of their demonstration trials, he'd probably never be heard of again. As far as the Russians were concerned, it seemed likely that the Mullett case was closed.

That didn't mean it was closed for me, of course. I no longer felt academic about the murder—I felt violent. I might be able to make a bit of trouble for someone, even if I couldn't help Nikolai. Nothing would give me deeper satisfaction than to be able to confront the real murderer with solid evidence of his guilt. At least I might as well make a few inquiries.

I suddenly saw myself as a kind of "private eye" in the Soviet Union, and the notion was so absurd that, for all my distress, I had to laugh.

All the same, there *were* one or two small matters that called for attention. I had a little business with Perdita, for instance. I went along the corridor and found her room—470—and she opened up at once in response to my knock. She was wearing rather more make-up than usual, but otherwise the shattering events of the night seemed to have had remarkably little outward effect on her.

"May I come in for a moment?" I asked. "I've something to give you."

She seemed somewhat surprised, but she was quite affable and I followed her in. There was a typed sheet on her table, similar to the one Zina had brought to us, and she had evidently been studying it with the help of a dictionary. No doubt a copy had been sent to each of the delegates.

I handed over the letter. "I met a chap from the Radio Station and he asked me to deliver it," I told her.

"How sweet of you." She opened the envelope without noticing that it had been tampered with. I glanced casually round the room. It was smaller than mine, but—as Gain had said—it was quiet. The narrow lane below the window was a pleasant contrast to the roaring square. Some of her photographs lay scattered around, and on her dressing table were two small china busts of Lenin and Stalin. "Presents from Moscow," I thought. It was a wonder they didn't make rock.

She said, "Well, that's all right," and put the letter down, and then she smiled at me in her infuriating way. "So they've found out who killed Mr. Mullett!" There was a challenge in her voice. There always was, either political or sexual. She just couldn't resist being provocative.

I said, rather wearily, "I suppose you believe that twaddle?"

"Naturally I believe it. You don't imagine they'd have published a thing like that if it hadn't been true?"

"Why not? A few weeks ago they said American airmen were dropping Colorado beetles on eastern Germany! They'd say anything if it suited them—*anything*. Black's white, and all men have four legs. You know that."

"Nonsense! Anyhow, this waiter confessed."

"It's something I'm trying to forget. I happened to know him rather well. He was a fine old chap."

"Possibly, but it seems he was also a class enemy, a traitor. I've just had the whole story from Mirnova. With his background, it's not surprising that he allowed himself to be used."

I felt the blood beating in my head. "Look," I said, "do facts mean anything to you at all?"

"Of course."

"Then listen! Nikolai had a known record as a servant of an *ancien régime* family. Would he have been chosen for this sort of job by anyone but a half-wit? He had struggled and sweated for years to give his son a decent chance in spite of that record. Would he have thrown the whole thing away and imperiled his family for an idiotic, pointless political crime?

He's supposed to be a conspirator. Wouldn't he have provided himself with a weapon that didn't shatter in his hand? He drew attention to himself by reporting the murder. Would he have done that if he'd committed it? Great God, in any decent court the case against him would be ripped to pieces in a moment. There's not a scrap of positive evidence. It's pathetic."

"This happens to be a matter of State security," said Perdita, "not a game for clever counsel. Or," she added nastily, "for amateur Sherlock Holmeses. Pray who do *you* think did it, if the waiter didn't?"

"I haven't the least idea."

"Then aren't you rather wasting your time?"

"That remains to be seen—I might find out something. I did think of making a few inquiries about where people were last night while all this was going on."

I thought a flicker of uneasiness crossed her face. "People? You mean the delegates?"

"Who else? No harm in checking their stories. No harm in checking yours."

Her blue eyes opened wide. "My dear crazy man, you're surely not accusing *me* of murder?" She gave me a lazy smile. "I assure you I was here in my room all the evening."

"Then you managed to wake up surprisingly quickly when the row started."

"What do you mean, 'wake up'? I wasn't asleep."

"Are you sure?"

"Quite sure."

"Most interesting. You see, you had a visitor last night—just before Mullett was killed. He knocked loudly several times, but he couldn't get an answer. There was no one here."

She stared at me, evidently at a bit of a loss.

"Of course," I said, "that doesn't mean that you were hitting Mullett with a bottle, but after a murder it's customary for innocent witnesses to tell the police the truth."

"You're not the police. I don't see what business it is of yours."

I shrugged. "Professional curiosity, perhaps. Or perhaps I just fancy myself as the sword of Nikolai! Anyway, I have a notion to make a study of this case and write it up for my newspaper when I get home."

"Aren't you forgetting the law of libel?"

"Hardly! But it isn't libelous to accuse anyone of murder—not, of course, if you can prove it!" I moved toward the door. "I realize, naturally, that I've got a long way to go, but at least I've made a start. 'Miss Perdita Manning lied about her whereabouts at the time of the murder. No explanation!' How's that for a first entry in the book of facts?"

"I think you're crazy," said Perdita.

" 'Miss Manning was known to have quarreled with the dead man, who had obstructed her in the fulfillment of a great ambition.' "

She flushed a little. "You know, you're making a positive fool of yourself. I tell you I was in my room all the evening."

I shrugged. "We shall see. What's happening about the delegation, by the way? Are you carrying on?"

"We're meeting this afternoon to decide," she said coldly.

I nodded, and went off thoughtfully along the corridor. I hadn't the least doubt that she *had* lied, and that she'd been somewhere she didn't want people to know about. However, I could think of half a dozen explanations more likely than that she had been busy murdering Mullett.

At the top of the stairs, I ran into Joe Cressey. He wore an expression of bewilderment and gloom.

"Hello, Mr. Verney," he said in a voice of muted welcome. "This is a fine how d'ye do, isn't it? Have you heard it was the waiter who did it?"

"I've heard," I said. "What do you think about it?"

He shook his head solemnly. "The fellow couldn't have been in his right mind, to do a thing like that. . . . I wish now I hadn't said what I did about Mr. Mullett. He wasn't so bad, really—I think he meant well. You could have knocked me down with a feather. When I got in last night and they told me what had happened, I thought I must be dreaming."

"I don't wonder. Ah, well, no good worrying about it. How did you like the Kremlin by moonlight?"

"Very nice, Mr. Verney. I was watching the cars coming out. They ring a bell first, did you know?—and then the cars shoot straight out across the Red Square with all the big shots in. I must say Moscow's a very interesting place, but I'll be glad to get home now. This business has spoiled everything."

I nodded sympathetically, and continued on my way. There was no reason, I reflected, to suppose that he *hadn't* been round the Kremlin—it was one of the best short walks in Moscow, and I'd heard someone recommending it to him a day or two earlier. All the same, these things were almost impossible either to prove or disprove. In England, detectives would have been checking up on all the delegates' stories, and with the necessary authority it would have been fairly easy to get a true picture. I could just imagine them questioning Cressey, for instance: "What time did you leave the hotel?"—"Which way did you go?"—"What did you see?"—"How long did you watch the cars?"—"How many came out?" But *I* couldn't ask questions like that, and, if I didn't, nobody would.

I comforted myself with the thought that perhaps there wasn't so very much point in checking alibis after all, when there were so many people who didn't even claim any.

I went down into the vestibule, thinking I'd try to have a quiet word with Ivan, the commissionaire. Tranter was just coming away from the reception desk.

I said, "Morning, Mr. Tranter. Shocking business last night."

He gave me a rather curt nod. There was a pretty strained look on *his* face, too. "A terrible affair, Mr. Verney. It's appalling to think that such a valuable career has been cut

short so unnecessarily. If people would only realize the futility
of violence!"

I wanted to continue the conversation and lead up to a
question, but he began to move off and I had to fling the
question after him. "When did you hear about it?"

He turned, with one eyebrow slightly raised, and his frosty
blue eyes bored into me. I thought he was going to brush me
off, but he didn't. "When I got in from the pictures."

"Oh," I said, "you were at the pictures? We wondered what
had happened to you. How do you like the films here? Personally I never think these Russian pictures are much fun
unless you understand the language. Or was it an American
film?"

Again he treated me to that cold stare. "I'm sorry, Mr.
Verney—I've no wish to be interviewed." The lift gates
opened and he stepped in.

So there I was again, with all the vital questions unanswered. At the pictures, Mr. Tranter? What cinema? What
was showing when you went in? What seat did you sit in?
What was the newsreel about? What time did you come out?
. . . No, it was hopeless. I was just wasting my time.

Ivan was busy bringing in some luggage from a truck outside, so I hung about. The vestibule of the Astoria was a bit
like Piccadilly Circus—you met everyone there eventually.
Presently Potts came in from the street.

"Hello, George," he said in his thin voice. "You've heard
the news, I suppose—about Nikolai?"

I nodded.

"It's a bit startling, isn't it? Waterhouse says they'll probably follow up the statement with another one accusing Attlee
and Eisenhower and John Foster Dulles of planting Nikolai
here! Surely they can't get away with this?"

"Can't they?" I said grimly. "You go into the streets and do
a little polling on the subject. Ask people if they think Nikolai
killed Mullett and wave *Pravda* at them. You'll get a hundred

per cent 'Yes'—not a single 'Don't know.' Hell, they've already got away with it."

Potts shook his head slowly. "One feels so helpless—I must say this is a most difficult place to get information. Even the delegates aren't very co-operative."

"You're telling me! I've just been trying to find out where Tranter was last night. He says he was at the pictures."

"At the pictures?" said Potts, musingly. "Let me see—I saw him somewhere. Oh, I know—it was when I was collecting that material on the second floor landing. Just before I came to the party. He got out of the lift and stopped to talk to the floor manageress. I suppose he went to the last house."

"I suppose so—he won't talk, anyway. What's doing at the Press Department—anything?"

"Not a thing—it's as quiet as a funeral parlor. They're holding all messages. Jeff saw Ganilov, but I haven't heard how he got on. Ah, well, see you at lunch." He went on upstairs.

I strolled slowly toward the revolving doors and stood looking out at the snow. It was a sparkling day, dry and much colder. Almost all the passers-by had their earflaps down. Presently Ivan returned to his post by the door.

I leaned back against the wall. "Morning, Ivan," I said nonchalantly. "Nice day."

He bowed. "Very nice, *gospodeen*."

"Cigarette?" I said. I handed him a full packet of Players and he fumbled for one. "You can keep them," I said. "I've got plenty."

He cast a nervous glance toward the reception desk, and then practically prostrated himself before me. I don't suppose he'd ever had more than one cigarette at a time in his life.

"Ivan," I said, "do you know Mr. Cressey by sight? One of the delegates—the one with the big chin."

He said he did.

"Did you see him go out last night?"

The commissionaire pondered. "I think I did, *gospodeen*—yes, I'm sure he did."

"What time?"

Ivan pushed up his tatty fur hat and scratched his grizzled temple. "I can't say, exactly—in the evening, sometime."

"Did you see him come back?"

He shook his head. "I don't think so, *gospodeen*. I don't know. There were so many things happening—all the excitement. I'm sorry. I would tell you if I could."

"What about Mr. Tranter? Did he go out at all?"

Ivan's puckered face cleared. "Indeed, yes, *gospodeen*. He went out at half-past eight. He returned just before eleven." The commissionaire's eyes flickered again to the reception desk.

"You're sure about that? It's not very easy to recognize people in their outdoor things, I know. You're sure it was Mr. Tranter?"

"Without doubt, *gospodeen*. He told me he was going to the cinema. He is the gentleman with the lame leg. At half-past eight he went, and at eleven he returned. That is the truth."

I wondered.

VIII

THE REST of the morning passed in an atmosphere of busy frustration. I could see no real hope of making progress on the case, and yet I found it impossible to switch my mind off it. At about eleven I put a call in to the Embassy to ask if H.E. had any views. He was engaged, but the First Secretary told me that they'd asked the Soviet Foreign Office for full particulars of the tragedy and that meanwhile they knew less than we did. I gathered from his tone that the Embassy, while extremely interested, was bearing Mullett's loss with fortitude.

I sat down and wrote a long letter to my office, which I hoped Jeff would carry with him when he left in a few days' time. I couldn't give them much information, but at least I was able to let off some steam, and I felt better as I sealed it up. Then I strolled across to the Press Department, expecting to find Jeff there. In fact I just missed him, but Waterhouse was still there and we had a long talk. He was amused—and secretly admiring, I think—because Jeff had been trying his American newspaper technique on the Department. He'd brushed aside all opposition, forced his way into Ganilov's office, and deposited written applications for interviews with the Chief of Police, the M.V.D., the prisoner's counsel, and the prisoner. He'd also left a long list of questions about Nikolai's whereabouts, and the date of the first hearing, and so on.

"When Ganilov came out," said Waterhouse, "he looked tired."

I laughed. If we could do nothing else, we could show a little spirit. I borrowed somebody's typewriter and wrote a careful story about Nikolai which would give offense without actually getting me thrown out, and left it with the censor. Then I walked back with Waterhouse.

I hadn't been in my room more than a couple of minutes before Jeff burst in and I saw at once by his face that he had some unpleasant news.

"Have you heard about Tanya?" he asked.

"No—what's happened?"

"They say she's ill. She's been sent off to the Crimea."

"Good Lord, really? I say, I am sorry. What's the matter with her?"

"That's what's so vague. Kira—you know, her sister—says she's been working too hard with the delegation, and that this Mullett affair brought on a nervous attack during the night, whatever that means. I asked her if it was serious, and she said 'No.' Anyway, Kira's taking Tanya's place with the delegation—she's already moved in next door. That's how I happened to find out about it."

"Pretty quick work," I said.

"The whole thing's a damn sight too quick for my liking, and the Crimea's a hell of a way to send anyone to get over an indisposition."

"It *is* a health resort, of course," I said. "All the same, it's queer they should have bundled her off like that."

"I think it's all darned fishy. It's true Tanya had a bad shock last night, but she got over it. She was all right when the police were questioning us and she was okay when I stuck my head in last thing. If she'd suddenly felt a nervous collapse coming on after that, surely she'd have come and told me—I was only two doors away."

"Doesn't Kira know what happened?"

"She says she doesn't know any details. She's given me an address in Simferopol, and I've sent off a wire, though God knows if it'll ever be delivered. Apart from that, all Kira can say is that Tanya will soon be better; and that there's absolutely nothing to worry about."

"I dare say she's right. What exactly is on your mind, Jeff?"

"I'd just like to know what happened here after we turned in, that's all. The police and those M.V.D. boys must have been around most of the night, working on that phony story about Nikolai. Well, I wondered—suppose Tanya was asked some more questions, and spoke out of turn. She liked Nikolai—she wouldn't have wanted to believe that story. She may have seen something, or heard something, that didn't square with the official version."

"Wouldn't they just have told her to keep quiet about it?"

"They might have thought it safer to put her on a plane for the Crimea. They'd know that she and I were pretty close—they might have thought it too risky to leave her around."

I sat silent for a while, thinking it over, and I didn't much like the look of it myself. Tanya had known that Jeff was leaving Russia in a few days' time, and unless she had suddenly become very ill indeed it was hardly conceivable that she would have left voluntarily for the south without saying good-by. Her abrupt departure by night was unpleasantly reminiscent of incidents that had happened before. The Soviet authorities, of course, cared nothing about personal feelings, and if it suited them they'd move people around like railway trucks. Their girl "contacts" would be allowed—indeed, instructed—to develop the closest possible relationships with foreigners, and then without a word of warning or explanation they'd be whisked away to Archangel or Tashkent or Vladivostock, and after that all efforts to trace them would fail. Letters and telegrams would go unanswered, and officials would stall, and finally the anxious—and on occasion heartbroken—foreigner would have to leave the country, and that would be that. It was, of course, a risk that every instructed foreigner knew about and took into account, but that didn't make the severance any more pleasant when it came.

However, it seemed a little early to take so gloomy a view in Tanya's case. "You may hear from her tomorrow or the next day," I said. "No point in losing sleep unnecessarily."

He said, "I guess not," and went off moodily to keep a lunch date.

Directly after lunch the delegation met to discuss its future plans, and afterward Bolting held an informal press conference in his room, with all present. He didn't look at all happy— the hoarseness that I'd noticed in his voice at the VOKS party had got worse and he was wearing a silk scarf round his throat. The others weren't exactly on top of their form, either. Mrs. Clarke was pale and blotchy, as though she'd just come out of the world's worst hangover. Cressey still seemed slightly incredulous that he could have become involved in such a drama, and Tranter was mum. The Professor doodled remotely, giving the impression that he didn't even know what was being discussed, and Islwyn had a dreamy, faraway look, as though recollecting his love-life in tranquillity. Perdita's expression suggested haughty disapproval of the whole proceedings. Mullett might not have been very popular, I reflected, but his death had certainly taken all the color and vitality out of the delegation.

Bolting began by reading a short prepared statement about the great loss everyone had sustained, which nobody bothered to take down, and then he said that after consultation with VOKS it had been agreed that what he called the "educational" part of the delegation's schedule should be completed according to plan, but that the social part should be curtailed out of respect for Mullett's memory. They would be leaving for home in just under a week.

The correspondents were no longer in the least interested in the delegation's schedule, but we were all interested in Mullett and how much the delegation had been told.

"Are you satisfied," Jeff asked, "with the official version of what happened last night?"

Bolting toyed for a moment with a gold signet ring he wore on his left hand and I felt that plain horse sense was warring with discretion. Then he gave a faint shrug. "Presumably the police know best," he said. "I'm not prepared to discuss the matter."

"*I'm* perfectly satisfied," put in Perdita, and there was a murmur of acquiescence from those around her. "I hope they hang him," said Mrs. Clarke viciously. The Professor continued to doodle.

We tried several more questions, but it soon became apparent that Bolting knew as little as we did about the circumstances of Nikolai's arrest and his present whereabouts, and what the next steps were going to be, if any. Only in one respect was he informative. Waterhouse asked him if there had been any medical report on Mullett, and Bolting said that as a matter of fact it was all rather tragic because it had been found that Mullett had an unusually thin skull. But for that fact, the blow with the bottle would probably not have killed him.

That was all, and soon after we dispersed. I gathered from Cressey, whom I managed to nobble in the corridor, that the earlier discussions about plans had been very bad-tempered. No doubt nerves were pretty raw all round. He himself would have preferred to pack up and leave right away, and so would Bolting and the Professor, but Tranter and Perdita had argued strongly that they'd come out to do a job and that they oughtn't to go before they'd finished it. As the VOKS people also had been most reluctant to see the delegation break up, this view had prevailed.

There was a telegram waiting for me when I got to my room. It was from my Foreign Editor, and it said: "MOST INTERESTED ALL DETAILS MULLETT AFFAIR." It was the sort of daft telegram that Foreign Editors do send to correspondents in Russia—a worthy successor to such classics as "INTER-VIEW FIRST LADY OF KREMLIN" and "SEND DETAILS RUSSIA'S NEW SECRET WEAPON EARLIEST." I walked gloomily across to the Press Department and sent off a reply: "SO AM I." Several correspondents from Eastern European papers were dispatching lengthy cables enlarging on the vicious record of the waiter Skaliga. It seemed that poor Nikolai was to go down in Iron Curtain history with the great assassins. It was pitiful.

When I got back to the hotel, I found that the guard on Mullett's room had been changed. The new man was a short, broad-shouldered moronic-looking type, with a lugubrious countenance. He was seated on a chair just opposite Mullett's door, and he gave me a jaundiced nod as I passed him. I went and tried Jeff's door, but got no reply.

"He's gone out," said the watchdog mournfully.

I nodded, and went in to have a sleep. The past twenty-four hours, with their tension and frustration, had been exhausting. When I woke up, I rang Jeff. There was something wrong with my telephone and I had difficulty in getting through, but I heard his bell at last. He didn't answer, though, and I remembered that he'd been going to a party at one of the Legations. A long evening stretched ahead.

I tried to settle down with a book, but I couldn't concentrate. My thoughts kept reverting to frail old Nikolai, who was probably on his way to some labor camp in Karaganda if he was lucky, and to the possibility that Tanya was in some sort of trouble, and to that room next door, and to what had really happened there the night before. The case was becoming a mental treadmill. The more I pondered, the more I felt not merely that the *official* story was ridiculous but that the whole episode as we knew it somehow failed to carry conviction. I still couldn't see how anyone could have got hold of the bottle and taken Mullett unawares. What were we to suppose that the victim had been doing at the time?—sitting at his table, taking no notice, with his back conveniently turned? Yet if he'd been paying the slightest attention to his visitor's strange behavior he'd have seen the attack coming, and a raised arm could easily have warded off the fatal blow.

As I dwelt on the case, I wished again that I had had more time to examine Mullett's room. There might well have been something there that I'd overlooked. There might still be something there. Why else, at this stage, were the authorities maintaining such a careful guard over the place? I turned over in my mind the possibility of luring the guard away and getting Mullett's key from the floor manageress by some subterfuge, but the prospect was poor, and I certainly couldn't do it without help.

I paced up and down restlessly for a while, and then stopped by the French doors and looked out upon the square. Dusk had fallen. The windows were steamed up and dirty outside, so that all I could see was the glow of the street lamps opposite and the intermittent flashes of the trolleybuses.

Suddenly I had an idea, and it jolted me right out of my gloom. A slim chance, perhaps, but worth investigating. Anything was better than inactivity. I slipped quickly into my *shuba* and fur hat, grabbed a torch, and took a firm grip on the handle of the French doors. It would mean resealing them afterward, but that was a minor matter. I braced myself, turned the handle, and gave a couple of sharp jerks. At the second pull the brown paper strips over the cracks came away with a tearing noise, and the door stood open. The outer doors were not sealed and presented no difficulty, and a moment later I was standing on the balcony.

It was devilish cold outside, but what I saw warmed me. On this side of the hotel there was one balcony to every two rooms, and the one I was standing on also served Mullett's room. I was in luck. A couple of steps, and I was outside Mullett's doors. The frozen snow crunched under my feet.

I felt a little conspicuous, as though a hundred eyes were on me, but in fact I was fifty feet above the street and there wasn't really much danger of being spotted. I turned the handle of the outer of the double doors, which again wasn't sealed, and slipped into the space between them. Then I gripped the handle of the inner door and shoved hard.

It opened so easily that I almost fell into the room, and for a hectic moment I feared that the watchdog out in the corridor must have heard me. I listened, holding my breath, my heart beating madly. I thought I heard the sound of a chair leg scraping, but nothing happened.

It was eerie, standing there alone in the darkness of the murder room, and my pulse leaped as the curtain by the bed suddenly stirred and rattled on its rings. I told myself it was only the draft blowing in through the open doors, but my nerves tingled in the guarded silence. I closed the doors softly behind me, tiptoed across the carpet, and switched on the light. It was with quite absurd relief that I satisfied myself that the room was empty and that there was no one waiting for *me* with a bottle. I'm no hero, and I've never pretended to be.

At first glance, the room looked exactly as it had done on the previous evening, except of course that the body had been taken away and the broken glass removed. No attempt had been made to wash out the big bloodstain on the carpet or to tidy up Mullett's belongings, which were scattered about the room just as he'd left them. The wastepaper basket was still half-full of rubbish—though when I probed deeper, in almost idle curiosity, I found that the copy of *Pravda* had gone, and so had the tin. That made me think a bit.

I prowled around for a while, hoping that I might have the luck to come across one of those little objects that detectives always seem to find—an unusual coat button or a scarab brooch or an initialed handkerchief. There wasn't really a chance, of course—even if the murderer *had* left any personal traces, the police would surely have discovered them. Afterward I went quickly through Mullett's personal possessions, thinking that I might stumble upon some better indication of motive than that unconvincingly exposed wallet. Again, there was nothing of interest. I riffled through the papers on his desk—mostly notes of the various trips the delegation had made. There was one rather odd thing amongst them—an envelope with a Moscow address on it in pale green ink and a Ceylon postmark. I couldn't quite fit it into the Mullett picture, so I slipped it into my pocket for later consideration.

Otherwise, the room was disappointingly barren. I was just going to switch off the light and return the way I'd come when I noticed that the velvet curtain which hung down on the left side of the French doors had been torn from two of its wooden rings. I didn't think I had done that myself, during my entry. Any suggestions of a struggle, or marks of a possible disturbance, were of interest, so I went over to examine the curtains more closely. As I did so, my attention was suddenly caught by the brown paper strips that had been used to seal the doors, and that I'd broken on my way in. They looked damp! I ran my finger along one of the strips, and it *was* damp.

Fascinated, I went and examined the paper strips which sealed the cracks in one of the other window frames, thinking that for some reason the whole room might have been freshly sealed that day. But they were tinder dry. There was no doubt about it—these French doors had been specially opened and resealed during the past twenty-four hours. I realized now why they had swung back so easily at my push. The paste was still tacky.

I thought at first that the police must have opened the doors during their investigation, though I couldn't imagine why. Then, as I dwelt on the puzzling details of the murder and tried to fit this new discovery into the pattern, a more interesting idea occurred to me. Here, surely, was a possible explanation of how the murderer had managed to strike that fatal blow without arousing Mullett's alarm. Suppose he'd succeeded in slipping into Mullett's room—taking advantage, perhaps, of a door temporarily left open—and concealed himself in the space between the two sets of French doors, having first armed himself with the bottle. Then, on Mullett's return after the broadcast, the intruder would have been in a position to catch him completely off guard. That at least made more sense than any alternative we had thought of so far.

At the same time, though, it left a lot of things unexplained. If the murderer *had* done that, presumably he'd sealed up the doors again before leaving—because they'd certainly been sealed when I'd glanced at them immediately after the discovery of the body. But how could he have managed that? If he'd been very provident, he might conceivably have equipped himself beforehand with paste and strips of paper, but in the ten minutes or so between Mullett's return and our entry into the room there certainly wouldn't have been sufficient time for him to have renewed the seals and cleaned up the mess.

However, I felt a glow of satisfaction at having taken even one step forward. I switched off the lights and returned to the balcony. There was no means by which *I* could reseal Mullett's doors, and I could see myself getting into serious trouble when the police discovered that their carefully-guarded room had been entered; but then serious trouble was an occupational risk in this country. In any case, I was too interested now to care.

Back in my own room I threw off my outdoor clothes, chafed my tingling ears, and poured myself a stiff drink. The first thing was to get the cracks in my own doors sealed up again, for the temperature of the room had already become unpleasantly low. I remembered that Potts had a roll of gummed brown paper which would do the trick for the moment and I tried to ring him, but the damned phone had gone completely dead. It was always happening, and it was not the least exasperating feature of life in the Astoria, for the phone was one of the few things that prevented one from feeling entirely cut off.

I flung down the receiver and went to see if Kira was in, and if I could use her phone to call the engineer. It was a long time since I'd seen her, but I had no difficulty in recognizing her when she opened the door. She was a little taller than Tanya, and instead of a page-boy bob she wore her hair in close peroxide curls, but she had the same rather sweet expression as her sister and she was the same type—an attractive, amenable girl groomed for contact with foreigners.

I'd expected her greeting to be quite warm, because I'd got on with her pretty well in the old days, but it seemed to me that her "Hello, Mr. Verney—how are you?" was formal and unenthusiastic. She was wearing quite a snappy number in negligees, and when I looked past her into the room and saw a couple of male legs protruding under the table I put two and two together and decided that I'd chosen a bad moment.

"My phone's gone wrong," I said, "but it doesn't matter now, you're busy." Kira didn't attempt to detain me, but as I was turning away, the legs suddenly moved and I saw, of all things, Joe Cressey's head peering toward the door. "Hello, Joe," I called.

Kira stepped aside then. "Of course you can use the phone," she said. "Please come in."

I said, "Well, thanks," in a suitably diffident tone, and followed her in. Cressey was sitting on a settee with an exercise book on a table in front of him. "We're just having a Russian lesson," he explained. He looked rather sheepish, and I recalled his remark that Mrs. Cressey wouldn't like it. Kira had evidently taken over where Tanya had left off.

"Sorry to butt in, Joe," I said. "I won't be a minute. I can't even get the operator on my phone." I wanted to say something about Tanya but decided that the moment wasn't really appropriate.

The telephone was on a little table by the window, and as I

crossed over to it Kira rejoined Cressey on the settee. I could smell her perfume across the room, but neither that nor the provocative V of her drapery seemed to worry the stolid Joe. Incredibly, he was *really* concentrating on Russian. I heard him repeating after her in an earnest tone, "*Ya znayu*, I know; *ti znayesh*, thou knowest; *on znayet*, he knows." I only wished he was right!

I lifted the receiver and waggled the hook. The operator was slow in responding, and my eyes roved idly over the French doors. I frowned. It *must* be my imagination. Here, too, the brown paper seals looked damp! "Hello," I said, "this is *Gospodeen* Verney. My telephone isn't working. Room 434—could you tell the engineer, please?" My back was toward the settee, blocking Kira's view of the French doors. I scratched with my thumbnail at one of the strips of paper and it crinkled up in a moist lump. "Thank you," I said, smoothing it down again.

For a moment I stood still, my hand on the receiver. Fantastic ideas were racing through my mind. I recalled the appearance of the long row of balconies. Each was separated from the next by a gap of perhaps three feet—a gap across which an unusually agile and daring person might have passed. With a slightly sick feeling I remembered Tanya's mountaineering exploits in the Caucasus. For someone who could negotiate half Mount Elbruz, a three-foot gap fifty feet above the street would have been child's play!

IX

AS SOON as I got back to my room I struggled into my *shuba* again and went out on to the balcony to examine the snow by the light of a torch. There were no footprints except those which I had made, but there was something just as telltale. In a broad band all down the middle of the balcony the snow had lost the smooth, iced-cake look that a virgin fall has. There was a sort of track where the surface had been disturbed, and it stretched right along to Mullett's room in one direction and right to the end of the balcony in the other.

I stared across the gap which separated my balcony from Tanya's. It was not, after all, quite three feet wide, but it seemed a hell of a long way to me. I looked down, and fifty feet below, almost exactly underneath me, there was a spiked iron fence protecting an area. I gave an inward shudder. I have never had a particularly good head for heights, and I've always regarded impalement as one of the less attractive deaths. Whoever had made the transit had been moved by no trivial impulse.

I flashed my torch across the gap, but the beam was not strong enough to show the state of the snow on the other balcony. It was reasonable to assume that it had been disturbed there, too, but there was too much at stake to be careless about evidence. I wanted to be certain—I *had* to be certain. I also wanted to find out how difficult it was to make the crossing.

My *shuba* would have been dangerously hampering, so I changed it for a polo-neck sweater and a woolen scarf. Then I went out again to size up the job. It ought to be pretty straightforward, I decided, provided I could keep my mind concentrated and forget the space beneath. The iron railings which surrounded the two balconies were hip-high and smooth along the top, and it would be simple to put a leg over. On the outside of the railings there was a rather crumbly two-inch cement coping on which it should be possible to get a toe hold. After that, it would be merely a question of stepping across. My nerve almost failed at the thought of that moment, and I decided that the sooner I got moving the better.

On the street corner opposite, the inevitable loud-speaker was blaring away, and down the hill from Lubianka Square a squad of Red Army girls were approaching, their uniformed bosoms outthrust and their shrill voices raised in excruciating martial song. I let them go by, and then took a firm grip of the rail. It was so cold that it almost burned me, but gloves would have weakened my hold. A spot of moisture dripped from my nose and froze solid on my upper lip. I must be quick!

The crossing proved much less terrifying in fact than in imagination, and a few seconds later I stood on Tanya's—now Kira's—balcony, breathing rather hard. I bent to the snow and shone the torch, and, as I'd expected, the track continued. I followed it silently to Kira's French doors, and there it stopped. Beyond, the snow was virgin. There could be no possible doubt, now. A transit had been made from Tanya's room to Mullett's room across the gap, and the marks of the passage had been deliberately obliterated. I remembered the wet newspaper that I'd discovered in Mullett's basket. Folded, that would have been just the thing.

I was overconfident on the way back and nearly came to grief. As I swung across and put my weight on the corner of the ancient coping a triangle of cement cracked clean off. Just in time I tightened my grip on the rail and scrabbled wildly for a new foothold. The broken piece fell with a smack into the area below and I pressed myself to the rail and prayed that no one had been passing underneath just then. I waited a second or two, my heart pounding, but there was no alarm. A moment later I was safe back in my room, and I must say I'd never been more thankful to see it. I went downstairs to borrow the sticky paper from Potts and stayed to have a drink with him. When I got back it took me fifteen minutes to make a satisfactory job of the resealing, and then I dropped into a chair and lit my pipe.

The events of the previous night looked very different now in the light of this new discovery. It still wasn't possible to be sure what had happened in Mullett's room, but it was possible to have a theory that fitted a lot more of the known facts. For instance, the resealing of Mullett's doors could now be explained. The murderer had presumably entered the room via the balconies while Mullett was still away broadcasting, and must have sealed the doors before his return. To do that, he must have carried the paste with him—and the wet tin in the wastepaper basket might well have been the container. Then he had lain in wait for Mullett, with the bottle in his hand—why he had failed to arm himself with a more reliable weapon was still a mystery. Anyway, he had struck his victim down and slipped out by way of the corridor.

I saw now why he had left the door ajar instead of shutting it. Having broken in by way of the balcony, he would naturally seek to give the impression that the murderer had entered by the door. He was obviously no fool.

He?—or she? Reluctantly I forced myself to face the facts, and whichever way I looked at them they were so unpleasant that I didn't know how I'd begin to tell Jeff. Indeed, after a few minutes' reflection I had almost begun to wish that I hadn't poked my nose into the business at all. Jeff's relationship with Tanya might not be very deep—he was much too sensible to get deeply involved with a Russian girl—and in the ordinary course of events he'd have left her with no more than a pang of sentimental regret. All the same, in his warmhearted way he was fond of her, and his anxiety about her that afternoon had been very real. I awaited his return from the Legation party with misgiving.

He came swinging along the corridor at about eleven, and he sounded very cheerful. He stopped by the watchdog, and I heard him say, "It's good to be alive—you ought to try it some time," with a chuckle and a complete disregard of the fact that the man didn't know what he was talking about. It seemed a shame to damp those spirits, and if he'd gone to his room I'd have turned in and left the revelations till morning. He didn't, though—he came and banged on my door.

"What, all alone, you old misanthrope!" he exclaimed. He slipped off his outdoor things and dropped into a chair. "Look what I've just collected." He handed me a slip of paper. "I guess you were right, George."

It was a telegram from Simferopol, in English, and it said, SORRY I RUSHED OFF WITHOUT SAYING GOOD-BY AM FEELING BETTER ALREADY ALL LOVE TANYA. It had been dispatched at noon, and presumably had crossed Jeff's own wire.

I read it through twice, very puzzled. "Well, that's fine," I said. Things were getting extraordinarily complicated.

Jeff looked at me in surprise. "You sure sound delighted, bud. What's on your mind?"

"A hell of a lot," I said. "I've been making discoveries." I went on to tell him about the two lots of balcony doors that had been forced and resealed, and the track in the snow, and the newspaper and the tin. I didn't make any direct reference to Tanya. I just waited, and let the facts sink in.

A look of bewilderment settled on his face, and there was a short silence. He fumbled for a cigarette and lit it and blew smoke across the room. "Well, I guess that's pretty conclusive," he said at last. "Mighty smart of you to find out. Some guy obviously got into Tanya's room when she wasn't there and used her doors." He was mentally stalling, and he knew it, and I knew it.

"They don't hand out room keys to any Tom, Dick or Harry," I said. "Besides, Tanya was in her room all the evening, working."

"She may have slipped out."

"She may, yes."

He suddenly looked truculent, and I thought for a second of the night we'd scrapped about the two Wills's. "Are you suggesting that Tanya bumped off Mullett?—because it darned well sounds like it."

"If I'm raising the possibility, I'm not doing it for pleasure. Look, Jeff, what do you say we drop the whole thing? We'll be up to our necks before we know where we are."

"Drop it, hell! We're going to get it straight now we've started. I think you must be as screwy as the Russians. Tanya's not the bottle-bashing type—look at the size of her, for one thing. She'd have had to stand on a chair to hit Mullett, and then he wouldn't have felt it. It's fantastic."

I puffed unhappily at my pipe. "Perhaps so—but Mullett's skull was thin, and if she's tough enough for mountaineering I'd say she was tough enough for anything. I know it sounds damned unlikely, but that evidence takes a bit of getting round."

Jeff gave an exclamation of impatience. "For Pete's sake!— what would *she* have had against Mullett?"

"Nothing that I know of. She must have met him when he was out here during the war, of course. She must have met everybody. I suppose there could have been something between them—though I confess I never heard that Mullett was interested in women."

"And I never heard that Tanya was interested in Mullett! What could he have given her that other people couldn't? I just don't believe it. Anyway, look how she behaved. A woman who'd just cracked a man's skull with a bottle wouldn't fall in a faint when she saw the corpse a second time."

"She might pretend to."

"Look, bud, *I* brought her round. She was out—clean out. I'd stake my last nickel that the first she knew of Mullett's murder was when she saw him stretched on the floor." He pulled savagely on his cigarette. "There's another thing, too—she wouldn't have had time to do it. Why, I was with her myself until somewhere around quarter after nine. Mullett was probably dead by then. Anyway, we know he was dead ten minutes later, and if there's one thing certain it's that Tanya couldn't have gone to his room and killed him and sealed up his doors all inside ten minutes. You're sure backing a loser."

I suddenly felt immensely relieved. It was true—she couldn't have done it. That last point of his clinched it, and I'd been slow not to see it before.

"Stupid of me," I said. "Sorry, Jeff! I had to raise the thing—it was on my mind—but don't misunderstand me. I couldn't see her in the part, either."

He brightened. "Well, thank God for that! Let's have a drink."

I said, "I'm afraid it doesn't let her out, though."

"What do you mean?"

"The murderer reached Mullett's room through her room—through her French doors. *Who sealed up her doors after him?*"

He sat very still, groping for an answer as I had done. "Well," he said at last, "I guess the guy who unsealed them must have got in again, somehow, and sealed them up. There was such a to-do last night, anything could have happened."

"What about the time in between? You might as well face it, Jeff—Tanya must have known. It's inconceivable that she could have sat in her room and not noticed what had happened. For one thing, there'd have been a hell of a draft."

"There wasn't a draft when I took that drink in to her."

"Exactly. That was because she'd already resealed the doors."

He clutched his hair. "Christ!" he said. "This is horrible."

He sat for a while, plunged in thought. "Okay," he said at last, "maybe she did know, but there must be some explanation. I can see Tanya as a lot of things, but not as a murderer's accomplice. And we're back where we were—why did she faint?"

I shrugged. "It's one thing to know a murder's going to be done, and another to see the results before your eyes."

"I don't believe it," he said stoutly. "I damn well don't believe it."

There was a long, gloomy silence while we both sought afresh for some chink in the evidence. There wasn't one, though—that resealing of Tanya's doors was damning. She must have been in it up to the neck.

Presently Jeff gave up groping and started off on a new track. "What beats me," he said, "is how the police came to miss this balcony business."

"I suppose they were concentrating on the corridor angle and didn't bother to look any further."

Jeff grunted. "If a man's found murdered in a room, you don't just accept the obvious. Even if it did seem likely that the murderer had come from the corridor. I'd have thought they'd have had a look round to make sure. Hell, they were in there long enough." He gave me an odd look. "Anyway, why did they bother to take the tin and the newspaper away with them?"

I didn't get it. "I suppose they thought they might be clues."

"What, an old tin and an old newspaper? Those things, bud, were only clues in relation to the balcony doors."

I stared at him, and a creepy feeling ran slowly up my spine. "Good lord!" I said softly. "You mean perhaps they did find out about the balcony!" I thought about it, and suddenly all doubt disappeared. "Why, of course they did—what a fool I am! That's why they wanted to look in my room—the explanation they gave seemed phony at the time. They'd discovered that Mullett's doors had been forced from the outside and as I shared a balcony with him they wanted to find out if mine had. Don't you see?"

"I'm ahead of you," Jeff said grimly. "They'd discover that your seals were intact. Then they'd do what you did—they'd realize that someone must have climbed from one balcony to the other. They'd examine the marks in the snow. They'd go to Tanya's room and they'd discover that her doors had been resealed that evening." With a set face he took the telegram from his pocket and read it again. Then he screwed it up and flung it into a corner. "*She's* gone to no health resort. I guess they could easily have arranged to have that sent. Oh, God!"

I couldn't contradict him.

"All the same," he said, frowning, "I don't get it. She'd have told them everything. She'd have told them who the guy was who went through her room—she'd have had to. They must know who the real murderer is, and they've arrested an innocent man instead. That's a swell set-up. What the hell do they think they're playing at?"

"It sounds to me," I said, "like Murder Through the Looking Glass."

X

ONCE IT became clear that the Russians were covering up for the murderer, anything seemed possible. Jeff said: "Maybe the M.V.D. killed Mullett themselves. They could easily have fixed it."

I thought about that, and of course he was right. If they'd wanted to get rid of Mullett they could have sent a man through Tanya's room, and instructed her to seal up behind him, and rushed her off afterward to some place where she'd be safe from curious questions until the affair had blown over. Tanya might simply have been the obedient young Soviet citizen, carrying out orders. In that case, though, surely they'd have removed her from the hotel before the murder was discovered? And anyway . . .

"Why would they have wanted to bump off Mullett?" I asked. "That really would have been killing the goose that laid the golden eggs."

"It seems that way, I agree," Jeff said slowly. "But then, what do we really know of Mullett, except that he was a pain in the neck to everybody? A lot of queer things happen to people with Soviet connections. You were suggesting just now that he might have got mixed up with Tanya—well, he might have got mixed up with the Russians. I know it sounds pretty crazy, but suppose he was a British agent, and the Russians found out. That pro-Soviet line of his could have been an act. Maybe he's been spying all this time."

"You've more faith in the British Intelligence Service than I have, chum," I said. "I don't believe that people who were dumb enough to let that atom man Fuchs get by would be smart enough to plant a man like Mullett. Besides, that stuff he talked had the ring of conviction. If he was putting it on all that time, he was a genius."

"Okay—it was just an idea." Jeff probed around for further possibilities. "Suppose he was a *Russian* agent, and for some reason they'd come to the conclusion that he wasn't reliable any more. Plenty of guys have been bumped off for that. Maybe they asked him over here with the deliberate intention of killing him."

I could sympathize with Jeff's eagerness to exculpate Tanya, but I thought he was being a bit fanciful. "They're capable of it, of course," I said, "but there's not a shred of evidence. Frankly, I don't believe the authorities had a hand in it—not in the actual killing. That bottle business was too crude for an official job. It smacks of the amateur to me."

"Then why are they covering up?"

I shrugged. "Search me. They must feel they've got *something* at stake. I suppose if some important Russian had done it, someone they couldn't bring to trial because he was too useful, they'd have covered up for him."

"Would they have covered up for a delegate?"

I felt a sudden stir of excitement. "That's a thought! You know, I believe they might have done that."

"It sure would have wrecked their campaign if they'd had to arrest Bolting or Schofield or Tranter on a murder rap. Hell, though, it's still only surmise. This whole theory is only surmise. How do we prove it? What are we going to *do?*"

"Well," I said, "we could try to break Kira down and get some confirmation from her—she must know a lot more than she's admitted. Or we could follow up the address on that envelope I found—you never know, it might have something to do with the case. Or, of course, we could pipe down and forget the whole thing—that's obviously what they'd like us to do."

"And let them get away with murder? Not on your life! I think Kira's the best bet."

"I think so, too. We'd better not both see her together—she'll think it's a hold-up. Shall I talk to her?"

"I guess you might as well—*I* didn't get much change out of her. Anyway, you British have a smooth line of talk when you want something."

"There's just one other thing," I said, as I got up. "How's it going to affect Tanya if we ask a lot of questions?"

"I figure it can't make things any worse for her," he said glumly, "and there's *just* a chance it might make them better—if we can get at the truth. You see, I still don't think she'd help in a murder. Maybe I'm just a sap, but that's the way it is." He picked up his coat. "So long, George."

As soon as he'd gone I turned in, but it was some time before I slept. I had to decide what would be the best approach to Kira, and it was a bit tricky. I didn't know how much she'd been told, or how tough she was, or what sort of strain she was under. I thought I'd go easy to start with and see how she shaped.

It was a few minutes after nine on the following morning when I knocked on her door. This time she was fully dressed, and all set for a day with the delegation. If she was surprised to see me she didn't show it, but there was still a hint of reserve about her manner. I had a feeling that she must have been specially warned against newspapermen. She was trying hard to be natural but not quite succeeding.

I told her there was something particular I wanted to talk to her about and that it wouldn't take long, and she threw a glance over at the watchdog and let me in. "I'm afraid I've finished all the coffee," she said.

"Thanks—I've just had some." I came straight to the point. "Kira—Jeff's still worried about Tanya."

She smiled, showing pretty teeth. "I know," she said. "He's

very foolish to do so. I told him yesterday that there was nothing to worry about."

I nodded. "It's just that—well, you know how things are here. Girls do kind of disappear sometimes. He's rather fond of Tanya and she left so very suddenly."

"He will hear from her, I am sure."

"He's already heard, if a telegram can be called 'hearing.' He's not satisfied, though. For two pins he'd rush off to the Crimea himself."

She smiled again. "Americans are so impetuous. He is a nice man—I like him. Of course, he could apply for a permit to visit her before he leaves."

I regarded her narrowly. "He could apply," I agreed, "but he wouldn't get it—do you think? Kira, did you see your sister before she went away?"

"I didn't see her myself, no, but Madame Mirnova looked after her and saw her on to the plane and she is quite all right, just rather upset. It is very natural that she should be. I assure you, Mr. Verney, that all this anxiety is quite unecessary. I, too, am fond of my sister. Should I not be the first to worry, if there were anything wrong?"

She was completely composed now. Indeed, her blue-eyed candor was disarming, and I had to remind myself that we'd got precisely nowhere. If she was putting on an act, it was a good act. The only hope was that shock tactics would make her forget her lines.

I walked across to the French doors and ran a thumbnail down one of the seals. It still wasn't quite dry.

"Does it mean anything to you," I said, "that these balcony doors have recently been opened?"

She struggled hard to control herself, but the very effort betrayed her. Her face lost all its color. A written confession couldn't have told me more.

She still remembered her lines, though. "I don't understand," she said. "Perhaps they have been opened—I don't know. It has nothing to do with me."

"It has a great deal to do with you. Mullett's murderer went through those doors and Tanya's all mixed up with the murder and the police are holding her and you're covering up. That story about the Crimea is a lie, and you know it."

She gazed at me in horror. "You must be out of your mind. You'd better go."

"Not yet. I want to know the name of the murderer. You can tell me."

"It was Nikolai, the waiter. You saw the papers. That's all I know." Her voice was high and scared.

"Kira, you're just repeating a lesson—you're saying what they told you to say. You've been put here to keep us quiet. Why are you doing it? Is it because they've threatened to take it out of Tanya if you don't?"

She looked at me with eyes full of anguish, and it seemed to me that she gave an almost imperceptible nod. *"Please go,"* she whispered.

"You poor frightened kid!" I said. "All right—I'll go."

I turned at the door. "Don't worry, Kira—I asked questions but you didn't answer them. You tell them that. Good luck!"

XI

I WENT in straightaway to tell Jeff what had happened. It was something to have confirmed—as I felt I had—that our thinking had been on the right lines and that the Russians were indeed engaged in a complicated maneuver to conceal the truth about Mullett. All the same, I had singularly little sense of achievement. Rather rashly, perhaps, I had shown our hand—and we still didn't know who the murderer was. I was depressed, too, by my glimpse of the police state at close quarters. I loathed the idea of anyone being made to act under duress, particularly out of fear for someone else's safety, and it would be a long time before I forgot that look on Kira's face.

Jeff took the news rather hard. I think he'd been hoping against hope that Kira would somehow succeed in reassuring me about Tanya. His exit permit had just arrived from the Press Department and with only a few more days in the country it looked as though all his anxieties would go unrelieved. I felt very sorry for him, but there wasn't much I could say.

Waterhouse popped in soon after breakfast and brightened us up a little. He'd written a story a week or two before about some outdoor demonstration which Vishinsky had attended, and it had been held up by the censor although it had been both objective and harmless. Now he'd just heard the explanation. Apparently he'd mentioned some incident which had occurred "within a stone's throw of Mr. Vishinsky," and the censor had taken umbrage. "Who," he had asked indignantly, "would wish to throw a stone at Mr. Vishinsky?" The phrase had now been amended.

Waterhouse had no fresh news on the Mullett case except that, after telegraphic consultations with the next-of-kin in London, the funeral had been fixed for the following morning at eleven and that—as he said—it had been decided *not* to bury Mullett under the Kremlin wall with the heroes of the Revolution! This decision evidently implied no posthumous disrespect, for the newspapers that day were full of fantastic eulogies of the dead man. The editorials were still roundly denouncing Nikolai and his "ring of conspirators," but no fresh persons had been named nor were any new details given.

As Jeff had some business of his own to attend·to, I went off alone with the delegation to visit a couple of schools and an establishment for juvenile delinquents. It was an interesting trip, but the delegates seemed to have only half their minds on it. The shadow of Mullett hung heavily over them. Bolting had stayed indoors to nurse what had turned out to be a mild attack of quinsy. Perdita was snappish, and Schofield preoccupied. Even Mirnova had lost some of her suavity, and Kira was careful to avoid my eye.

In the afternoon I went off with Jeff to a skating rink in Gerzena Street and tried out some new skating boots which I'd brought with me from London. The ice was in fine condition and we worked off a good deal of our depression. When we got back to the hotel, however, messages were waiting for us that seemed to spell trouble. The Press Department had rung up, and would be glad if Mr. Clayton and Mr. Verney would go across right away to see Mr. Ganilov.

There was a glint in Jeff's eye, as though he foresaw battle. "If I happen to choke that guy today," he said, "will you let it be known that I did it for humanity!"

The atmosphere in the Department when we walked in a few minutes later was distinctly hostile. The news always seemed to get around when a particular correspondent was in disgrace and even the secretaries looked down their noses. Ganilov himself, however, was no different from usual. He got

up and gave us both a fishy handshake and motioned us
politely into the two leather chairs. Then he sat down again
behind his massive desk, his heavy shoulders up round his
neck and his eyes unfathomable behind their bull's-eye lenses.
He had, I reflected, neither the presence nor the manner of a
high executive, but I didn't underrate his intelligence and cunning, or the wholesome respect in which he held his own
safety. Whatever he had to do, he would do it skillfully and in
complete accordance with his instructions.

He began with a sardonic comment on our work. "I trust,"
he said, "that you have both enjoyed your trips with the delegation."

"It's been a way of getting around," said Jeff. "The only
way."

Ganilov gave a little nod, as though he were noting a point
without accepting liability. "At the same time, you do not
appear to have sent many dispatches to your papers." He
made a pretense of fumbling around in a tray. "Not a single
one, I think."

We didn't comment. He knew the form, and we knew the
form, and there was nothing worth sparring about yet.

"Perhaps," he said, thoughtfully nibbling a fingernail, "you
have been too interested in the regrettable calamity which
overtook Mr. Mullett. Now on that, I see that you have both
filed."

"You should know," said Jeff. "You're the guy that's been
sitting on the stories."

Ganilov smiled. His smile was like one of those electric
radiators with imitation coal that look warm and aren't. However, he never made a personal issue of these things unless he
had to. I think he neither liked nor disliked us. If he'd been
told to fix a banquet in our honor he'd have done it in the
same unemotional way.

"In the Soviet Union," he said, "we do not believe that the

speculations of reporters on individual crimes are of any public interest."

"We weren't writing for the Soviet Union," I reminded him. "In our countries, there's a lot of public interest in these things."

"Nevertheless, Mr. Verney, I have always understood that even in your country a case may not be commented on while it is *sub judice.*"

I smiled. "A case can't be *sub judice,* Mr. Ganilov, unless it's going to be tried. This one isn't. It's all been fixed beforehand by the M.V.D., as you very well know."

Ganilov shook his head in sad rebuke. "When we allowed you to come back to the Soviet Union, Mr. Verney, we were under the impression that you were an objective observer. It seems we were mistaken."

That didn't seem to require comment either.

"In fact," Ganilov went on, "you seem to have allowed yourself a quite abnormal license in invention, even by the standards of anti-Soviet correspondents. I am told you have been saying that the waiter, Nikolai Skaliga, was not the murderer of Mr. Mullett, and that the whole affair is what Mr. Clayton's compatriots would call a 'frame-up.' I gather you have been expressing this opinion rather freely."

I shrugged. "Why not? It's what I think."

"And what you also think, Mr. Clayton?"

"Sure," said Jeff.

Ganilov sat back as though he'd reached a marked passage that he'd got to get included in the record. "It is an intolerable insult to the Union of Soviet Socialist Republics to suggest that our judicial system is corrupt." He spoke with simulated anger.

Jeff stirred restlessly. "Look, Mr. Ganilov, I don't know why you asked us down here, but can't we quit this fencing? You know what we think of your judicial system—we don't have to pretend with each other. What exactly is on your mind?"

Ganilov got up, went over to a corner of the room, spat carefully into a spittoon, and resumed his seat. "I understand that Mr. Verney has been acting as a kind of amateur detective," he said. "Is that not so, Mr. Verney? You have been making discoveries?"

"I have, yes. I know that Mullett's murderer came along the balcony, and I know that the police know."

"Ah! Leaving aside, for the moment, the impropriety of your breaking into a room which the police had closed, has it not occurred to you that it may be rather dangerous to interfere in these matters?"

"Is that a threat, Mr. Ganilov?"

"A threat?" He managed to sound genuinely shocked. "Why, certainly not. It is possible, of course, in view of your attitude of open hostility, that we shall have to consider whether after all you are *persona grata* here. We could withdraw your press card. At the same time, we should much prefer that you yourself saw the unwisdom—the *danger*—of your attitude."

"I don't think I quite understand you," I said. "Danger to whom?"

"I will explain." He took another nibble at his nails. "You see, it is possible that our police have made a *bona fide* mistake."

I sat up with a jerk. This was something quite unexpected.

"Yes," said Ganilov, "even *we* make mistakes! In the first instance, it appeared certain that the waiter Skaliga was the criminal. A little later, new evidence came to light—the evidence which you, Mr. Verney, have discovered for yourself. It is difficult to be certain, but it does now appear possible that Skaliga, after all, was not the perpetrator of this crime."

"I thought he confessed," said Jeff nastily.

Ganilov was quite unperturbed. "That is so, Mr. Clayton,

and he has undoubtedly been concerned in an anti-Soviet conspiracy. He has admitted that. His confession to the murder of Mr. Mullett, however, may have been due to an overanxiety to placate his accusers. Such things have happened before. As I say, we cannot be sure, but there is no denying the fact that this new evidence does seem to point to someone else."

"To whom?" asked Jeff.

The thick glasses gleamed. "To you, Mr. Clayton."

Jeff nearly sprang out of his chair. "Why, you son of a . . . !"

"Easy, Jeff," I said. "Let's hear what the gentleman has to say."

Ganilov sat back with his finger tips together, recalling his brief. "It seems, Mr. Clayton, that you and Mr. Mullett were old acquaintances. As it happens, he and I were discussing you a few days before he died—at the reception for Miss Manning, to be exact. He told me about an article you had written—a rather scurrilous article, he said—and of some unpleasant exchanges which followed."

"Go on," said Jeff contemptuously.

"You had, in fact, a grudge against him. Last Sunday evening, you saw an opportunity to square the account. You were, if I am rightly informed, giving a little party in your room. At about a quarter to nine, however, you left the party, ostensibly to take some refreshment to the young lady who was acting as interpreter for the delegation—Tatiana Mikhailovna. You were away for about half an hour. Is that correct?"

"Sure—I was with Tanya."

"That is what you say. It seems quite possible, however, that what in fact you did was to climb from one balcony to the other, enter Mr. Mullett's room, wait for him to come in, and take your revenge before rejoining the party. The police found a tin in Mr. Mullett's room which has been identified as similar to some still in your possession. There was also a newspaper which had been used to obliterate footmarks, and in one corner of it your name was faintly penciled—a guide, no doubt, for the morning delivery. That, Mr. Clayton, was an unfortunate oversight."

Jeff started to say something, and checked himself.

"Of course," Ganilov went on smoothly, "if by any chance this reconstruction is correct, you would have needed an assistant. Your relations with Tatiana Mikhailovna were, I believe, of the closest. You might well have persuaded her to cooperate to the extent of sealing up her doors behind you. Unfortunately she is not well enough at the moment to be questioned, but in due course she may see the advisability of confirming that that is, in fact, what happened."

My heart sank. I glanced at Jeff and there was sweat on his forehead. It was the thought that they'd got Tanya at their mercy that was so ghastly. Of course they could make her confirm it if they wanted to. They could reduce her to such a state that she'd come into court and swear Jeff's life away. Such things had happened before, and to tougher personalities than Tanya. Everyone had a breaking point.

Ganilov toyed with his papers. I think he was rather bored by the whole business.

After a while Jeff said quietly, "That's quite a case, Mr. Ganilov, but there's not a shred of truth in it. The motive's ridiculous, of course—Mullett never seriously bothered me and I had hardly any dealings with him. It's true that Tanya and I were friendly, but she wouldn't have helped me do a murder —that's fantastic. The fact that I've got cans like the one that was used means nothing—so have other people, and anyhow I've given quite a few of them away. As for the newspaper, it was an old one—anybody might have got hold of it."

"Oh, quite so, quite so," Ganilov agreed quickly. "I was only outlining the case. I agree that *so far* it is by no means conclusive."

There was an awkward pause—it still seemed to be Ganilov's move, but he sat back almost as though the interview were over. At last Jeff said, "Well, what do you propose to do about it?"

"Do about it?" echoed Ganilov innocently. "Why, nothing—at the moment. As I say, the case is not complete. Then again, relations between your country and mine are already difficult—we should be most reluctant to have to indict an American citizen for murder." He got up. "We must try to avoid unpleasantness all round. Now that I have explained our point of view, I am sure that you will both see the advantages of forgetting all about the Mullett case."

"Why, you goddamn blackmailer . . . !" Jeff burst out.

Ganilov withdrew the limp hand which he had extended in farewell. He seemed unable to believe that the oblique and tortuous methods of Soviet negotiation could have been described by so harsh a word.

XII

JEFF'S LANGUAGE when we got outside the building was quite unprintable, and the flow went on for an astonishingly long time. If he'd been in a position to do so I'm sure that at that moment he'd have dropped an atom bomb on the Kremlin with pleasure. He blinded away about police states, and people who used women as levers, and people you couldn't argue with because they didn't recognize any sort of morality, and I agreed with every word he said. We were still left, however, with the problem of what we were going to do about it, if anything. I was frankly worried.

"The point is," I said, "that if they did force Tanya to give evidence against you, you'd be in for it. You could get a life sentence."

Jeff gave me a derisive look. "Like hell I could! They're bluffing—they'd never get away with it."

"I wouldn't be certain of that. They're obviously determined to prevent the truth about Mullett's death getting out, and it looks as though they'll go to any lengths. Jeff, I'm not exaggerating—I believe you're in real danger. They've jailed foreigners before now on a damn sight thinner evidence than there is against you."

His face was about as grim as I'd seen it, and he didn't look as though he were open to argument. "They're simply trying to scare the pants off me," he said, "and it's not going to work."

"What about Tanya?"

He fell silent. With a hostage in the hands of the police, we were really quite powerless. They'd got us where they wanted us, because they were callous and we weren't. It was a filthy sort of pressure.

"I think we'd better admit defeat," I said. "You're leaving in a day or two—and the sooner the better. Once you've gone, they'll have no reason to turn the heat on Tanya. You'll be helping yourself and her too."

"It means playing their game," he said savagely. "It means they get away with blackmail and everything else. I feel more like handing my exit permit back and sticking around."

"Don't be a fool—it's not worth it. They've got all the cards—every single one."

He gave a violent kick at a piece of frozen snow and plodded on morosely for a while.

"I guess you're right, George," he said at last, "but, by God, it hurts. I never thought I'd take a licking from these people."

"For that matter," I said, "we were pretty well licked before we saw Ganilov. We've practically reached a dead end. We know how Mullett was killed but we don't know who did it and I don't see how we can hope to find out."

"There's that Russian address you've got—you might as well go along there before we call it a day. There's no risk—no one will know you've been if you're careful."

I said, "Perhaps I'll do that." I glanced quickly around. "Are you game for a walk?"

He looked surprised. "You don't mean you're going right now?"

"No—I just want to try a little experiment."

"Okay—I'm with you."

We set off briskly toward the "A" circular road. The pale yellow sun was sinking in a clear, frosty sky, and we had to move fast to keep warm. A thermometer on the corner of a building showed minus eighteen centigrade.

I said, "I once cut my face on my pocket handkerchief."

Jeff grinned. "I'll buy it."

"It was in Stalingrad, about this time of year. It was so cold the tears ran from my eyes and I dabbed them with my handkerchief. It froze in my pocket. Next time I used it I gouged my face with it. It was thirty-eight below."

He looked at me suspiciously. "Isn't that what you guys call 'shooting a line'?"

"I was only trying to keep you interested."

"Ah, shucks! Where are we going?"

"Any quiet spot."

We stepped smartly up the Tverskaya, weaving in and out of the home-going crowds. After we'd crossed the circular road they began to thin out a bit and presently I grabbed Jeff's elbow and steered him into a side road. There was no one in sight but a girl walking away from us about a hundred yards ahead.

"Right," I said, "this'll do." I stopped and pulled out a cigarette. "Give me a light, will you, and keep your eyes skinned."

He perked up, and snapped on his lighter. He'd cottoned on now. He was just lighting his own cigarette when two men turned the corner and walked past us, paying no attention. They were like a million other Russians—sturdily built, short-necked, and broad in the face. One wore a cloth coat with a fur collar and a brown fur hat, and the other a short padded jacket and astrakhan hat. Both carried brief cases. They could have been any two Russian functionaries going about their business, and perhaps they were. In this quiet district, we should soon know.

We waited a moment to make sure that no one else appeared, and then turned in our tracks and set off quickly down the Tverskaya the way we had come. Being "tailed" was a new experience for me—the four-letter boys had never bothered with correspondents in the ordinary way. It was the diplomats who always had someone at their heels, ostensibly for their own protection, and I remembered one of them describing to me during the war the various techniques he'd perfected for throwing off pursuit. His favorite method, I recalled, was to hire a rowing boat on the Moskva River and row upstream for five miles at full speed. He was, of course, an Englishman! Some of the things he'd told me might come in handy now.

After we'd walked about fifty yards we stopped in the dusk to study a copy of *Pravda* that was being displayed in a big glass-covered frame for the benefit of those citizens who couldn't get a copy of their own and liked to keep *au fait* with the timber-gathering and house-renovating campaigns. Peering round the edge of the frame, I saw our two men reappear and stand hesitating on the corner. As soon as they spotted us, they turned in our direction.

That was all I wanted to know, and we walked back to the hotel without bothering any more about them. Jeff had become rather thoughtful—I think he was convinced at last that Ganilov had not been bluffing. He was even more thoughtful when he returned that evening from a talk with a man named Dowson, a career diplomat at his Embassy who had had a lot of experience in the Iron Curtain countries. Dowson had reeled off a hair-raising list of recent cases where Westerners had been jailed east of the Curtain on fabricated charges. Some of them had been pretty tragic, and in most of them a woman had been concerned. His advice had been emphatic—to get out on the first plane.

There was nothing more I could do that day, for I didn't want to go searching for my Russian address in the dark. The best time, I thought, would be the afternoon of the next day and I made my plans accordingly.

Mullett's funeral took place on the following morning and of course all the delegates went, so the hotel was pretty quiet. I wrote a few innocuous letters and typed out some notes, and just before lunch I went down to borrow a plan of Moscow which I'd seen in Potts's room. The address on my envelope—printed rather laboriously in block characters, as though it had been copied from a letter by someone unfamiliar with the language—was Pushkinskaya 137, and the name of the addressee was A. A. Liefschitz. I located the street on the plan and mentally organized the journey. Just after three in the afternoon, when the homeward rush of workers was beginning to get under way, I left the hotel on foot. The same two M.V.D. men I'd seen the day before were hanging about in the vestibule, and there was an M.V.D. car near the entrance with two more men in it.

I walked slowly to the Metro station in Teatralni Square and took a ticket for Arbat. The man in the brown fur collar was a few yards behind me. He didn't bother to take a ticket—he just murmured something and passed through. He knew that I knew who he was and he obviously didn't mind. I gave him a broad wink and stepped on to the crowded escalator. A few moments later we were both swept on to the platform by a surging tide of humanity.

Fur Collar was beginning to look a bit worried, and with reason, for there is no more congested place on earth than the Moscow Metro and the behavior of the public is not such as to assist a sleuth. A train comes in, packed to the doors, and stops at a crowded platform. The automatic doors slide open. Those inside fling themselves out. Those outside fling themselves in. There is a frightful melee for perhaps half a minute, and then the doors remorselessly close. Fifty per cent of those who want to alight are carried on; fifty per cent of those who want to get on are left behind. This keeps the trains up to schedule and the service working efficiently.

As my train came in I pushed and elbowed forward with the rest, cursing and being cursed in accordance with the custom of the country. When I had forced my way sufficiently deeply into the coach to be safe from ejectment, I looked around for Fur Collar and saw that he also had made a lodgment. I moved the sharp end of a hoe from between my shoulder blades, leaned heavily on a sack of potatoes which later turned out to be a small peasant woman, and relaxed.

Successive assaults on the train at intermediate stations left the distance between myself and Fur Collar substantially unchanged. As we approached Arbat, I began to work my way slowly toward the doors by the simple and traditional expedient of exchanging places with anyone in front of me who wasn't proposing to get out. I saw that Fur Collar was bracing himself for a renewal of the chase.

"Are you getting out, comrade?" I asked a burly worker who was already very near the doors. *"Da!"* he said. I smiled at Fur Collar and the train slid to a halt.

The platform at Arbat was jammed solid. As the doors opened, everyone went into action at once. The burly worker was shoving nobly just in front of me and I wedged my twelve stone against him and shoved too. Fur Collar was having his own troubles and for the moment his attention was diverted. It was touch-and-go whether we got out or not. As the doors began to close amid howls of protest from all, I suddenly turned and tried to push my way in again. Somewhere down the train a woman screamed, "I've lost my galosh!" But you can't have war without casualties and no one took any notice. With a final thrust I just managed to squeeze between the doors before they made contact. I caught Fur Collar's eye as we moved off, and it was plaintive. He was being carried implacably away toward the escalator.

The woman who had lost her galosh screamed all the way to the next station without a break—she couldn't have made more noise if she'd lost her leg. I traveled on for two more stations after that, and then fought my way out and changed into a train going in the opposite direction. A quarter of an hour later I emerged from the Metro near the Central Market, and set out briskly for Pushkinskaya.

XIII

HAVING THROWN off my pursuer I assumed that my difficulties were pretty well over, but I was wrong. I found Pushkinskaya quite easily, but I couldn't find Liefschitz's residence. It simply wasn't there. Number 135 Pushkinskaya was an apartment house, number 139 was an apartment house, but number 137 turned out to be a squat, new-looking building of two stories which, from its lack of chimneys and its blank walls, I judged to be some kind of warehouse. Its heavy doors were locked, and there was no one about.

I thought perhaps I had made a mistake, and checked with the address on the envelope. On closer scrutiny, and with the help of a little imagination, it seemed just possible that the figure "7," which had no stroke through it, might have been intended for a "1." I walked back to number 131 and tackled a woman who was just coming out. No, she said, she didn't know of a Liefschitz there. I showed her the envelope, and explained my difficulty about number 137.

"*Oy yoy,*" she said, looking at me as though she thought me rather simple, "you won't find that. Number 137 was bombed during the war. There haven't been any apartments there for nine years." And she went on her way.

I felt baffled, and more than a little aggrieved. Probably not more than a couple of dozen buildings in the whole of Moscow had been seriously damaged by bombs, and mine had to be one of them. Liefschitz's correspondent was evidently as out-of-date as I was.

Well, there was nothing for it now but to apply the old reporter's technique. There was a newspaper kiosk fifty yards along the road and I strolled along there and browsed for a minute or two and finally bought a paper-backed edition of Stalin's *Problems of Leninism* for twenty-five kopecks. "I've had a journey for nothing," I grumbled to the vendor while I waited for my change. "I hoped to visit someone at number 137, but I'm told the place was bombed."

"Ah, yes, citizen," he said with a shake of his head. He was an oldish man, with white hair and a pointed beard. "You're behind the times. A stranger in Moscow, I dare say?"

"Yes, I'm from the Ukraine. I had a relative, a cousin, who used to live at number 137. Name of Liefschitz. It's very disappointing."

The man nodded understandingly. People in Russia were always trying to trace missing relatives. "The Bureau might be able to help you," he said, without much confidence.

The Bureau was a tracing agency for people who had been lost sight of during the war, and it was about the last place I wanted to visit. I said, "Thanks, comrade," and was just turning away when he called after me. "I've just remembered— they moved some of the families from 137 into that big red building across the way—number 128. Those that weren't killed. You might learn something there."

I thanked him again, less perfunctorily, and crossed the road to 128. It was a very tall, very narrow-chested apartment house of the cheapest brick, with a rusty fire escape zigzagging down one side and ferro-concrete balconies that had never been properly finished off—a typical example, I reflected, of "Five-Year-Plan-in-Four-Years" architecture. It looked as though it might have been flung up in about a fortnight. However, by Moscow standards it was a desirable residence, and if Mr. Liefschitz had been squeezed in there he could count himself lucky.

I climbed the crumbling front steps, pushed open the paint-less door, and stepped into a dark hallway. There was a strong smell of cabbage and *makhorka,* but no sign of life. I peered up the well of the stone staircase. No doubt most of the residents had just got home from work and were busy indoors preparing their afternoon meal. I estimated that there were about twenty flats in the building, and was just thinking of starting a door-to-door inquiry when I heard someone coughing a few yards along the hallway. I investigated. In a poky little room hardly bigger than a cupboard I found an old crone with a shawl over her head, warming herself at an iron stove and nibbling a hunk of black bread. This, presumably, was the janitor.

She gave me an indifferent glance. *"Da?"* she said.

"I'm looking for a Citizen Liefschitz, who used to live at 137. Does there happen to be anyone of that name here?"

"Yes," she said, "but he's just gone out."

I drew a sharp breath of relief. I had been lucky after all.

"He's gone to the market to buy potatoes," she supple-mented.

"Which flat does he live in?"

"Number 8." She gave me a slightly more curious look, but I must have appeared indigenous enough in my fur hat and *shuba* and felt *valinki* for I obviously passed her scrutiny. "The market is very near by," she said. "You would probably see him there."

"What is he like?"

"He wears glasses."

That was certainly as good a distinguishing mark as any, for in Moscow I don't suppose that one person in a hundred wears glasses. Nothing would be lost by looking for him and indeed it might be safer to establish contact with him outside than in. I told her I'd be back in about fifteen minutes if I failed to find him, and set off up the street again.

As always, the market was fascinating. It was a place where

you saw Moscow in the raw, and I felt rather sorry that Joe Cressey wasn't with me. Although it was now late in the day there was still a considerable crowd, and an incredibly drab crowd it was. Most of the people were home-going workers of the poorer sort, but there were also peasants from near-by collective farms, many of them dirty and bearded, and numerous beggars, and not a few ragamuffin children selling odds and ends that they'd probably stolen, and an astonishing proportion of the halt and lame. Here and there were neater, more respectable figures—members of the bureaucracy and the intelligentsia who had popped in to make a quick purchase for the afternoon meal—and it was among these that I looked for Liefschitz.

Inside the main building, where milk, vegetables and meat were being legally traded, a shuffling crowd moved between the stalls, buying little and fingering much. No one hurried, since almost all were trying to sell something privately and illegally while pretending not to. There was an undertone of muttered offer and request—"For whom soap?"—"Who has bread?"—and from time to time a swift, surreptitious transfer of money and goods. I saw no one in glasses.

I passed through into another building where a notice on the wall read: "Trade in household goods, food products or industrial goods is forbidden." Just beneath it, a shawled woman offered a saucepan and a battered samovar. Other vendors held out a variety of trifling objects—a pair of darned socks, a screw driver, a handful of pencil stubs, and two small apples. Scruffy militiamen looked on, pouncing quite arbitrarily to collect a fine from this person or from that, or to intervene with futile temper in the squabbles that repeatedly broke out.

In the dirty, trampled snow outside, more illegal salesmen were lined up. A man offered me three cardboard-tipped cigarettes as shiftily as though he were trading filthy pictures, and another a revolting piece of fruit tart in a scrap of newspaper.

A small girl piped repeatedly, "For whom an egg?" holding out a single hen's egg in a grubby paw. Further along a man was trying on a jacket, his eyes watchful for the approach of authority.

Markets are usually cheerful, colorful places, but this one wasn't. It was shabby, furtive and extremely grim. But it was still fascinating.

After I'd walked round twice, I decided that I'd missed my quarry and that I might as well go back to number 128. I was just leaving the enclosure when a little man passed me carrying a string bag through which potatoes bulged. I quickened my pace and caught him up. He was wearing glasses.

"Excuse me, citizen," I said, "but is your name Liefschitz?"

He glanced up in surprise. He was a man of about forty, a white-collar type, except that his collar was pretty soiled. He wore a black overcoat, shiny round the seat, and a pointed astrakhan hat. He had a lively, intelligent face.

"Yes," he said. "Who asks?"

"You wouldn't know my name if I told you, but I should be very grateful if I could have a few minutes' talk with you."

He looked me up and down. "What is it?" He was friendly but cautious.

I produced the envelope. "I think this must have been sent to you."

He put down his bag in the snow, took the envelope, and gazed at it for a long time, turning it over and over. He seemed very puzzled, and I had no doubt it meant something to him. "Are you a foreigner?" he asked.

On the whole, it seemed better to be frank with him. "Yes," I said, "I'm an Englishman."

I half expected him to snatch up his bag and rush off, but he didn't. Instead, his face broke into a smile and he seized my right hand between both his. "An Englishman! I am delighted to meet you. I speak a little English." And there and then he began to do so.

I interrupted him. "Better talk Russian!" I said.

Belatedly, he gave a nervous glance around. "You are quite right. We will walk a little." He thrust the envelope back into my hand and picked up his bag, and we moved off. "It is indeed pleasant to talk to an Englishman. During the war, when we were allies, I met many of your countrymen—at official functions, you understand. At that time, we could talk more freely. It was even possible to visit. Now . . ." He shook his head. "Now we are all afraid, and in any case there are few foreigners left in Moscow. You are a diplomat?"

"A newspaper correspondent."

"A correspondent! That is splendid." He gripped my arm with long, pale fingers, as though he feared that I might slip away. "I also am a journalist. I am the assistant editor of a magazine—*Classical Literature*. It is a comfortable back-water—quiet, and safe! What is your paper?"

I told him.

"The *Record?* Yes, I have seen it once, many years ago. It is not like your *Times,* but it is a lively paper, an interesting paper." Again he smiled. "Not like *Pravda.*"

"You are very daring, my friend."

He shrugged. "Safety is not everything. A backwater can become tedious. To meet someone from the outside world, the Western world, that is worth a risk. Come, we shall have some tea together. My apartment is quite near. You will come?"

For the fraction of a second, I hesitated. I would have liked to know something more of the connection between Mullett, the envelope, and this friendly, naïve, uninhibited little man before committing myself entirely to his care. Disappointment hovered on his face.

"Please!" he said.

"I don't want to get you into trouble."

"Don't worry—we will be careful. You look very like a Russian." He gave me a quick, confidential grin. "Like a rising young commissar! You know, you have the accent of the south—how is that?"

"I once lived in the Ukraine for a while," I explained. "In Moscow, the accent helps to conceal the fact that I am a foreigner."

"Of course—you are clever." He halted at number 128. "This is where I live. I am a bachelor—we shall not be disturbed once we are in."

He led the way up three flights of stone stairs and unlocked the door of flat number 8. "Follow me," he murmured. "Do not fear—it is all right."

I kept close behind him. The smell of cabbage was stronger now, and there were other smells as well—of humanity too closely packed. The flat had four or five rooms, and each room evidently housed at least one family, for there was a clatter of talk from all sides and the sounds of many children. At the end of the passage Liefschitz unlocked another door and ushered me into a small room.

"This," he said, "is my home. It is not, I fear, what you are accustomed to. I must apologize for it."

"Not at all."

He smiled. "You know how it is with us. Please take off your coat and be comfortable."

I glanced around. The room was about ten feet square. There was a single divan bed, a dresser piled with books and belongings, a chest of drawers also piled with books, a bureau, a small table and a solitary wooden chair. There was barely space to squeeze between the furniture.

"You will find that the bed is not too hard for sitting," he said. "By comparison with others, I am fortunate. At least I have a room—many, as you know, have only space for sleeping. It is a concession to me, because I am an artist and need quiet for my work. Quiet!" He gave a wry smile, and began to put a cloth on the table. "There are some, on the other hand, who live like millionaires. Especially those who write books which find favor. I, too, have written books, but they are not popular with the publishers. They are romantic, idealistic—that is a mistake. In our country, no idealistic book is approved unless its author has been dead for at least fifty years."

I picked up a battered, paper-backed volume from the bureau. It was a copy of *Pride and Prejudice* in translation. Its yellow pages had been lovingly sewn together and almost every sheet showed some sign of careful repair.

"A favorite, I see."

He nodded. "I have many books from the old days. The difficulty is to keep them in one piece. My friends all borrow them. In our country, it is only works on dialectical materialism which have shiny covers and crisp pages." He opened a cupboard and began to forage.

I put the book down. "Please don't go to a lot of trouble for me," I begged him.

His eyes twinkled. "My friend, occasions such as this occur rarely. We will eat, we will drink, and we will talk." He suddenly became anxious. "Or are you, perhaps, in a hurry?"

"No, no," I assured him, "I'm in no hurry, but I don't like to see you depleting your cupboard on my account."

"It is a pleasure," he said simply, and I knew that further protest would be useless.

Well, he produced everything he'd got. I wasn't hungry, but he pressed me to partake of crabmeat and herring and sausage, and he opened a bottle of wine, and when that was finished he found some sweets, and made tea in a kettle over an electric ring. All the time, we talked. He was avid for news of the outside world, for information about people and happenings. We talked of books and newspapers, of the cinema and theatre, of the coming Festival in London and of my last visit to Paris, of ballet and women's fashions and music, of Marshall Aid and Korea and the chances of war and peace. Half the time I was out of my depth, and he was amazingly well-informed within the limits of his opportunities, but he listened to me as attentively as though I were an oracle. It was pathetic.

The time passed quickly, and it was after ten o'clock when he gave a long sigh, as though of mental repletion, and switched the conversation to the circumstances of our meeting. "The envelope," he said. "You wanted to ask me about that?"

I nodded, I'd almost forgotten it myself.

"May I see it once more?" I passed it across to him and again he fingered it thoughtfully. "Where did you get it, my friend?"

"I found it at the Astoria Hotel. I thought I would like to have a talk with the person to whom it was addressed."

At that, he looked very surprised. "But you are making a mistake—a big mistake. This envelope is not addressed to me. I am Stefan Alexandrovitch Liefschitz. This is addressed to my father, Alexander Alexandrovitch Liefschitz. It is a very old envelope. See, the date is 1931. You thought it was new?"

I had another look. The postmark was by no means clear. Now that I examined it more closely, though, I saw that the figure indicating the year, which I had automatically read as 1951, was indeed 1931. Moreover, the royal head on the stamp was that of George V, not George VI. I had been grossly unobservant.

I stared at Liefschitz in some bewilderment. "But that's extraordinary. . . ."

"No, it is quite simple," he said, smiling. "You see, though my father was by profession a curator of museums, his hobby was collecting foreign stamps. He had correspondence with other collectors all over the world. This envelope is no doubt one that he received in that way."

I felt a stir of excitement. It was as though I had suddenly come upon an entirely new panorama, a country unknown, unsuspected, but full of possibilities.

"Is your father still alive?"

"Unfortunately, no. We were living together at number 137 when the bomb fell. He was at home, and I was not. He was killed, and I was transferred here."

"Yes, I see. How do you suppose this envelope got to the Astoria Hotel?"

"That I can tell you, if it interests you. During the war, it was very hard for us in Moscow. You know about that, of course, for you were here. There was very little to eat, and prices in the commercial shops and in the market were high. It was difficult to keep alive, and we all sold what we had in order to buy food. I had nothing but my father's stamp collection. One could not eat stamps, and one could not sell them —at least, so I thought. Who would pay good money for bits of paper when with the same money it was possible to buy eggs and meat? However, I was wrong. One day I was at a *vecherinka,* a party, at which most of the foreign colony were present. It was in the spring of 1942—the first big celebration, I think, after the German retreat. There I got into conversation with a girl—a Russian girl—or perhaps she got into conversation with me. She mentioned the name of an acquaintance of mine who had told her that I had a collection of foreign stamps. She said she knew someone who would perhaps buy them from me. Naturally, I was delighted. I met her in Sokolniki Park one Sunday afternoon and she took the collection away with her. A week later I met her again. She returned the bulk of the stamps, but a few of them she had set aside—perhaps fifty or sixty—and these she said she would like. We discussed payment, and arranged where I was to receive it. She took away the loose stamps in an envelope, for safety, and because of the green ink I remember that this was the envelope. It had been preserved, I suppose, with the rest of the collection, for my father hated to throw a stamp away."

"Can you tell me what the girl was like?" I had to ask, though it seemed hardly necessary.

He threw out his hands, rather wistfully. "Young, pretty,

with fair hair—long on her shoulders and cut in a fringe. A nice girl—I was sorry our relationship was so commercial. I never learned her name. She worked, I think, for VOKS."

I nodded. "I suppose you don't happen to know who the stamps were for?"

"Obviously for a foreigner, but the name . . . ? No, I don't know."

"Did you get a good price?"

He smiled. "I am not a philatelist—until then I had never been interested in the value of postage stamps. I can tell you this—*she* was satisfied with the bargain, for she asked me if I knew the names of other collectors in Moscow, and I was able to give her one or two from a notebook of my father's. Yes, and I was satisfied, too. I received a tin of American butter, nearly a kilo, and four tins of meat—Spam, I think it was called, very good indeed—and two pairs of nylon stockings which I sold for a fabulous sum in rubles, and a pair of trousers, which I wore. As a matter of fact, I still have the trousers."

"You have! Would it be possible, do you think . . . ?"

He laughed. "You would like to see them? *Pazhaluista!*" He rummaged in the chest of drawers and presently produced them. They were an ordinary pair of cloth trousers, of a light herringbone tweed, and at one time had no doubt been part of a suit. Now they were threadbare, patched and darned, and a little stained. By the cut, I judged they were not of Russian make. There was no tailor's mark, but just inside the waistband there was what looked like an old laundry or dry-cleaning mark, now barely decipherable.

Liefschitz held them up against him. "They were too long for me," he said, "but that was not difficult to remedy. They have given me good service. Now, alas, they are no longer fit to wear."

"They would still be of great value to me," I told him. "If I paid you enough rubles to buy a new Russian pair, would you allow me to take them?"

"But that is absurd," he said. "If you want them, you can have them with pleasure, but do not talk of payment. They are worn out, my friend."

"You know I can't take them for nothing, and there's no reason why I should. As it is, you will be doing me a great favor."

He shrugged and smiled. "Very well, if you insist." He folded them up carefully and then turned to me with a slightly worried look. "All this makes me very curious."

"Yes, it must." I debated what to say. "The thing is, I'd like to tell you what it's all about, and if you insist I will tell you, for you have the right to know. It will be better, though, if I don't. You see, in some strange way this envelope and the girl who took it from you and these trousers have all got mixed up in a case of murder."

"Murder!" He looked at me with a startled expression and then shook his head. "You are right, I am not interested in murder. There are enough problems already. Better not to tell me." He stood hesitating. "Shall we meet again, perhaps?"

"It would be unwise. I'm immensely grateful for your hospitality and your help and it's been delightful to talk to you— but to see each other again would be most dangerous. For you, and for me. You must believe me."

"Of course," he said sadly. "It is always the same. We open a little window, and a breath of fresh air comes in, a ray of light, and then quickly we have to slam it lest something horrible happens to us."

He wrapped up the trousers in an old newspaper and I put a thousand-ruble note on the table. I don't think he even noticed. He helped me on with my *shuba* and I thanked him again and we walked to the outer door.

"Good-by, my friend," he said, leaning over the stair rail as I began to descend. His voice dropped to a murmur. "You are very fortunate—to be English."

XIV

WHAT LIEFSCHITZ had told me seemed to put a very different complexion on the case. Until now, I had taken it for granted that the motive for Mullett's murder had been a personal one—hatred, perhaps, or revenge, or fear. Now there was a hint, if no more, of a possible financial angle. I was far from seeing how this new element fitted into the known picture, but as I scrunched my way back through the snow to the Astoria I certainly had plenty of food for thought. I wondered just how much money *had* been at stake.

All that I knew about philately would have gone easily on to a pinhead, but you didn't have to be an expert to know that stamp collections could be valuable, and Liefschitz's foreigner had had exceptional opportunities. Russia had for years been virtually cut off from normal interchanges with the outside world and there must have been an unusually rich treasure house to rifle. The fact that Liefschitz had been no haphazard contact but one of a systematically exploited chain showed that the enterprise had been on a considerable scale, and the care with which the collections had evidently been sifted was the mark of an expert who knew his values. The business must have been all the more lucrative since the stamps had been obtained in return for what, to a foreigner, must have seemed trivia—the surplus items of wardrobe and larder which he could have replenished with no great difficulty. For that negligible outlay, it seemed to me, he might well have amassed a collection of hand-picked stamps which would have been worth a small fortune after the war in the free market of the Western world.

He had been, evidently, a discreet as well as a not over-scrupulous person. A foreigner, making his own contacts and doing his own trading with Russians on such a scale, would most likely have drawn unfavorable attention to himself in the end. The authorities, quite understandably, had never liked the "trinkets for copra" method of trade. But with Tanya to act as his go-between, he would have been able to sit back securely and wait for the wealth to pour in. I wondered just how much Tanya herself had got out of it all. No more, prob-ably, than a good share of imported luxuries, but to a young girl in wartime Moscow that would have meant all the dif-ference between privation and affluence.

The main thing now was to discover what, if any, the con-nection had been between this nine-year-old racket and the present murder. That there was some link, I felt sure. Tanya had been deep in the stamp business; Tanya had allowed the murderer to pass through her room; and an envelope that related to the stamp business had been found among Mullett's papers. Surely there was significance in that chain of events? At the same time, it was very much in my mind that the stamp racketeer's loot would have had no value as long as it was kept in Russia, and that he would therefore have taken it out with him at the first opportunity—and sold it. If the treasure had been liquidated, where did the financial motive come in?

There was another thing. If the stamps had been removed from the country and sold, by what strange accident had that old envelope reappeared in Moscow after all this time? Had it perhaps been tucked away in some old wallet or suit and been brought to light again more or less fortuitously? It was possi-ble, but surely unlikely? Again, how had Mullett, of all people, come to be connected with it? One explanation was obvious; but I found it even more difficult to imagine a man of Mullett's character and interests as an avaricious buyer-up of underpriced goods than as an agent of M.I.5.

All the same, the possibility that he had been a secret philatelist had to be explored, and the only place to search for indications was, once again, his room. I noticed, as I approached along the corridor, that the watchdog had been withdrawn. Presumably the police felt that they no longer had anything to hide.

Getting into Mullett's room was now simple routine. I broke my seals just before midnight and a few moments later I was standing once more on the bloodstained carpet. No one had taken the trouble to seal Mullett's doors up again, and the appearance of the place was, if anything, more untidy and neglected than when I had last been there. Apparently the hotel people proposed to leave the room undisturbed until the time came for the delegation to depart.

My search of Mullett's effects was far more leisurely and detailed than on my first visit. I was necessarily a little vague about what, specifically, I was looking for; I simply had the feeling that it was somehow unlikely—supposing Mullett to have been interested in stamps—that that one envelope would be the only sign. Philatelists, like other enthusiasts, tended to carry some signs of their hobby around with them. If there had been any of the heavier impedimenta—catalogs or magazines or albums—I should already have seen them, but I thought that there might be some notebook among his effects, with telltale entries; some reference in a diary, perhaps, to a successful purchase; even, maybe, a loose stamp or two. It took me more than an hour to turn out all his drawers and cases, with their now familiar contents, and to examine all his small possessions one by one. At the end of it, I'd drawn a complete blank. Apart from that nine-year-old envelope, there was nothing.

I felt baffled. After my talk with Liefschitz I'd really begun to feel there was a chance that I might break the case open, but now I seemed to have lost the trail again. I sat down moodily on a chair arm and lit a cigarette, thinking that quiet contemplation of the scene might assist the flow of ideas. Almost with exasperation, I saw in my mind's eye that envelope lying among the papers. It had been as out of place there as an inkstand on a luncheon table. *Who* had put it there, and *why?*

When I stubbed out my cigarette ten minutes later I was as far from an answer as ever and there seemed no point in sticking around. Perhaps Jeff would be able to suggest something in the morning. I crossed the room and was just going to switch off the light when, as my eye traversed the enigmatic countenance of Stalin above the divan, something about the picture struck me as odd, and I paused. The heavy gilt frame, which before had hung slightly askew, was now quite straight. Of the many objects in the room which had contributed to the general appearance of disorder, only the picture of the Great Leader and Teacher had received attention.

I smiled. Perhaps one of the policemen had had an unusually precise eye, or had sensed lese majesty in the crooked frame. It was a small thing, but as I considered it I felt intrigued. In any ordinary room I wouldn't have given the matter a second thought, but this was a murder room, and the tiniest thing might be significant. A picture, after all, might hide something—or, shifted out of place, reveal something. My thoughts at this stage dwelt vaguely on concealed microphones, which were reputed to be sprinkled about the Astoria in fair numbers, and on camouflaged cupboards, and similar melodramatic devices. Anyway, there was no harm in looking. Standing on the divan, I lifted the picture off its hook and laid it carefully face downward at my feet. Then I examined the wall, tapping the plaster with my finger tips in the hope of discovering a hollow place. I was very thorough, but found nothing at all suspicious. My imagination was running away with me, I decided,

I bent to lift the picture, and was about to rehang it when something else caught my attention. The frame was old, with the dust of years gathered in its moldings; the glass was dirty. Everything spoke of neglect. But the back of the picture, which consisted of three widths of thin plywood held in place by sprigs driven lightly into the frame, looked as though it had recently been opened. There were marks on the wood where some tool had been used to gouge out the sprigs—and the marks were definitely fresh.

My curiosity was now thoroughly aroused. Not merely was this no ordinary room, but the picture, evidently, was no ordinary picture. The straightening of it on its hook no longer struck me as a touching tribute to the Leader—it suggested, rather, a desire to make the thing as inconspicuous as possible and so to conceal the fact that the back had been opened. Obviously I had to investigate further.

I fetched a pair of scissors from Mullett's toilet set and got to work. After a little difficulty, and some more scoring of the wood, I managed to dig out enough of the sprigs to release one section of the plywood. What I saw, when I cautiously eased it from the frame, drew a low whistle from me. Clearly outlined against the gray-white back of the canvas was a slightly paler rectangle about twelve inches long and nine broad. On the inside of the plywood itself, corresponding in position to the rectangle though with less sharply defined edges, was a faint but unmistakable indentation. Some large, flattish object had evidently been held there under pressure between the canvas and the plywood—and for a very long time. Only the passage of years, of many years, could have produced those marks.

I thrust aside the temptation to leap ahead, and tried to look at the facts squarely. Something had been cached here for a long while. It had been taken out very recently and a murder had occurred, so there was probably some connection between the two things. About the time that it was removed, the stamped envelope had appeared on Mullett's table. The object concealed could have been, from its size and shape, a large packet filled with stamps. There was no other kind of secret hoard that I could think of from which that incongruous envelope could have been detached. The chain of argument seemed sound. To all appearances, and against all reasonable expectation, the racketeer's stamp collection had been hidden behind this picture since 1942. As it had now disappeared, the conclusion seemed inescapable that the murder of Mullett had resulted from an attempt—a successful attempt—to steal it or recover it.

I turned that over for a while. To steal or recover—which? My thoughts reverted to the possibility that Mullett himself might have been the original racketeer. This was his first trip to Moscow since the war, and he might have come with the specific intention of regaining his booty. He might, for that purpose, have asked to be put back into the room he had occupied during the war—as Islwyn Thomas had done in the case of *his* room, for less concrete reasons. Having achieved that, he might have told Tanya, his former associate, that the stamps were in his possession again. She, in turn, might have told someone else and helped that someone to plan a theft and murder.

It was a possible theory, but I didn't much like it. I couldn't see either Mullett or Tanya in the roles for which it cast them.

The alternative—and more likely—explanation was that Mullett had been given, quite fortuitously, the room which had been occupied during the war by the stamp racketeer, and that this man, after enlisting Tanya's help, had killed Mullett in the course of an attempt to recover his own stamps from the place where he'd put them.

Once I'd begun to think on those lines, two conclusions leaped at me. The first was that the murderer was definitely one of the delegates. The stamps had been hidden by a foreigner in 1942, when several of the delegates had been in Moscow. They had lain untouched for nine years, until the arrival of the delegation, which was the only new factor. No one but a delegate qualified.

The second conclusion was more startling. I remembered that the period chosen for the attempt had been one when Mullett had been out of the way and the room had been empty. It had been a period, moreover, when Mullett was supposed to be broadcasting, and when the intruder could therefore consider himself safe from interruption. In those circumstances, it surely followed that *this man had not intended to commit murder at all.* If Mullett had not returned unexpectedly that night, he might still have been alive.

Now at last I began to understand something which had long puzzled me. With his unsealed doors, his balcony approach and his clumsy paste pot, the murderer had appeared to take quite unnecessary risks in order to bring about Mullett's death. A straight entry and a straight assault would have been simpler and safer. But if he had not intended to kill Mullett at all, there should have been no risks to speak of. If everything had gone according to plan he would have recovered the stamps and departed in good order before Mullett's arrival, and no one would ever have had any suspicion that anything out of the ordinary had occurred. Mullett wouldn't have missed the stamps, for he hadn't known they were there. He would certainly not have thought of examining the seals of his French windows on his return; and before long the paste would have dried. He would have been equally unlikely to investigate the contents of his wastepaper basket. All traces of movement on the balcony would soon have been covered by fresh snow. It should have been a cinch. Instead, by sheer bad luck, it had been a disaster.

There were almost enough facts available now for me to attempt a reconstruction of at least a part of that evening's events. The murderer must have passed through Tanya's room, I estimated, not later than half-past eight, because Jeff had gone in to her at a quarter to nine and by then her doors had been resealed. In all probability, the murderer had collected the tin of paste and the strips of brown paper on his way through. He might have picked up the newspaper there, too. One of Jeff's old *Pravda*'s could easily have come into Tanya's possession.

He had made the transit of the balconies, covering his tracks as he went. He wouldn't have needed to hurry, for as far as he knew he had plenty of time in hand. Then he had broken into Mullett's room. That was all clear enough.

The precise order of his actions after that could be a matter only of guesswork. His first impulse must surely have been to satisfy himself that the stamps were still where he had left them. He would, I imagined, have gone straight to the picture, recovered the loot, fastened up the back of the frame, and rehung it. I doubted if he would have opened the package, but it was possible. He would probably have laid it on the divan or the table.

Next, I thought, he would have sealed up the doors behind him—a rather lengthy job, requiring care. There might have been surplus strips of paper to dispose of—he could have stuffed those into his pocket. Afterward, he would certainly have needed a wash, and while he was in the bathroom he would probably have taken the opportunity to wash out the paste tin. Having no cause to expect any investigation, he would have felt quite safe in slipping the tin and the wet newspaper into the bottom of the wastebasket.

By now, the time must have been getting on—well after nine, I thought, with all those jobs behind him. Mullett's voice would have been booming reassuringly from the loud-speaker opposite. Then suddenly, without the formality of a knock, a key had scraped in the door.

The scene was so vivid to me, sitting there in the room reconstructing the pattern of events, that I felt the sharp panic of that moment almost as a physical sensation. If the intruder had had time to think at all, he would no doubt have supposed that a chambermaid was about to enter, but I couldn't imagine that he had had a second for thought. His reaction would have been instant. He had done, surely, what anyone would have done in the circumstances—retreated behind the bed curtain. From there, peering out, he had seen—of all fantastic, impossible things—Mullett!

Then what had happened? Somehow, I had to account for the presence of that stamped envelope on the table. Perhaps Mullett had been responsible for that. If he had seen a strange packet lying on his table, he would have opened it. He would certainly have been interested in the contents. He might well have drawn up a chair and settled down to examine them.

On that assumption, how would the intruder have acted? He had been in a fearful position. In a few moments, his unauthorized presence would inevitably be discovered. It could not possibly be explained away, for he had not even made his entrance through the door with a borrowed key—he had broken in, and tried to conceal the fact. An explanation would be demanded. He would have to admit everything to Mullett —tell him the whole sordid story of the stamps. It would mean humiliation. Far worse, perhaps, it would mean the loss of the stamps. Mullett might agree to forget the episode in the interests of the delegation, but he was not a man to surrender ill-gotten booty. All this must have flashed through the intruder's mind.

On the instant, he would have had to make a decision—to lose all, or to silence the man at the table. Not necessarily to kill him—just to creep up unnoticed and hit him hard enough to knock him out, and then slip away. By morning, the episode would have shrunk to a mere bump on Mullett's head.

And so he had gripped the nearest weapon, the only available weapon, a bottle, and he had stepped out and slugged Mullett. And because the old man had had an exceptionally thin skull, it had caved in against all the rules, and he'd rolled lifeless to the floor.

The shock to the killer must have been severe. Nevertheless, he'd managed to keep his head. He had gathered up the stamps—all except the solitary envelope which Mullett must have pushed accidentally among the papers. He had ransacked the dead man's pockets to leave an impression of petty theft, and he had left the door ajar behind him to suggest an entry from the corridor.

A cool hand, evidently; but developments since the murder must have put an almost unbearable strain on the strongest nerve. An innocent man accused, an appalled accomplice whisked away. The knowledge that the Russians had discovered everything; that they were sitting tight and blaming others only because they thought he might still be useful; that he was wholly in their power. The fear, surely, that they might change their minds about him. I didn't envy him his thoughts.

On one score, I felt immensely relieved. Tanya's part in this affair had evidently been very different from what I, at least, had feared. She had, it was true, made it possible for her former principal to get secret access to his cache of booty, but that appeared to be the limit of her moral involvement. Not for a second could she ever have contemplated the possibility that murder would result, and it was plain that the shock had overwhelmed her. No wonder she had fainted!

Thoughtfully, I rehung the picture. It had told me a great deal—it had filled in all the gaps in my knowledge about "How?" and "Why?". But about the most important thing of all—the identity of the murderer—I still hadn't a clue. Except, of course, the trousers.

XV

WHEN I told Jeff the news next morning, I could almost see the burden rolling from his back. In spite of his stout defense of Tanya, I think he'd been even more depressed by the thought that she might actually have had a hand in the planning of the crime than he had been about her personal safety. Anyway, he certainly cheered up remarkably. In fact, he was now inclined to go to extremes and exonerate her completely.

"Mind you," he said, "I'm not kidding myself that that stamp business was exactly ethical. Kind of borderline case, maybe. The thing is, it wasn't Tanya's show. She was obviously under this guy's influence, and I bet she didn't get much of a cut. Even if she did—well, hell, look how the women in this town were starved of decent things—look how they still are. I figure any girl around here would have done the same thing."

I agreed. I certainly wasn't passing any moral judgments on that score. "At the same time," I said, "helping the fellow to break into someone else's room was going a bit far."

"Sure it was—the kid ought to have her head examined. Still, even that wasn't as bad as it seems to us now. This guy would have claimed that the stamps belonged to him—there wasn't any question of theft. If there hadn't been a murder, it wouldn't have amounted to so much."

"I imagine the Russians would have taken a dim view," I said, "murder or no murder. It would have meant a jail sentence for Tanya anyway."

"So what? They jail you here at the drop of a hat. What's that popular crack that Waterhouse was telling me about?— 'Everyone here has been in jail, or is in jail now, or will be in jail soon.' If it hadn't been for this it would have been for something else." He looked at me a little aggressively and then, slowly, he began to grin. "Okay, she shouldn't have done it, but she's a sweet kid all the same. Look, George, now that we've got this far surely we ought to be able to clean the case up? Then maybe they'll let her go after a few months' timber-cutting or whatever it is she's doing."

"What about Ganilov's threat?"

"Hell, that's all old stuff now. What you found out yester-day puts me right in the clear. I wasn't here during the war, and I don't know the first thing about stamps. With all this fresh evidence, they haven't got a hope of making a charge stick."

I was inclined to agree about that. "The trouble is, *we* haven't much hope of making a charge stick, either. The delegation's leaving in a couple of days or so and we haven't the hint of a case against any of them."

He grunted. "What *have* we got? Just the pants?"

"They're the only bit of solid evidence."

"Well, let's have a look at them."

I fetched them from the drawer in which I'd locked them away, and he held them up to the light. "I guess these were a swell pair of pants once," he said, "but they've sure seen their best days. What about the size? It's a pity we can't go around trying them on all the delegates."

"I've done the next best thing," I told him, "I've tried them on myself. With the legs turned down to the original position they're a pretty good fit."

Jeff regarded me thoughtfully. "In that case I'd say they'd be right for Bolting—his figure's the dead spit of yours. Islwyn Thomas, too—just right. They'd be a bit loose on the Prof, but he may have lost weight. No good for Tranter, no good for Cressey."

"I worked that out, too," I said. "There's a snag, though. The trousers might not have been bought for the murderer."

He looked surprised. "How come?"

"Well, he may have had the idea of this stamp racket in his mind when he first heard he was coming to Russia. If so, he'd have stocked up with suitable garments and it wouldn't have mattered what size they were—in fact, a variety of sizes would have been all the better for his purpose."

"He was mighty smart if he saw that far ahead," Jeff said. "It's much more likely he wouldn't have realized the opportunities till he got here. Anyway, these pants have been cleaned—and not in Russia, either. You're not suggesting he brought in assorted sizes of *used* clothes?"

I had to agree that that was hardly likely. "We still can't be sure the trousers were his, though—he could have got them from someone else while he was here. There was a lot of bequeathing—anyone who left the country for good would always pass on his old stuff to a pal, and believe me, nobody bothered much about the fit. If the legatee couldn't wear the things himself, there were always secretaries and girl friends clamoring for castoffs for their relatives. In those days you took what was offered and were grateful."

Jeff digested that. "Okay, but it still seems more likely than not that the pants belonged to the guy who traded them."

I conceded the greater likelihood. "Even so," I said ruefully, "it's going to be difficult enough to trace them back after all these years."

He examined the threadbare garment again. "I guess you're right. What about this laundry mark?—it might come up with a bit of care. Any chance of getting a line on that back home, do you suppose?"

"An outside chance, perhaps, if I could get some help."

"What about the other stuff that Tanya traded to your

friend Liefschitz—doesn't that tell us anything? It sounded
as though it was all American stuff—is that an angle?"

"I don't think so. As far as the tinned food's concerned, this
hotel was full of lend-lease stuff during the war—everybody
had some. And the fellow could have brought the nylons in
with him—most people bought a few pairs in Cairo or Teheran
on their way through."

"Yeah, I see." He puffed thoughtfully at his cigarette for
a moment or two. Presently he said, "What beats me, George,
is how this guy came to go off without the stamps, after taking
all that trouble. It seems crazy."

"That's what's bothering me," I said. "I can see everything
up to that point. He'd completed his collection and he wanted
a safe temporary hiding place more or less under his eye and
I imagine he chose the picture because that was about the one
place where light-fingered chambermaids wouldn't go poking
about. He would certainly have intended to take the packet
away with him—and then he didn't. There must have been
some damn good reason."

Jeff screwed up his face in thought. "It was wartime, of
course—I guess lots of unexpected things happened to people
around 1942. Didn't you tell me something about Mullett
having to beat it practically overnight to Kuibyshev in the
evacuation?"

"I did, yes—but that was in 1941. And he was the victim,
not the murderer."

"Sure, I know—I was just illustrating. If *he* had to rush
off, why shouldn't some other guy have had the same kind of
experience?"

That rang a bell at once. "Why, of course," I exclaimed,
"there *was* someone else who left at very short notice—Islwyn
Thomas. He was put under arrest for striking a senior officer.
I don't know exactly what happened afterward, but if he was
brought back here under escort he might not have had a
chance to collect his haul."

"What was he doing at the hotel, anyway?"

"Oh, just a spillover from the Mission. It did happen from time to time."

"Any idea which was his room?"

My moment of excitement passed. "Of course, yes—the one he's in now. He was announcing the fact with great glee the day the delegation arrived."

"Oh, he was! Well, maybe he was trying to throw dust in our eyes. Maybe the room he really had was Mullett's, and he was building up an alibi before he got to work."

"It's possible," I agreed. "So's the other thing, though. He's a shocking sentimentalist."

"He's nuts about that country of his. I'm all for self-determination, but he talks a heck of a lot of drivel. Maybe he ran the stamp racket to raise funds for the Welsh national revolution!"

I grinned. "There'd be precedents for that over here. Uncle Joe Stalin started his secular career robbing banks for the Cause."

"Sure! Thomas is just the type to have done this job, too. A guy who'd slap his commanding officer wouldn't hesitate to hit Mullett with a bottle if he was in a tight corner. And he's active enough to have made that balcony crossing."

"I suppose Tanya never dropped a hint that she'd known him before?"

"Not a word. She may have." His forehead wrinkled in a frown. "Funny, I never liked that guy."

I laughed. "Well, we seem to be making a bit of progress, anyway. Now what about the others who were here in 1942? What about Schofield—would he have gone off in a hurry, I wonder?"

"I'd guess he'd have been more likely to get left behind. Besides, those official missions usually work to a comfortable schedule—you can bet he'd have had twelve hours' notice, at least."

"I'd like to know more about what he was doing over here, all the same. If he was a key man on that mission—I'm just thinking aloud, now—I suppose he might have been called home suddenly for consultations in the middle of the talks and . . . No, it won't do. He'd have managed to get a few minutes alone with the picture, somehow."

"Pity!" said Jeff. "He's the type that would understand about the values of stamps—keen mind, good at figures, that sort of thing. Familiar with markets. Quite a likely suspect, in some ways."

"Do you think so? I'd have said myself that he lived in a much too rarefied intellectual atmosphere to run a private racket like that. As long as he had tobacco for his pipe and some comfortable old clothes and a pile of books, I think he'd always be content. I've never seen anyone who seemed to care so little for the fleshpots."

"That could be misleading," said Jeff. "What about those miser fellows who keep millions of bucks in old chests and live like beggars? Maybe it's just because the Prof has salted so much away that he looks so scruffy. He was certainly handy for the job—right across the corridor from Tanya. Slipping in and out of those rooms would have been less risky for him than for anyone. He's pretty active, too, in a stringy sort of way—I imagine he could have negotiated the balconies."

"Can you see him getting on those confidential terms with Tanya?"

"As a purely business deal, I guess I can. There'd have been plenty of opportunity, too—I dare say she was attached to that economic mission of his the same way she was attached to Mullett's crowd. Still, we've nothing on him really. What about Bolting?—he was here in 1942. I wonder if *he* left in a hurry?"

"He said something on the train coming in about having fractured his skull skiing. I don't know what happened to him after that. It would bear looking into."

"It sure would, bud. Now he *is* the sort of guy who might tie a woman round his fingers. It wouldn't surprise me to know he likes the fleshpots *and* the flesh."

I nodded. "Both expensive tastes, too."

"Oh, he could use the dough, all right. There's another thing. Any guy who walks around with his head wrapped up in a balaclava needs watching!"

I chuckled. "Damn it, the fellow's got a bad throat."

"So what? Maybe he got it playing hide-and-seek on the balcony."

"He had it before then. Don't you remember?—he was beginning to get hoarse at the VOKS party."

"Okay—he made it worse on the balcony, going out without his coat. Anyway, he's acting suspiciously. Who wanted the delegation to pack up and leave after the murder? Bolting. Well, if he'd just killed Mullett and recovered the stamps, that's exactly the line he'd have taken. He'd have wanted to beat it from here at top speed and never come back."

"So he would if he simply had quinsy and felt like hell and didn't want to look at any more nurseries."

"Have it your own way, George. Anyway, there's as good or as bad a case against him as there is against the other two. What we need, of course, is more information."

"Waterhouse will be here soon. Perhaps he'll be able to fill in some of the gaps."

"Let's hope so," said Jeff. "This case is just a goddamn sieve at the moment." He got up and took a turn or two across the room and then he suddenly stopped. "Say, if we're on the right lines and this guy *did* have to leave in such a hurry that he couldn't take the stamps with him, wouldn't he have been working like the devil ever since to get back here? Maybe that gives us a lead?"

I wasn't quite sure what was in his mind. "You mean like Islwyn Thomas parading his Welsh nationalism to attract favorable notice and hook an invitation?"

"Something like that."

I pondered. "It seems to me they're all in the same boat there. Bolting, for instance—getting into Parliament and putting the Russian case day in and day out. Even Schofield—he's been making himself delegation-prone in an academic sort of way. What's to choose between them? Anyway, I don't think we can safely draw conclusions from pro-Russian activity. Most of the people who were sent out to Russia during the war were 'pro'—it was their golden age—and when they got home they'd naturally continue on the same lines—even more so, because they'd have special knowledge to exploit."

"Still, this guy might have made an extra effort."

"He might. On the other hand, he might have written off his haul. Then when a stroke of luck brought him back here he'd naturally look around for the picture and once he'd found it he wouldn't be able to rest. It could have happened without planning."

Jeff nodded. "Okay, no lead." He looked at me speculatively. "There is one other approach, of course. Whoever recovered those stamps must have them with him in his room right now. That's a teasing thought."

I smiled. *"I'm* not breaking into any more rooms. Forget it, Jeff—it's too risky. Mullett's was accessible but the others aren't, and it's impossible to get the keys."

"I guess you're right," he said reluctantly, "but it sure would be a short cut to a solution if we knew where to look."

At that point Waterhouse arrived. Jeff made some coffee on my electric stove and on the principle that three heads were better than two I again outlined the position as we knew it. The whole business was getting pretty complicated by now, and Waterhouse seemed a little puzzled once or twice. He hadn't been milling over it the way we had, of course.

"The key to the whole thing," I told him finally, "seems to be the answer to this one question—who left Moscow in a tearing hurry?—and that's where you come in. You're the man with the memory. Do you happen to remember the precise circumstances in which Thomas, Schofield and Bolting got out?"

Waterhouse took his coffee and settled himself in a comfortable chair. "Well, now," he said, "as far as that flamboyant Welshman is concerned I don't know anything, except that he left in disgrace. I hardly think he was under arrest, except in a technical sense, perhaps, and I'm sure he'd have done his own packing."

I nodded. That, on the whole, was my own feeling.

"Schofield?—now let me see, he was on Watson's supply mission and—yes, they *did* go off in a rush. I remember that very well, because I was giving Watson luncheon at the Aragvi and he had to dash away with his *shashlik* almost untouched. There was a Catalina flying out by the northern route and they were given about ten minutes to pack. You know how difficult transport was in those early days—people had to take what there was without argument, even V.I.P.'s."

I knew very well. "All the same," I said, "Schofield would surely have managed to grab the stamps, however short the notice? Unless, of course, someone was with him all the time, and that seems unlikely. You don't happen to remember which room he had, do you?"

"Hardly, dear boy. I am not the Recording Angel."

"Ah, well, let's leave him. What about Bolting? I gather he had an accident."

"That's right, he did. He was out skiing with a girl and tried a slope that was too steep for him. If I remember correctly, he crashed into a tree." Waterhouse gave a sidelong glance at Jeff, who had already opened his mouth to speak. "I do *not* know who the girl was."

"Too bad," said Jeff, and relaxed.

"All I can tell you is that he was badly hurt—he wasn't around at all after that. They took him to the hospital here but he didn't completely recover—loss of memory, or something—and he was sent home by plane. He must have got over it in the end, of course."

"Loss of memory?" I echoed. "Now that *is* something. Why, he might not have remembered about the stamps until he was back in England. I wonder how complete it was."

"I doubt if there's anyone here now who could tell you—except the Russians, of course, and they won't."

"Well, it's very intriguing. Did you know much about him, Waterhouse, at that time?"

"Not a great deal. He wasn't a particularly prominent member of the colony. His accounts job at the Embassy was a very minor one, and he just mixed in with everybody. He's blossomed out quite a lot—I know I was rather surprised when I heard he'd been elected to Parliament."

"How did he manage to get here in the first place?"

"Oh, I think he was seconded from the Army on account of his Russian. Yes, I remember now, he was in the Desert—he came in from the Middle East."

Jeff grinned at me. "As you said, laddie—complete with nylons!"

"It adds up to this, then," I said. "The choice seems to lie between Bolting, Schofield and Thomas, with Bolting slightly in the lead. Tranter, Cressey and Mrs. Clarke have never been to Russia before, and Manning wasn't here during the war—so they're out. Right?"

Waterhouse gave a rather preoccupied nod. I considered the proposition again and there didn't seem to me to be a way round it. Presently, though, I recalled a remark that he'd made a few days earlier.

"At that VOKS party," I said, "you seemed to think that you'd met Tranter before. Could you have?"

"I still think so," said Waterhouse slowly, "but for the life of me I can't remember where. Perhaps it'll come back to me." He sat frowning for a moment. Then he suddenly looked across at me with an odd expression and put down his cup.

"I've just thought of something else, though—I'm afraid there may be a weakness in your chain of argument, gentlemen. You've been assuming that the murderer-to-be must have left suddenly in 1942 because otherwise he'd have been able to take the stamps with him. That isn't sound, you know. A picture on a wall isn't a fixture, especially a picture of Uncle Joe. Suppose that a few days before this villain of yours was due to leave, the picture was removed to grace some banquet—perhaps in the hotel, perhaps outside? In those circumstances, your man might very easily have been unable to lay his hands on it."

I gave an exclamation of disgust. Waterhouse was dead right, of course—we'd completely overlooked that possibility. A rather sterile silence followed.

"Well," said Jeff finally, "there seems to be no point in wasting any more time over that quick exit business. I guess we ought to have had Waterhouse K.C. in on this earlier. The best thing we can do now is to try and find out who occupied this room of Mullett's in 1942—work at it from that end. Somebody might remember."

I was still thinking about the mobility of the picture, and now another snag occurred to me. "That's all very well, but how do we know that the picture was in that particular room when the fellow was collecting his stamps? In nine years, it may have been switched all over the place. Our man may have had quite a different room. What do you think, Waterhouse?"

"It's possible, of course," he said. "At the same time, I've known this hotel for nearly thirty years, and there've been remarkably few *permanent* changes. Once a picture was hung, I'm inclined to think it would remain *in situ* except in the sort of case I mentioned—a special removal for some function. Even then, I think the chances are that it would be put back in the same place afterward."

I nodded. "Well, it's no good speculating any more. I'll

make some inquiries about the history of the picture, and if it seems that it hasn't been moved about I'll do as Jeff suggests and try to get a line on who had Mullett's room during the war. It's a long shot, but it might come off."

"If it turns out to be the Welshman," said Jeff, "I'll stand you a bottle of champagne. Now *that's* what we need in this case—to catch someone out in a thundering big lie."

XVI

I SPENT the rest of the morning chasing chambermaids. I realized that they would probably chatter afterward about my questions, however concretely I appealed to their discretion, but that couldn't be helped. We knew enough now to go full speed ahead with all possible lines of inquiry even at the cost of secrecy, and there was no other way of getting the information I wanted.

It was Katya, a maid recently transferred from the fourth to the third floor, who proved most useful. She said she was sure that the picture of Stalin had hung in room 435—Mullett's room—ever since she could remember, which was from well before the war. When I pressed her, she agreed that she couldn't really be certain that it hadn't been removed temporarily for a conference or a banquet, but she insisted that if so it had been restored afterward to its rightful place. Waterhouse's view seemed fully confirmed. Each room, apparently, had its allocation of furniture, its special inventory, and I gathered that the necessity of making any changes always rocked the hotel bureaucracy to its foundations. I remembered the trouble there had sometimes been over moving a chair from a colleague's room without permission of the management, and the ritual over Potts's request for the hotel cat, and I could believe what Katya said. For once, I felt thankful for such rigidity. I presented her with a couple of cakes of toilet soap and she was so overcome with gratitude that she bowed until her forehead almost scraped the floor.

What the maids couldn't tell me was who had occupied

Mullett's room in 1942, and that was now the most vital question of all. One or two of them professed to have vague recollections, particularly when they saw Katya's soap, but their accounts were so conflicting that it was obvious no reliance could be placed on them. Several of the waiters were equally obliging but equally unhelpful. The information would, of course, be buried somewhere in the hotel archives, but short of breaking and entering the manager's office, I saw no way of getting hold of it.

I lunched with Jeff and Potts in the restaurant. Beyond indicating that I had made only slight progress I steered away from the topic, for the delegates were within earshot. The indefatigable Potts had been out with them that morning to a factory meeting where a unanimous resolution had been carried condemning the American "aggression in Korea" and where he had made a note that sixty-eight per cent of male workers appeared to shave only every other day. On other matters, he was more usefully informative. It seemed that the delegation's program was to be completed that evening; that the following day—Sunday—would be devoted to pooling their findings and drafting a report, and that they would be leaving by air first thing on Monday morning. Bolting, who had been receiving medical attention and was still confined indoors, was expected to be sufficiently recovered by then. We had little more than a day left to come to some conclusion on the case.

After lunch the three of us retired to my room and I brought Potts up to date with the latest developments. Soon afterward Waterhouse joined us again, eager to know the results of my inquiries that morning. We talked for a long while and went over a great deal of old ground, but in the end it became clear that we were doing no more than marking time. It was all rather melancholy.

Jeff gave us a short pep talk. "We haven't done so badly for a bunch of tyros," he said. "Hell, it's only a few days ago that we were grilling that guy Gain about his relations with Mullett. We've come a hell of a distance since then."

That was true, of course. I'd almost forgotten the Gain interview. "What a chap, eh?" I said. "Gosh, he was scared."

"I think he must always look rather frightened," said Potts. "I saw him again yesterday—he was just coming out of the Lux Hotel. When he saw me he scuttled away like a rabbit."

"What were *you* doing there?" asked Jeff. "Collecting bus numbers?"

Potts gave him a pallid smile. "I was just interested in the people who live there."

"You'd be a darned sight safer scaling the Kremlin wall with a ladder," I told him. "That Lux outfit gives me the shivers."

The Lux was a small hotel set aside exclusively for the use of foreign Communists. In the old days, most of the Comintern people had lived there, and during the war many of the Party members who were now running the Iron Curtain countries in Eastern Europe had stayed there during their periods of training. I'd visited the place once, many years earlier, and it had seemed to me more like a prison than a hotel. Visitors had to fill up a form before they could get past the porter, and even residents had to show their passes as they went in and out.

"It looked ordinary enough to me," said Potts.

At that moment Waterhouse, who had been sitting with a perplexed frown on his face, suddenly gave a sharp exclamation. "I've got it!" he cried, snapping his thumb triumphantly against his fingers. "I've got it at last!"

"What have you got?" I asked eagerly. We badly needed an idea.

"I know where it was that I saw Tranter. *He* was coming out of the Lux."

I stared. *"Tranter!* When?"

"Oh, it was during the war—early in the war. I *knew* I'd seen him. His hair's much whiter now and he's filled out, but he had that same limp. I can see him perfectly—he was with a man I'd met at some VOKS affair, a French Communist named Leclerc, and that's how I came to notice him."

Jeff was leaning forward intently. "I'd sure like to think you were right, John, but it's pretty queer. Wouldn't other people have remembered if he'd been around during the war?"

"Not necessarily," said Waterhouse slowly, as though he were still mentally resolving a jigsaw. "Of course, there were some well-known Communists at the Lux whom we all knew about and even ran into occasionally. Leclerc was one of them. But there's no doubt at all that there were others whom we never met—undercover men. That was one of the functions of the Lux—to segregate them. They mixed with the Russians a bit, but mainly they kept to themselves, and the more important the jobs they were being trained for, the less they had to do with anybody. The idea, of course, was that when the war was over they'd be ready to go back to their own countries and take up all sorts of duties in the interests of the Party, and no one would know that they were Communists or be able to say for certain what they'd been doing."

"You know, Waterhouse," I said, "I believe you've put your finger right on the spot. Look at the job he's doing—everything fits. He slips back home after the war, gets quietly into touch with the peace societies, appears to be overflowing with good will and Christian pacifism, and the next thing is that he's given a big post in the movement. He's doing a wonderful job for the Russians—and this trip he's making now is just a continuation of it. He comes out here, ostensibly for the first time, posing as an impartial, nonpolitical observer, and he goes back and tells everyone how friendly and peace-loving the Russians are, and people listen because they think he's unbiased. And all the time, he's just a professional revolutionary. Wonderful!"

"He must be a clever man," said Potts thoughtfully. "I

suppose all that pretense of not knowing any Russian is part of his disguise. He's certainly kept it up very well."

"Hold your horses!" I said. "That's something we ought to be able to check. I'll see if he's in." I·went over to the phone and asked for his room number. A moment later there was a click, and a soft voice said, "Tranter here."

"The hotel manager is speaking," I said in Russian. "Can you please come down to my office at once. Comrade Goldstein wishes to talk to you urgently."

There was another click, and the line went dead.

"What's going on?" asked Jeff impatiently.

"I asked him to visit the hotel manager."

"Well, what did he say?"

"Nothing. He hung up." I went to the door and opened it an inch or two. "Listen!"

Another door had opened and closed at the end of the corridor. Presently we heard the sound of quick footsteps approaching—quick but irregular—the unmistakable steps of a limping man. They turned off toward the lift and gradually died away.

I looked at Waterhouse. "That seems to settle it."

"The dirty, double-crossing son of a so-and-so!" murmured Jeff. "When I think of the stuff he's talked on this trip . . . !"

Waterhouse was smiling sardonically. "Peace on his lips and hatred in his heart? A familiar paradox in these parts, dear boy."

Jeff looked pretty mad. "Anyway, this puts Tranter right in the picture as far as Mullett's concerned. He's a twister, and he was here in 1942. Why shouldn't he be the killer?"

"Do you think," said Potts, "that a professional revolutionary would get involved in such a disreputable private affair?"

"Sure—why not? Even among black sheep, I guess some are blacker than others. These guys have their weaknesses like everyone else. Why, only yesterday Zina was reading me an account from *Pravda* about six big private rackets that had just been exposed here. One fellow held down four different jobs and drew a paycheck at each one without anyone cottoning on. He was a big-shot local administrator, too. Tranter's human, even if he is a Communist. We can't rule him out."

"We can if he lived at the Lux in 1942 and not here," said Waterhouse.

"We don't *know* he lived at the Lux. You saw him coming out, but he may have been visiting. Maybe there wasn't room for him there at the time. Maybe he was accommodated here, and had Mullett's room."

Waterhouse looked dubious. "It's possible—I wouldn't put it higher than that. In any case, I understand he was at the cinema when Mullett was killed."

"It wasn't a very satisfactory alibi," I reminded him. "It struck me at the time that the commissionaire remembered everything a damn sight too clearly."

"Exactly," said Jeff, "and it's not difficult to drop *that* piece into place. If Tranter did it, and the Russians found out, isn't he just the kind of guy they'd be most keen to cover up for? He's right in the center of an important propaganda campaign —they just couldn't afford to discipline him at this moment. I think they found out the truth, and that between them they concocted this story about his going to a movie and told the commissionaire to say 'Yes' to it. Whereas Tranter, instead of being at the movie, was in fact hanging around the hotel waiting to carry out his plan."

"When *I* saw him," said Potts, "he was hanging about the second-floor landing. Remember, George, I told you? Considering all we've found out about him, I'm just wondering if he might not have been going to that meeting some of the big shots were holding."

"Potts could be right," I said. "The Russians would want to cover up for that just as much as for a murder. Suppose he was at the meeting and came out knowing nothing about

Mullett. Naturally he'd be asked where he'd been. He couldn't tell the truth, because his association with the Party had to be kept secret, so on the spur of the moment he'd say he'd been to the pictures. Then he'd get in touch with his bosses and explain the awkward situation and the M.V.D. would fix the commissionaire."

"It's all pure supposition," Jeff objected. "He could just as well have been doing the murder."

I was about to agree that either of the theories would fit when suddenly I remembered Tranter's disability. "We're a lot of dopes," I said. "Of course he couldn't have done it. With that stiff leg he couldn't have made the transit of those balconies in a million years."

"Hell!" exclaimed Jeff. He looked quite deflated, and subsided gloomily into the depths of his chair with his hands in his pockets and his legs thrust out. "I was sure looking forward to getting that guy."

"At least," said Waterhouse, "we haven't been wasting our time. I should think that when you get back to London, George, you'll be able to damage Mr. Tranter's nonpolitical position quite a bit."

I was just going to assure him that I should leave no stone unthrown when Jeff shot out of his chair with a look of jubilation on his face.

"You guys think you're smart, don't you? Tranter couldn't have done the murder because he couldn't have crossed the balconies, eh? Well, suppose he didn't need to? Suppose Tanya climbed across and broke into Mullett's room and fixed the latch from the inside so that Tranter could walk in from the corridor, and then went back to her own room the way she'd come? Well, what about it?"

We all paid him the homage of silence. We'd been pretty dumb.

XVII

FOR ABOUT ten seconds, it seemed as though we had found a reasonable answer to all our questions. Here was a man whose very profession was plotting and scheming; a man of nerve, accustomed to taking risks. He had been in Moscow in 1942 and could certainly have known Tanya. After the long asceticism of Party work, he might well have been tempted by the prospect of big money. He, more than anyone, would have needed a go-between, for he would have suffered more than most had he been found out. Some act of Party discipline—moving him suddenly, perhaps, from the Astoria to the Lux—might have prevented him from collecting the stamps. He had a dubious alibi for the material time, and he was physically capable of having done the deed. He was, to say the least, right back in the running.

Then I began to realize the new possibilities that had been opened up by our discovery of Tranter's duplicity.

"Look here," I said, "we've been assuming all this time that certain of the delegates could be ruled out as possible suspects because they weren't in Russia during the war. Tranter was one of them. Now we find that Tranter has been taking us all in, and that in fact he *was* here. Well, how do we know the others weren't? Any of them—Cressey, for instance?"

"Hell!" said Jeff. "You're surely not casting Joe Cressey in the role of a master mind?"

"I don't know. He's certainly not as dumb as he sometimes seems—not by a long shot. I wouldn't think it likely, but frankly my faith is a bit shaken after this Tranter business.

How can we be sure that Cressey isn't another of these under-cover men?"

"I understood," said Waterhouse, "that he was elected by his workmates."

"That's what he told me, and I dare say it's true, but you know as well as I do how expert the Party boys are at fixing elections. It might be the old story—a small minority knowing its own mind and a large majority divided. Cressey's rather independent attitude may be just a clever pose. He certainly saw plenty of Tanya when he got here, and all those Russian lessons he had with her and with Mullett may have been an elaborate blind. Perhaps he knows as much Russian as Tranter."

"I doubt that," said Waterhouse. "Tranter was very careful not to talk it at all. That should have made us suspicious. Cressey, on the other hand, tries, and makes a shocking mess of it. If he'd been here during the war, I don't see how his accent *could* be as bad as it is."

"There's another thing," said Potts. "Hasn't Cressey a sort of alibi? I thought he was seen leaving the hotel."

"It's no better than Tranter's," I pointed out. "Ivan says he saw Cressey going out, but on the assumption that Cressey is an undercover man and valuable to the Russians, they'd have covered up for him just as much as for Tranter."

"Okay," said Jeff, "maybe Cressey isn't quite in the clear, but there's absolutely no evidence that he was here during the war. In Tranter's case there is evidence. Anyway, who else do you want to drag in while we're about it?"

I smiled. "If we're going to be thorough, Miss Manning. She's been out of the picture for quite a while because we thought she wasn't here in 1942, but again, we've only got her word for it. She'd probably think it frightfully clever to have a secret political life. She'd adore it."

"You're not suggesting she wore those pants, are you?" said Jeff.

"No, but I still say she could have got hold of them. She certainly enjoys the good things of life—with her taste in clothes, some extra money would always come in handy. What do you say, Waterhouse?"

"Well," he said with a twinkle, "I confess that I find the picture of la Manning as a commercial philatelist a trifle bizarre."

I laughed. "You may be right about that. Still, all I'm asking is that we don't neglect her. She's a pretty cool customer; she disliked Mullett, so she'd probably have hit him with gusto; and what's more, being a sculptress she'd have known just where to hit. *And* she lied about being in her room."

Jeff snorted. "She was probably having a cozy time with Islwyn Thomas or Bolting and was too coy to say so. That genteel type never likes to come clean about sex. I bet that's where she was—in someone else's room. Anyway, let's get this over. What about Mrs. Clarke, George?"

"She's the one person who couldn't have done it," I said. "She was heard talking to Mullett on the landing just before he went into his room, so she certainly couldn't have been inside his room pasting up windows."

"Who says she was talking to Mullett?"

"Why—the floor manageress."

"Just so—and the floor manageress might have been covering up for Mrs. Clarke. Now let me tell you something, since you're so darned keen to widen the field of suspicion. As far as I can see, the murderer need never have been in Russia before. He might simply have been the agent of someone who was."

Potts said, "I don't quite follow you."

"Why, it's easy. There's a guy somewhere back in England who was in Russia during the war and worked this stamp racket with Tanya and for some reason had to leave the haul behind. Well, he reads or hears that a delegation's going out, and he approaches one of the delegates with his story. 'Somewhere in the Astoria Hotel,' he says, 'probably in room 435 which is where I lived, there's a packet of stamps behind a picture, worth $50,000. They belong to me. If you can get hold of them and bring them back to me you can have a fifty per cent cut in the proceeds.' Wouldn't that tempt anyone?"

"It would have been a pretty difficult assignment for a stranger," I said. "Getting Tanya's co-operation, for one thing."

"Not if the stranger had all the facts at his or her finger tips. Tanya could hardly have refused to co-operate, anyway, with so much known against her. She was wide open to being blackmailed into helping. Besides, she'd have got something out of it, too. Once Mullett was settled in that room, I imagine the job would have been pretty straightforward for any resourceful person."

I felt disheartened. We'd been making good progress eliminating people, and now we'd been set right back on our heels. Personally I still thought the idea of the murderer being a commission agent was less likely than the other, but it certainly complicated everything.

Waterhouse seemed to feel the same way. "Now that our suspicions are spread impartially over the whole delegation," he said, "what is the next move?"

I couldn't think of a thing. Even the trousers seemed to have lost some of their potential value as a clue. Nobody else had any ideas, either, and soon afterward we dispersed.

That evening I had supper down in the restaurant, and the delegates were all there. I watched them with a kind of helpless fascination. One of them—and I had to keep telling myself or I still wouldn't have believed it—one of them had killed Mullett, and now had the secret locked away inside him. But which? There was nothing in the outward behavior of any of them to give a hint of such a thing. Bolting looked very peaky, but he was listening attentively to something Tranter was telling him and neither of them showed any sign of that preoccupation which might have been expected to go with the consciousness of recent crime. Schofield, thoughtfully scraping out his pipe, could have been looking back on murder, but then he always had that rather absent air when he wasn't talking. Perdita and Islwyn Thomas were bickering playfully. Mrs. Clarke was telling Cressey about a speech she'd once made at a Labour Party conference, and Cressey was listening with his customary politeness. Murder? It seemed ridiculous. But after all, I reflected, it was probably only a very unusual sort of murderer who would show his feelings afterward. A clever one would hide them with artistry and a cunning one with satisfaction. A calloused one would have none to hide. It was really a waste of time to watch faces and behavior.

What about the characters of these people? I mentally listed some of the qualities that the killer had shown before and during and since the crime, and tried to measure up the delegates against that list.

First, the initial interest in philately—the expert knowledge that had made the stamp racket possible. Well, it was impossible to be dogmatic on that. All sorts of people had a passion for stamps—kings and schoolboys, judges and explorers, men of action and men of letters. Some collected for pleasure, and some for gain. Of the seven at that table, Schofield, Bolting, Tranter and Cressey seemed the most likely. Perdita would surely have been too superior; Thomas too impatient; Mrs. Clarke too busy.

Second, the inventive skill that had been needed to think out that complex and ingenious method of approach. Schofield, certainly—he'd have worked it out like one of those price graphs in his textbooks. Perdita, too—she was calculating, and she must have something of a creative imagination as well. Perhaps Cressey—he was slow, but skilled mechanics often had ingenious minds. And Tranter had certainly shown no lack of inventiveness and resourcefulness!

Third, ruthlessness, to crown a man with a bottle. Bolting, perhaps—he'd always impressed me as a man who wouldn't easily be stopped if he'd set his mind on something. Schofield, Tranter, Thomas—almost all of them were possibles. Even Perdita. You didn't line up with the Soviet Union these days if you hadn't some ruthlessness in your system. Not, I would have thought, Cressey.

Fourth, a heartless realism, a complete indifference to the fate of others. Thomas, I thought, would have been too chivalrous, unless a cause had been at stake. But Perdita wouldn't; basically, she cared only for Perdita. Tranter. Perhaps Schofield.

Fifth, nerve, physical and moral. The murderer had quite probably climbed across the balconies. He had behaved with swift competence after the murder. He had sat tight since and shown not a glimmer of fear or panic. A tough character, the murderer! Bolting seemed to qualify, in part—the man who made reckless ski runs. Schofield, too, perhaps—his nerve was probably inhuman. Islwyn Thomas?—well, courage, yes, but of the hot rather than the cold variety. Tranter, certainly—plenty of nerve there. Perdita, too—she was as cool as any woman I'd met.

Well, it was interesting, but the method didn't help much, I decided. Apart from Mrs. Clarke, who didn't seem to me to have the necessary intelligence, and Cressey, who was a dark horse but appeared humane, I could imagine any one of the other five having the caliber and qualities to make a murderer if the circumstances were right.

As snatches of their conversation came wafting across to me, I suddenly felt a deep hatred of the whole lot of them. Not because there was someone sitting there who had killed Mullett for personal gain—that wasn't my special affair. As Perdita had said, I wasn't a policeman. Not even because

Nikolai and Tanya were having to pay the penalty—I'd had my moments of savage anger on their account, but once you started knight-errantry on behalf of these poor devils of Russians, it was a job without end. No, what made my gorge rise was the thought that once again Moscow was going to put a preposterous story across, and get away with it. One more lie was going to be established, and we were all going to have to swallow it even though we knew it was a lie. The delegation would go gack to England with its smug fables, and Mullett's death would be shot and shell for them. The very person who'd killed him, the person with the loot in his pocket, would probably be the most vocal in denouncing the killing as a monstrous political assassination. I'd have done anything to put a spoke in that wheel.

The real trouble, of course, was the utter impossibility of coming to grips with the delegates individually. A hard shell of political unity covered them all, and they clung together beneath it. I didn't know them, except in the most superficial way, and I couldn't know them, for they had no desire to make my closer acquaintance. I could make no contact, have no impact. I hadn't the right to question them, or even the opportunity to quarrel with them. A little anger might have produced a little truth, but they were self-satisfied and not easily provoked. They would slip away, barely aware of my hostile interest and certainly indifferent to it.

At that point in my reflections Perdita caught my eye and it seemed as though she must have read my thoughts, for she gave me one of her mocking smiles. It was the last straw. I *couldn't* leave things as they were. I'd *got* to force a showdown. I sprang to my feet and walked swiftly to the fourth floor, bubbling with anger. Jeff's door was open and I banged on it and went in. He was mending the handle of one of his suitcases.

"Hello, George," he said, swinging round. He stared. "What's eating you? Has someone been unkind?"

"Look," I said, "if we're going to break this case we've got to do it before those people get back to England and disperse. Jeff, I'm going to confront them with the facts we've got. I'm going to give them the whole works, and see if they can still smile. That's what the police would have done in any other country, and that's the only way to jolt them."

"Now *just* a minute," said Jeff. "Cool off, will you. You need a drink."

"No, thanks. All I need is a flaming row."

"Look, pal," he said, "a day or two ago you were urging me to clear out of Russia to save my skin. You're a swell sort of adviser."

"You didn't clear out," I said.

"That was different. The danger was pretty vague—this isn't. One of those guys is a murderer, don't forget, and he's not likely to sit tight and do nothing if you stick your neck out."

"That's the whole point. There's just a chance he may give himself away if he's rattled enough. Anyway, it's the only hope we've got. I'll be on my guard, don't worry."

He looked at me for a long time and then gave a shrug. "Okay, when do we start?"

"We don't—this is something I'm going to handle alone. I just wanted you to know before I walked into the den."

"Nuts!—I might as well come along too."

"Much better if you don't," I said. "If we're going to provoke our man into action, things have got to be made simple for him. He's got to have one person, one target, to concentrate on. If I get into a bad spot I'll be glad to lean on you, but honestly there's no point in your sitting in at the conference."

He was only half-convinced, but I didn't give him the opportunity to argue. I went back to my own room and waited until I thought the delegates must be out of the restaurant, and then I rang Bolting.

XVIII

THEY WERE all gathered in his room when I went along there fifteen minutes later, and they had obviously been told what the session was about for there was a Star Chamber atmosphere about the place. Perdita, gracefully draped over one end of an old-fashioned chaise longue, regarded me with icy hostility. Islwyn Thomas had taken his cue from her and was scowling in sympathy. Joe Cressey was perched very straight on the edge of a hard chair and looked as uncomfortable mentally as physically. Mrs. Clarke was beside him, flushed and expectant in a ringside seat. The Professor had settled himself over by the window with a pad on his knee, and shot me a swift, curious glance before returning to his doodling. Tranter and Bolting had placed themselves behind a table like a couple of judges.

Bolting whispered, "Please sit down, Mr. Verney." He had a scarf wound round his throat and mouth and was almost voiceless. I couldn't help recalling what Jeff had said in jest—wrapped up like that, he did look a bit sinister.

I dropped into the chair that had evidently been left for me. I had brought the trousers along, done up in paper, and I put the parcel down beside me. I felt keyed up and thankful to be facing them at last.

"Mr. Tranter will do the talking," said Bolting huskily. "You'll forgive me, I know—throat!" He pointed to the enveloping scarf.

I nodded, and Tranter took over. "Well, here we all are, Mr. Verney," he said. In contrast to the others, his attitude was quite gentle and benign. "We're rather busy, you know—getting ready to leave—so we'd be glad if you'd come straight to the point. What *is* this urgent matter in connection with Mr. Mullett's death?" .

I ran an eye rapidly round the watchful company. "Only that one of you people killed him."

It was meant to be provocative, of course, and that was the way they took it. Tranter's eyes narrowed and Bolting's head jerked up and there was a chorus of angry protest. By and large, they looked about as friendly as a cage of cobras. From Perdita came a brisk "Ridiculous!" and from Mrs. Clarke an incredulous "Well, what a thing to say!" For six of the seven, I'd certainly caused a sensation, and the seventh wasn't giving anything away.

Perdita was the first to regain the power of consecutive speech. "This is going to be a pure waste of time," she said impatiently. "It's been plain for a long while that Mr. Verney hates our delegation and would like to make mischief. He's a thorough reactionary and this is a political move—or else he's trying to work up a story for his miserable paper. I suggest we report him to the Press Department and leave Mr. Ganilov to deal with him."

"You ministering angel!" I murmured.

Mrs. Clarke scrambled to her feet. "Mr. Chairman," she cried shrilly, "I support the motion. We all know poor Mr. Mullett was done in by that waiter chap, the same as the papers said. Why, this man's calling our Russian comrades liars. He's a Fascist, that's what he is."

"Just a moment, Mrs. Clarke," said Tranter gently. "We don't want to turn this into a public meeting."

"Well, tell him to take his lying gossip somewhere else."

"As a matter of fact," I put in, "that's exactly what I propose to do. To England. I thought, though, that you might all care to hear the case that one of you will have to answer."

"Very sporting of you," said Thomas disagreeably.

"Just a moment, *please!*" Tranter rapped on the table with his knuckles. "I must say that this accusation of Mr. Verney's sounds utterly fantastic to me, but I suppose we ought to hear what he has to say. What do you think, Bolting?"

"Obviously," said Bolting.

"Very well, Mr. Verney. We're all attention."

I sat back and proceeded to unwind my story. There was no barracking—after the first moment or two they all became far too interested. I started with the reasons why Nikolai couldn't have done the murder, and went on to my discoveries in Mullett's room, the disappearance of Tanya, the fact that the Russians knew everything and were covering up for someone, and the business of the stamps. I didn't, of course, mention Liefschitz, and I didn't discuss the relative claims of the various delegates to the role of chief suspect. I wanted the murderer to work that out for himself. I simply outlined the general case as lucidly and cogently as I could.

The recital wasn't without effect. Except for mutterings from Mrs. Clarke, who had probably failed to follow me, there was almost complete silence as I concluded.

Again, it was Perdita who spoke first. "Mr. Verney couldn't have made his motives clearer. As I said before, this is a political thing. He hates the Soviet Union, and he's trying to work up a story—a stunt story—for political ends. As though the Soviet Union would arrest a man they knew to be innocent! If you ask me, the whole thing's a farrago of nonsense from beginning to end."

"Very ably presented, though," muttered the Professor from the window. "You're a dangerous man, Mr. Verney."

Tranter seemed at a loss. "I must say that I find it all quite incredible. Apart from anything else, it seems to me most unlikely that a collection of postage stamps would be worth all that risk."

"Oh, they might be, Mr. Tranter," put in Cressey unexpectedly. He reddened, as baleful eyes were turned upon him. "I'm a bit of a philatelist myself, you know. There was a stamp once that changed hands for more than £7,000. Mind you, that's not common, but it's nothing for a stamp to fetch twenty or thirty pounds and a large packet would hold thousands."

"Thank you, Joe," I murmured. I'd completely forgotten his interest in stamps but I remembered, now, his knowledgeable comment when the subject had been mentioned at the VOKS party. He was either very simple, very honest, or very clever, to volunteer information at this stage.

Tranter's eyes dwelt speculatively on him, and it was clear that some at least of the delegates were wondering.

"Even if that is true," Tranter went on, turning again to me, "the accusation seems to me to be extremely vague and unsupported by tangible evidence."

"It might seem less vague," I said, "if we were to go round together now and search everyone's room. Somewhere in this hotel there's a packet of stamps."

There was another outcry at that, and the baying became louder when Cressey said, "I don't mind having *my* room searched."

"Well, I *do*," cried Perdita angrily. "I wouldn't think of allowing it." She glared at me. "What *right* have you to make all this trouble?"

"In a country where the police side with the criminal," I said, "I have every right."

Schofield looked up again from his doodling. "You talk recklessly, Mr. Verney. The Soviet authorities are not going to like this, you know."

"I don't suppose they're going to like the evidence, either, Professor. Certainly not the publication of it."

Bolting took a sip of water. "You couldn't publish that, my dear fellow," he croaked, "as you know perfectly well. No newspaper would touch it—not even the sensational sheet for which you work. . . ." His voice trailed off again into a painful whisper.

"You haven't had quite all the story yet," I told him. "There does happen to be one piece of material evidence." I unwrapped my parcel and held up the ancient trousers. "The man who built up the stamp collection traded this garment for stamps in 1942. Perhaps one of you gentlemen recognizes it?"

There was a bit of a stir. Perdita turned up her nose in disgust, and Mrs. Clarke cackled, but all the men got up and crowded round. And, of course, they all disowned the trousers with varying degrees of emphasis.

"Pity!" I said. "I'm not a detective, of course, and I'm afraid they're going to give me rather a lot of trouble. But when eventually I go home to England, I shall certainly take them with me and it's just possible I might be able to find out something about them. For one thing, they've been dry-cleaned—there's a cleaner's mark here. For another, they're a rather good quality tweed, and I believe cloth can be traced, with expert help. Then again, they have definite measurements. Finally, it's always possible that one of the murderer's friends or acquantances may recall a suit of this kind. I've a couple of contacts at Scotland Yard who might be interested in the case."

"You damned snooper!" said Thomas. He'd definitely written me off as an old pal.

"You realize, of course," put in Schofield, "that—supposing you're right in your general accusation, which frankly I doubt—the British courts would have no jurisdiction as regards a crime committed in the U.S.S.R.?"

"That," I said, "is a thought with which the murderer is no doubt consoling himself. There'll be precious little else he'll be able to comfort himself with. A reputation, if not a head, will roll!"

There was another uneasy silence as I wrapped the trousers up again. "We should get further, of course, if I had your co-operation. I suppose those of you who were here in 1942 wouldn't care to tell me what rooms you occupied in the hotel?"

I looked at Schofield. I didn't think he'd answer, but the morale of the party wasn't quite what it had been, and after a moment he gave a little shrug. "If it will help to disabuse your mind of baseless suspicions, I'll gladly tell you. My own room was on the second floor, at the end of a long corridor. Number 284, if I remember rightly."

I nodded—I had a rough idea where it was. "Thank you, Professor." I looked at Thomas. "And yours, I believe, was the same one that you have now?"

"Oh, go to hell!" he said. "Yes, it was."

"Since everyone is being so helpful," Bolting whispered, "mine was on the third floor. Number 370."

"You were fortunate," I said. I know that room, too—it was a particularly quiet and cozy one looking out on the lane and had been occupied in my time by one of the agency men. "And what about you, Mr. Tranter?"

Tranter's eyes were frosty. "What makes you think that *I* was here in 1942, Mr. Verney?"

"You've been recognized by someone who saw you then. You're an old Party worker, Tranter, an undercover man. A Communist wolf in pacifist clothing. Who do you suppose rang you up last night? I'm afraid you had your journey downstairs for nothing. It'll make a nice little story, won't it?"

He must have been expecting it, of course, and he didn't bother to argue. After all, he was among friends. But he sat very rigid, and he looked very menacing.

"The fact that it is sometimes necessary to be reticent about past events," he said slowly, "does not mean that one is a murderer."

I looked around. An amused, malicious smile curved Perdita's lips and there was a cynical gleam in Schofield's eye.

Cressey alone looked slightly shocked. The revelation had certainly fallen very flat in this audience.

"Ah, well," I said, "I'll have to try it on your peace society, Tranter. I'm sure *they'll* be interested." I got up. "By the way, Joe, I suppose *you* weren't in Russia in 1942?"

"Eh?" said Cressey. "Why, no, Mr. Verney, you know I wasn't."

"Okay, I just wondered."

Bolting leaned across to Tranter and there was a whispered consultation. Tranter nodded vigorously, and then turned again to me.

"Well, Mr. Verney, I'm afraid you haven't made much of an impression with your detective story. There's just a final question I'd like to ask you. Apart from those trousers, which are most unlikely to give you any results, have you a single piece of evidence pointing to any particular person? If not, you must see that you really have no case."

I glanced at Perdita. "I have one small piece of evidence—in reserve. I'm rather dubious about a statement which was made to me." I picked up my parcel. "Good night—comrades."

Thomas's scowl was the last thing I saw as I closed the door behind me.

XIX

I FELT pretty cheerful as I turned into Jeff's room to tell him how things had gone. At least I'd pricked the delegation's monstrous complacency and got some of the gall out of my system. Jeff listened to the story with obvious satisfaction, though his chubby face became a bit solemn at the end.

"Well," he said, "I guess you've done what you wanted to. How does it feel to be live bait?"

"No pain so far. I don't suppose anything will come of it."

"I wouldn't count on that. One way and another I reckon you've caused a lot of anxiety. Desperate men take risks."

"I know, but when you see them sitting quietly in a room they don't look desperate. It's hard to believe anyone could get violent. Still, I'll watch my step."

"You do that—and I'll watch it, too. What are you going to do with those pants?"

"I thought of chaining them to my bed!"

"You leave them here with me," he said. "Then when the murderer knocks you on the head, at least he won't get the evidence."

That was obviously sensible, and I watched him lock the parcel away in one of his cases. "What worries me more," I said, "is how I'm going to get them out of the country. Somebody's bound to give the Russians a full account of tonight's session, and when the time comes they'll be all set to take them from me."

"Then let me take them. I've been pretty much in the background since that day we saw Ganilov, and after what you

189

said tonight they wouldn't expect you to part with them. I'll leave them in London for you."

"Have you fixed up about going?"

"Not definitely—they say there may be a plane Wednesday. Ganilov's practically promised me a place, though you know what he's like."

"Is he bearing malice?"

"Not a bit. I guess he thinks I've had a change of heart or something."

"Why don't you ask him if you can go out with the delegation? Tell him you're needed urgently back home for a year's assignment to South America. He might be glad to speed you on your way."

"Hell, I don't *want* to go with the delegation. What's the point?"

"Only that when I traveled in with them I wasn't bothered by the Customs. It'll probably be the same going out."

Jeff shrugged. "Well, I guess I'm not all that fussy, if you think it'll make a difference. I'll ask him, anyway."

"Good man!"

I returned to my room and picked up a book on the Alger Hiss affair that I was in the middle of. It was fascinating, but somehow I couldn't concentrate—the actual tangle in this hotel was for the moment even more fascinating. I could still hardly believe that the murderer would take any fresh action, but I could see he was in a spot, all right. I'd certainly have thought so in his place. If he went home and the trousers *were* traced to him, the case would be just about complete. Even if he couldn't be prosecuted initially by the law, it was fresh in my mind that there was such a thing as forcing him to take action for slander, and he'd be ruined just the same in the end. I wouldn't have wanted to go home with those risks ahead. Yet obviously he'd got to return to England, because that was where his importance lay for the Russians, and if he wasn't

going to be important to them any more they might change
their minds about keeping the murder quiet.

I wondered what he was doing at that moment—what he
was planning.

A sharp rap on the door made me jump. I got up to open
it automatically, thinking it was probably Jeff with some fresh
idea, and it was only when my hand was on the knob that I
remembered the step I'd got to watch.

"Who is it?" I called.

"Islwyn Thomas."

I opened the door a fraction and peered out. His hands
were by his sides and as far as I could see he hadn't anything
in them. "All right—come in," I said. I stood back and let
him pass in front of me, and I left the door ajar.

"Nervous?" he asked unpleasantly.

"Fairly."

"You've good reason to be! Verney, I've come to warn you.
Keep Miss Manning out of this business, do you hear? If you
don't, I'll . . ." his hands clenched, and anger darkened his
swarthy face, ". . . I'll make you sorry you were born."

"Thanks for the warning. What will you use—a bottle?"

I thought for a moment that he was going to attack me
there and then, and I was thankful I'd left the door open.

"This isn't a joking matter," he said.

"I'm not joking—I'm serious."

"You're crazy if you think I had anything to do with that
Mullett business. All I'm concerned about is Miss Manning.
I'm not going to have her name bandied about, do you hear?"

"Have I bandied it?"

"No, but you damned well hinted. As it happens, she was
with *me* when Mullett was killed, as you've possibly guessed,
but she doesn't want it talked about."

"So she's sent you to threaten me into silence. How very
old-fashioned!"

"You damned swine!" he said.

"Look, Thomas," I said, "why don't you grow up? If Miss Manning was with you when Mullett was killed, that's her affair and yours and I'm not interested. But *was* she?"

"What do you mean?" His hands clenched again. He was longing to slug me.

"I mean there's no proof. She may be giving you an alibi. You may be giving her one. If it's her reputation you're concerned about, you can trot back now and tell her everything's all right. If you're trying to protect her from a murder charge, or she you, you're wasting your time. Now, do you mind going? I don't like threats."

For a moment we faced each other, glaring. Then he shrugged, turned quickly, and walked out. I shut the door behind him.

I prepared for bed in a rather somber frame of mind. There was more violence in the air than I'd been willing to admit. Of course, it was just like Thomas to go rushing off to battle for his lady's honor, and just like Perdita to send him. If that was all there was to it, and they'd really been together, both of them seemed to be absolved of murder. If it had merely been a try-on, then Thomas might be back.

I turned in soon afterward but I found it impossible to sleep. The scene with Thomas had unsettled me, and my imagination began to get out of hand. It had been one thing to face that bunch of fellow travelers and deliberately goad them into some kind of action when that had seemed the only way to get results, but lying in bed at night in a silent, unfriendly hotel waiting for that action to materialize was quite another. Moral courage and physical courage are very different things, and, as I said before, I'm no hero. The catch on my door was pretty old—a heave from a strong shoulder would be enough to break it open. I was soon straining my ears for footfalls in the corridor, ready to leap from bed and meet an aggressor. A straight scrap on equal terms wouldn't be so bad, but I had no mind to be attacked in my sleep with ugly weapons.

After a while, I began to feel uneasy about the balcony. If the murderer could somehow get hold of a key to Mullett's room—and he might be better placed than most to do so—he would be on me before I could stir. There was the approach through Kira's room, too—a route that had been used once could be used again. It might even be used by the M.V.D.—by now they might be as keen as the murderer to get me out of the way. I had talked too much for everybody's comfort. I began to think I'd been a bit of a fool. No one is at his best in the night watches.

In the end I got up and wedged a chair under the handle of the French doors, and just to be on the safe side I shifted the wardrobe so that it covered the door into the corridor. I felt rather glad that Jeff couldn't see me. Before getting back into bed, I took a skating boot out of my trunk and laid it on the little table beside my head. After that, my fears dissolved and I soon fell asleep.

In daylight next morning my precautions looked ridiculous, and I hastened to put the furniture back in its proper place. I'd hardly finished dressing when the phone rang. It was Joe Cressey, and he wanted to know if he could come along and see me. He said it was rather urgent. I told him to come right up. I couldn't imagine what he wanted, and I was still watching my step, but it was difficult to see any menace in Joe, particularly just after breakfast.

He arrived in a few minutes. His knock was diffident and his air oddly conspiratorial as he came in and shut the door behind him.

"I wanted to talk to you, Mr. Verney," he began uneasily. "I'm afraid I'm in trouble, and there's no one else I can go to."

"Why, what's the matter?"

"Well, it all comes of what you said last night. It's terrible—they're treating me almost as though *I* killed Mr. Mullett."

"Oh." I'd rather expected that something like that might happen. "Have they said anything?"

"Not in so many words, they haven't, but I'm sure that's what they're all thinking. They've been so friendly up to now, but last night after you'd gone they treated me like dirt."

"They'd have done that, anyway, because you sided with me over the value of the stamp collection. They're a spiteful crowd."

He looked a bit dubious. "I thought p'r'aps it was because I said I knew about stamps, and I seem to be the only one that does, and—well, if someone collected up that packet the way you said . . ."

"If you weren't here in 1942, Joe, you couldn't have collected the stamps, could you? You've no need to worry—they've got nothing on you. They're just being unpleasant. People of their persuasion divide all human beings into two groups, those who are for them and those who are against them, and you've got to be all one or all the other. You spoke out of turn so you're an 'anti' and they're taking it out of you, that's all. If they make faces, I should make faces back."

He still looked slightly disconsolate. "I only said what was true, Mr. Verney. You know, I think you're right—I think one of them *did* do it. I'll be glad when I'm home—I've no time for them. I was glad you talked the way you did. I'd have liked to do the same. Fancy that Tranter pretending all that time!" His heavy chin jutted out indignantly.

I smiled. It seemed absurd now that I could have suspected Cressey of being a murderer, even for a passing moment. He was such a straightforward, simple soul. "If you go back and give your chaps in the factory a plain account of what you've seen here," I said, "you'll be more than even with Mr. Tranter."

"I suppose so." He stood hesitating. "Would there be anything I could do to help you, Mr. Verney? About finding out who did it, I mean?"

"That's nice of you," I said. "I really don't think there is, though—I'm pretty well stuck till I get home. If I think of anything, I'll let you know."

He nodded. "I could take those trousers back to England for you, if you liked. I was thinking, now you've said so much about them you might have a bit of difficulty, and no one's likely to look in my luggage, seeing that I'm a delegate."

I stared at him. He met my gaze frankly, without the hint of an *arrière pensée,* but I wondered. *Was* he so simple? Or had he been putting on the biggest act of all?

Suddenly I knew I had to test him. I switched to Russian, and in Russian I told him I knew he was Mullett's murderer!

He looked at me in such perplexity that I had to laugh. "Sorry, Joe," I said, "it was just a thought. Thanks for your offer, but I think I'll manage about the trousers. I don't want them to go out of my keeping."

"All right, Mr. Verney, just as you say. Well, I'd better be going—we're supposed to be preparing a report today. They're all very keen to get it done before we get home."

"I bet they are! Don't you sign anything, Joe. Tell 'em you want to think it over. Good luck!"

"Cheerio, Mr. Verney, and good luck to you." He shambled out.

The rest of that day passed without incident. I had no more visitors, and as far as the delegates were concerned I might not have existed. They spent most of the morning and all the afternoon in Bolting's room, presumably drawing up their precious report, and in the evening they were all busy packing. About seven, Bolting and Tranter came along to Mullett's room and spent an hour or so putting his belongings together and packing them up so that they would be ready to be taken away with the rest of the delegation's luggage in the morning. Then the whole lot of them went down to the restaurant and

I saw them later having a subdued but still considerable fare-well banquet with Mirnova and other people from VOKS.

Jeff had seen Ganilov, contrived to give the impression that there was now nothing in the world he was less interested in than the Mullett case, and extracted permission to leave on the delegation plane. I sat around while Jeff did his packing, and then some of the boys came in and we had our own fare-well party. It wasn't as gay as some I'd known, but by mid-night when it broke up I certainly wasn't worrying about the delegation any more. I had no longer any fears that something might go bump in the night and I didn't even bother to shift the furniture. I felt pretty certain that the Mullett case was about to be shelved for good, and, frankly, I couldn't have cared less.

XX

I AWOKE next morning in a melancholy frame of mind, not wholly accounted for by a slight hangover. I had a strong feeling that this wasn't going to be one of my days. It was satisfactory, of course, that the delegation was clearing out—the hotel would certainly be the sweeter for their departure—but I knew I was going to miss Jeff a good deal and Potts, though well-meaning, was no adequate substitute. Professionally, my assignment was a washout. Now that I'd blotted my copybook with Ganilov, I shouldn't even get a pretense of help from him. I felt that I would have given a lot at that moment to be joining Jeff on his plane. I lay for a few indulgent moments wallowing in self-pity, and then I snapped out of it and took a shower. Something would be sure to turn up, even if it were only a new variety of trouble—and there was always Waterhouse.

My mood wasn't improved by the newspapers, which arrived while I was making coffee. They were full of the departing delegation. *Pravda* had a big photograph of them, all with unearthly grins in the flashlight, and there was about half a page of interviews and last messages. A banner headline declared, PEACE DELEGATION CARRIES GOOD WILL GREETINGS TO WORKERS OF THE WEST. Yes, someone was getting away with murder all right.

The corridor was already buzzing with the sounds of imminent departure when I emerged from my room. Mullett's door stood open, and Ivan was just coming out, his shoulders bowed under two heavy cases the contents of which I knew by

197

heart. Schofield, dressed for the road, was pacing slowly up and down, smoking his pipe and looking as unperturbed as ever. He gave me a brief nod but didn't speak. Mrs. Clarke, in her fantastic leopard skin, was standing by her door with a huge bouquet of hothouse flowers in her arms. Cressey was sitting on his luggage, lost in thought. Along the corridor, Bolting—looking like a dressed-up Invisible Man in his big fur coat and hat, his balaclava and his scarf—was bent toward Tranter.

I dropped in on Jeff and told him the address to which he should post the trousers. At that moment I felt it was most unlikely that I should ever want to take up the case again. Since none of the delegates had shown any further interest either in the trousers or in me, I could only conclude that the murderer was satisfied that they couldn't be traced to him. Still, we'd made our arrangements, and Jeff had to pass through London anyway, so he might as well take them. I told him he was a lucky dog to be going but he seemed in two minds about that. Presently Ivan came to see about his bags, and I drifted down to the vestibule to watch the preparations for departure.

There was a busy scene there, too—you'd have thought the whole hotel was on the move. "Like royalty!" exclaimed Katya the chambermaid excitedly, as she swept by with an armful of parcels. The delegation's luggage, it appeared, was being sent ahead to the airport in one big truck and there was the usual air of frenzied chaos that always marked these simple jobs. The vestibule was crowded with hotel staff and M.V.D. men and a big farewell committee led by the president of VOKS. Mirnova and Kira were having a frothy conversation with Perdita and Islwyn Thomas. Bolting had just come down with Mrs. Clarke. They all stared through me, and I sensed contempt. I was not merely a busybody who had tried to interfere—I was a busybody who had interfered without effect. They'd outsmarted me, and they knew it.

There was a lot of coming and going in the next fifteen

minutes. The delegates were all restless and tended to form into little knots and then break up and disperse for a while, as though they'd recollected last-minute jobs they'd forgotten to do. I heard Mirnova condoling with a speechless Bolting about his throat and telling him to keep it well wrapped up when he got outside; and a snatch of argument between Thomas and Schofield; and Tranter telling Mrs. Clarke that the weather was good for flying. I had a few words with Cressey, and then Mirnova called the delegates together and they all went into a huddle about something. The cars had not yet arrived and Jeff hadn't appeared, so I went up to the second floor to see if Potts had survived the party. He said he'd just been up to bid Jeff *bon voyage*. His hangover was rather worst than mine, so I only stayed a few minutes. I was just going down again when I remembered that I hadn't given Jeff the letter to my office which he had promised to take with him. It seemed a pity to miss the chance, so I went back to the fourth floor.

The corridor was deserted now. All the delegates' doors stood open, and somewhere a vacuum cleaner was at work. I wondered what on earth Jeff was doing and why he hadn't come down. I put the key in my door and went in. The letter was in a drawer over near the window. The room struck me as cold, and automatically I glanced at the *fortachka*, thinking that one of the maids had opened it. Then I saw something that froze me in my tracks. The seals of the French doors were broken. Someone had been in here!

I could have wept at my lack of foresight. This was the time, above all, when I should have been watchful—this period of confusion before the departure. I'd gone to all that trouble to set a trap, and then I'd been away when it was sprung. The murderer had been in here—he'd come through Mullett's open room, of course. He'd been searching for the trousers, and I'd missed him. Now I should never know his identity

Deeply chagrined, I turned toward the door. As I did so, something stirred behind the curtain of the bed annex. For a moment I stood as though paralyzed, my pulse racing. God, he was still here! I looked round for a weapon, but it was too late. The curtains parted and I saw the glint of a steel skating boot, the menace of an implacable eye. I gave a hell of a shout and dived for the murderer's legs. We went down by the bed with a fearful crash, dragging half the curtain with us, and struggled wildly in the narrow space. I was fighting mad. I knew that this was the reckoning, and that life itself was at stake. We rolled over on the floor, punching and clawing and still half-entangled in the curtain. Somehow we scrabbled our way through into the bathroom. We were both landing blows, but it was the skating boot I was afraid of. If only I could get that away!

Suddenly the wrist I was clutching was wrenched from my grasp. I lunged at a bloody face and dived out of range of the boot and then as I came up from the floor I hit my head a terrific crack on the underside of the wash basin and everything went blank.

XXI

THE DELEGATES had been excused even the formality of a call at the airport customs and porters had now begun to load their luggage into the Russian-built DC-3 which was to take them as far as Prague. Jeff Clayton, relieved that Verney had been proved right and that no one had shown any interest in the contents of his bags, was chatting cheerfully to Cressey in the comfortable waiting room. The rest of the delegates were gathered around Tranter and Perdita, who were drafting a last-minute message to Stalin of a kind which had become practically *de rigueur* for departing delegations.

Presently Mirnova put her head in. "You will be taking off in ten minutes," she announced. She looked around. "Oh, Mr. Bolting, could you spare a moment? Mr. Vassiliev has a little present for you."

Bolting detached himself from the group and followed her out.

"That guy sure looks sorry for himself," said Jeff.

Cressey nodded. "He ought to have gone home a week ago, when he wanted to. It's been miserable for him since."

There was a stir among the delegates as Perdita straightened up from the table with a slip of paper in her hand. "I think this will do," she said, and began to read: " 'On leaving the territory of the Soviet Union, we the undersigned wish to thank you, Comrade Stalin, for the hospitality and friendship which has been extended to us. We acclaim the efforts of the Soviet Union to strengthen peace, and we assure you that we will seize every opportunity to acquaint our fellow countrymen with the truth and to foil the plan of the imperialists, seeking to foment a new world war.' Is everyone satisfied with that?" She eyed the delegates in turn, challenging anyone to criticize.

"You could say, 'P.S. Sorry about the statue,'" Jeff murmured.

Perdita gave him a contemptuous look. "Then that's all right. We'd better see what Mr. Bolting says."

Bolting had just returned with a parcel under his arm. He read through the message and nodded. The delegates gathered round the table again to append their signatures. Cressey went across to Perdita and said diffidently, "Excuse me, Miss Manning."

"What is it?" she asked him, with a touch of impatience.

"I don't want to sign it."

There was a short, heated wrangle. Thomas finally suggested that as there wasn't time to bring Cressey to a sense of his responsibilities the simplest way out of the difficulty would be to say "this delegation" instead of "we, the undersigned," and that was agreed to. Mrs. Clarke sniffed indignantly, and told Cressey he ought to be ashamed of himself, but Cressey stolidly ignored her.

Schofield said, "What's in the parcel, Bolting?"

Bolting bent to his ear. "Caviar," he whispered. "A one-pound tin for each of us. Will you tell the others? From VOKS."

Schofield made the announcement.

"A most acceptable parting gift," said Tranter. He caught Jeff's eye. "I fear you're not included in this, Mr. Clayton."

"That's okay—I'm self-supporting," said Jeff.

Presently Mirnova reappeared. "Will you all come along now, please—the plane is ready."

She led the way out on to the Tarmac. The cold, away from the shelter of the building, was breath-taking. Cressey said, "Catch me coming here again!" as he hastened across with Jeff. A party of Russians, who were flying as far as Prague, brought up the rear. At the plane, there was a last pause for photographs; then Vassiliev and Mirnova and Kira shook hands all round, and a few moments later the aircraft taxied out to the runway and took off.

As it gained height and turned in a wide circle Jeff looked down with mixed feelings at the Kremlin's gleaming towers, the frozen line of the Moskva River and the galvanized iron rooftops of faded maroon. He was wondering if by any chance Tanya was down there, in one of those buildings. He felt for a cigarette and lit it with a set, expressionless face.

When the aircraft ceased to bank, Perdita called across the gangway, "Glad to be leaving, Mr. Clayton?"

"You bet I am!"

"I expected to see your friend Mr. Verney at the airport," she went on. There was a note of mockery in her tone.

"So did I," said Jeff gruffly. "I guess he was held up."

"I'm afraid he's a rather disappointed man. All that clever detective work, and no result!"

"The odds were too great," said Jeff. "You know that. Anyway, don't kid yourself that you're out of the wood yet. He's tough—he'll be after you."

"Surely *you* don't believe that ridiculous story of his?"

"You'd be surprised," said Jeff, and turned to the window again. He didn't want to talk to the woman—she was just being a bitch. He didn't want to talk to any of them. He drew his *shuba* more closely round his ears and wished the plane would warm up.

They were flying very low, but there wasn't much to look at. Conifers and bare birches and snow—that was about all. The route seemed to avoid most of the towns. There was little talking, for the noise of the engines made conversation an effort. Soon everyone began to doze. After a while Jeff became somnolent and dozed too. There was no better way to pass the time.

They landed somewhere in Poland to refuel, but took off

again as soon as the job was done. There would be another machine waiting for the delegation at Prague, and if this good progress were maintained they should be in London that night. People nibbled sandwiches and drank from flasks of coffee which the hotel had thoughtfully provided. The plane droned on.

At Prague airport, which they reached shortly after two o'clock, there was a small reception committee, appropriate to the brevity of the stay. A minor banquet had been prepared in the airport building, but it fell rather flat. Cressey announced that he wasn't feeling up to any more celebrations and sat in the lounge with Bolting, whose throat permitted him to take nothing more than a glass of warm milk. Jeff sat on a stool at the bar, drinking Pilsener and flirting with the barmaid. Excitement had begun to grip him. In a few hours now he'd be out of all this—over the Curtain—out of reach. It was hard to wait.

Just before three o'clock the banquet broke up, and they were all conducted out to the Czech plane which would fly them direct to Northolt. The Russians had gone about their business and there were no fresh passengers.

The delegates were drowsier than ever now and time passed unnoticed except by Jeff. It grew dark. Somewhere there was another refueling stop, a rather bumpy one, and Mrs. Clarke showed signs of nervousness until Schofield reassured her. No one got out. Perdita and Islwyn Thomas were settled comfortably in adjoining seats with a rug over their knees. Tranter was sitting alone by the door, apparently lost in thought. Jeff wondered what new instructions he'd received from Moscow now that his pose could no longer be sustained. Bolting was almost buried under a rug and nothing of him was visible but the top of his fur hat and the ringed hand that held the rug in place.

As the plane gathered speed for the last take-off, Cressey turned and smiled at Jeff. "Not long now, Mr. Clayton!"

Jeff grinned, and held up two fingers, crossed. "It's the last lap that always scares me, Joe." He didn't look scared, though—he looked as though he might become separately airborne with excitement at any moment.

Repeatedly he gazed out of the window, wondering where they were and trying to make out what sort of weather they were flying through. There was cloud from time to time but the ceiling was high—there was no meteorological reason why they shouldn't make it. He smoked a couple of cigarettes in quick succession. If only he could skip the next hour or two! The tension became unbearable. He tried reading, as some of the others had begun to do, but he couldn't concentrate. He tried counting up to a thousand and then starting all over again. *Anything* to take his mind off the interminable minutes. The plane could so easily be recalled. As long as it was in the air, it belonged to Prague, to Moscow. Every time one of the crew came out into the saloon, his pulse gave an uncontrollable leap of apprehension.

Suddenly there were no more lights from the ground. The aircraft was over the sea—this was really the last lap. Shortly after nine o'clock the great incandescence of London began to glow in the sky ahead. A stir ran through the delegates. The radio operator stuck his nose out. "Ten minutes," he said with a friendly smile.

Jeff felt a drop of moisture trickle down his spine. They were losing height now. He stubbed out his cigarette and groped for his seat belt. There were lights everywhere below— he could almost lean on them as the plane banked for its circuit. The runway swung beneath them. The passengers became suddenly quiet. The plane straightened out, dropped a little, and touched. It bumped once, then rumbled steadily along the concrete. There was a collective exhalation of breath. As it taxied up to the airport building, Jeff unfastened his belt and stood up. The engines roared, and died.

He stepped out into the gangway. "Okay, George," he said, "you can come out of that cocoon."

I threw off the rug and the fur coat, the hat and the bala-clava, and the horn-rimmed glasses that had given me a hell of a headache. "Hello, folks!" I said.

It was quite an entrance. For a second, everyone just stared. Then Mrs. Clarke gave a loud scream. Perdita turned very white and clutched Thomas's arm and Schofield said, "Good God!" As for Cressey, I thought his bottom jaw was going to drop right off.

The pilot came through with his crew. "Anything wrong?" he asked.

"Nothing," said Jeff curtly. "We'll be out in a moment."

It was Tranter who recovered himself first. "What *is* all this? What the hell have you been up to, Verney? Where's Bolting?"

"As far as we know," said Jeff, "he's lying in Verney's room at the Astoria with a hole in his head. Unless they've found him, of course."

"You mean—he's dead?"

"I guess not. I had to hit him with a skating boot, but he'll probably recover. His skull isn't as thin as Mullett's was." Almost as an afterthought he added, "Bolting killed Mullett, you know."

"Nonsense!" exclaimed Perdita, but at last the word had lost its ring of conviction.

"I'm afraid it's true," I said. "He attacked me in my room. He was looking for those trousers—remember?" Ruefully I fingered my swollen face. "You wouldn't like to model me instead of Uncle Joe, would you, Miss Manning?"

She turned away, gathering up her things. I think even she was shocked out of her complacency at last. Islwyn Thomas silently helped her. Mrs. Clarke, still on the edge of hysteria, was assisted from the plane by a grim-faced Schofield. Cressey descended in a daze.

Tranter's front had completely collapsed. "It's hardly credible," he said in a strained voice. "What a blackguard!"

"Even by *your* standards, Mr. Tranter?" I said.

He picked up his belongings and left the plane without another word. To him, of course, Bolting was now just another traitor to the cause.

"Come on," said Jeff, "we've got a lot of explaining to do." He gripped my arm. "Oh, *boy*, we've made it."

XXII

I PUSHED back my plate, took a sip of black coffee, and helped myself to a Lucky from Jeff's pack. We were in the airport restaurant—more or less on parole while the immigration people continued their inquiries about me—and I'd just had my first solid food in twenty-four hours.

I lit up, and sat back with a relaxed sigh. "That's better. Next time I impersonate anyone, I'm going to make sure beforehand that he's capable of eating and smoking like a normal person."

Jeff surveyed me dispassionately. "You still look a bit of a wreck. How's the head?"

"It could be worse. By the way, Jeff—thanks!"

"Forget it."

"He'd have killed me, you know. I could see it in his eyes."

"Me too. That's why I hit him with the skate."

"It must have been a pretty near thing."

"I'll say it was. By the time I'd registered your shout and tried your door and rushed through Mullett's room, you were out cold and Bolting was just raising the boot. I never want to see anything nearer."

"Thank God you were still upstairs, that's all. What were you doing, hanging about there?"

He looked a bit sheepish. "As a matter of fact, I was just penning a line to Tanya. I thought that maybe she'd turn up again one day, and that if I left a note Kira could give it to her. Kind of optimistic, but I didn't like the idea of just walking out."

"Well, it was lucky for me. In fact, things turned out pretty well altogether. We'd have been sunk if Bolting hadn't been wearing his outdoor things."

Jeff chuckled. "It sure was the perfect disguise. Of course, you're just his build and the glasses helped enormously, but all those wrappings were a gift. You almost had *me* fooled."

"There were some bad moments, all the same. I thought I was going to have to sign that message to Stalin and I hadn't the remotest idea how Bolting wrote his name. That shook me. And when the plane began to warm up, I thought someone might think it odd that I didn't unwrap at all. The trickiest moment of the whole lot, though, was when Mirnova called me away to see Vassiliev."

"That had me worried, too. Why didn't he bring the parcel in and make a little speech?"

"The parcel was only an excuse. I wasn't taken to Vassiliev. I was taken to the Customs."

"The Customs!"

"Yes. There were a couple of tough-looking birds there whom I hadn't seen before. One of them said, 'Keys!' and there was no fraternal nonsense about his tone either. I felt in one pocket after another, and I couldn't find them, and I thought to myself, 'You've had it, chum,' and then suddenly they jingled. It's a good job you were thorough. Well, they opened the bags, and the packet of stamps was lying right on top of one of them. They removed it without a word, locked the bags up again, and returned the keys. I was taken to Vassiliev, who handed me the parcel of caviar, and then Mirnova brought me straight back. I didn't open my mouth the whole time, and no one seemed to expect me to."

"Darned queer!"

"I thought so at the time, but I don't now. Put yourself in Bolting's place . . ."

"Not likely!" said Jeff.

I laughed, even though it hurt. "The thing is, he knew that the Russians knew everything he'd done. He knew that they'd decided to let him go, and why. But he must have had a pretty good idea, too, that they wouldn't let him get away with his loot. I imagine he'd realized all the time that they'd collect at the Customs, and that was why he'd put the stamps handy for them. Anyway, it all went off very smoothly."

"Well, I guess they're entitled to the stamps. I don't know what we'd have done with them."

"I'd have bought myself a new typewriter," I said ruefully. "Still, what the hell!" I lit a second cigarette from the stub of the first. "You know, Jeff, I've been pretty dumb. I ought to have realized that Bolting was our man. The evidence was there."

"I suppose it was, in a way," said Jeff thoughtfully. "Maybe we ought to have paid more attention to that job he had as an accountant. It showed his bent in the early years—you might even say it showed he was the sort of guy who might trade stamps as a sideline. Still, he wasn't the only one that could be fitted in."

"I didn't mean that sort of evidence. There was something concrete. You remember he told me that when he was in Moscow in 1942 he had a room on the third floor on the side overlooking the lane?"

"That's what you said."

"Well, that was the giveaway. When we were at that VOKS party, he told us a story—perhaps you weren't there at the time—about how he'd sat on his balcony during the war and watched the passengers in a trolleybus being sprayed with water. Well, he couldn't have seen any trolleybuses from the room he said he had. He'd forgotten that first story. Funny!— you said that what we needed was a thundering lie, and when we got it I didn't even notice."

Jeff shrugged. "He'd probably have talked himself out of it.

The only sure way was to catch him red-handed."

"You must have done that literally! I wonder what's happened to him."

"Maybe he threw himself off the balcony when he came round. Best thing he could do, I should think."

I pondered. "Somehow I can't see Bolting as a suicide. He's got too much self-confidence. I don't think he'd chuck his hand in as long as he had any chips left."

"Maybe not, but he hasn't any chips. He can't be any more use to the Russians—once this story breaks he'll be just a liability, and you can bet your life they don't love him. In fact, they must be pretty sore all round. . . ."

He broke off, and I guessed what he was thinking. We'd been so careful, all through, not to make things worse for Tanya, and then at the end events had taken control and we'd had to act without giving her a thought. When the full story broke, the Russians would lose a lot of face and they'd probably take their revenge where they could. It was a sobering thought. At that moment, neither of us had any sense of triumph.

"There's not much we can do about it now," I said sadly.

"I'm not so sure. Maybe I'm just crazy but I've got a sort of idea . . ." He was silent for a while. "Look, George, where are we going to get by spilling this story? The delegation's bust, anyway—Mullett's dead, Bolting's written off, and Tranter will have to crawl under a stone."

I looked at him in surprise. Hitting the headlines would normally have been a good enough reason for either of us. Besides . . .

"I don't quite follow you," I said. "It's a story that'll make a tremendous stir, here—I should think it'll be worth a division in the cold war. Soviet police framing an innocent man to protect a fellow traveler—why, it's terrific."

"Maybe, but there's Tanya and there's Nikolai. The way I figure it, a couple of decent people are worth more than the

bit we can add to the case against the M.V.D. We both hate
the Kremlin's guts, we'd both like to have a crack at them in
the headlines, but if two people go right down the drain as a
result, we're just playing things the Communist way—ideology
first and human beings nowhere."

"I'm with you there, of course," I said, "but I'm afraid
they're going to take it out of Tanya and Nikolai whatever
we do."

"Well, are they? Suppose we offer to keep our mouths shut
if those two are given a break?"

For a moment I was speechless. "They'd never make a deal
like that."

"They might if we handle it properly. Hell, look what they
stand to gain—complete silence on the whole unsavory episode.
And what do they lose? Nothing. They don't really care a hoot
what happens to Tanya and Nikolai—those two are just
pawns. They wouldn't even have to explain anything to anyone—you know that. They could simply let them go and drop
the whole thing."

"But, Jeff, if we tried this and by some miracle it worked,
we'd have Bolting back here, scot-free and full of bounce,
doing his stuff all over again and knowing damn well we could
never say anything because of the hostages in Russia. That
would be a hell of a thing after all that's happened. I'm not
sure I could stomach it."

"Bolting doesn't have to come back," said Jeff eagerly. "We
can make it clear that if he sets foot here again, the deal's off.
For that matter, I shouldn't think the Russians would be all
that anxious to let him go."

"He's still a British subject," I pointed out, "and an important one. The only way they can keep him is to indict him
for murder, and if they did that the whole story would come
out anyway, so they wouldn't benefit from the deal."

Jeff chewed over that for a while. "You're wrong," he said

at last. "They could easily keep him if they wanted to. They could tell him he'd be indicted if he asked for an exit permit!"

It was ingenious—I had to admit that.

"Anyway," I said, "are we in a position to make this deal? Suppose someone else talks?"

"Who can? Who would? Not that bunch of delegates—they're not going to foul their own doorstep if they can help it. They'll sit tight and see what happens—if they're asked about Bolting they'll probably say he's ill. That's my guess, anyway. We could make sure by giving one of them a ring. Apart from them, no one else knows that Bolting did it—those other guys in Moscow may have a shrewd idea, but they've no evidence. There are your officials here, of course, but *they're* not going to rush into print. George, let's give it a trial. If the Russians won't play, we'll be no worse off, and if they will—well, I'll feel a darned sight happier."

I gave him a rather lopsided grin. "I believe you really fell for that kid."

"None of your business, George. But I did kind of like her."

We left it at that.

XXIII

THAT NIGHT I rang Schofield and told him that, for our own reasons, we proposed to say nothing about Bolting for the time being and that no doubt the delegation would be glad to take the same course. He sounded puzzled but extremely relieved, and he undertook to take care of Mrs. Clarke whom he described, with one of his characteristic understatements, as "somewhat vocal." Apart from his misguided allegiance, he was a man I could have liked a lot.

Next day I called on the responsible authorities and got my personal position straightened out. I had to tell them pretty well the whole story, of course, and it was received with the greatest interest. It wasn't necessary to say anything about the plan that Jeff and I had evolved, for they took the view from the beginning that publication would be injudicious at a time when a crucial international conference was about to start; and I almost stunned them by agreeing.

Of course, I had to tell my Editor the full story to explain my sudden return, and he wasn't so keen on keeping quiet about it, but I won him round finally. So that was that.

The approach to the Russians was tricky. They're rather less fond than most people of anything smacking of an ultimatum —as we'd found, they like propositions to be well wrapped up. In the end, we managed to concoct a letter which satisfied us, and I myself saw that it was delivered in the right quarter. First, we set out the case against Bolting, with every detail included, right up to his assault on me. It was completely watertight and would unquestionably have won a conviction in any impartial court. Secondly, we showed how the Soviet authorities were implicated, from their discovery of the balcony route to their removal of the stamps from Bolting's case under my very eyes.

After that, we appended a hypocritical little piece about the importance of not worsening relations at such a dangerous moment in international affairs—very much on the lines that Ganilov had followed in that memorable and instructive interview we'd had with him. In the circumstances, we said, we were seriously considering not publishing these facts, but we pointed out that the return of Robson Bolting to England would make silence very difficult.

Finally, we said that as Nikolai had now been proved to be innocent, and Tanya to have been concerned only in a minor degree, we had the fullest confidence that justice and clemency would be shown to them.

It was an odd document, but so was the situation.

We heard nothing officially, of course, either then or later. The document wasn't acknowledged, and we didn't expect it to be. Very little came out of Moscow—only a brief paragraph to the effect that Mr. Robson Bolting had been prevented from leaving with the rest of the delegation owing to illness, and was now recovering in a Moscow hospital. The days dragged on, and soon Jeff had to go back to the States. I promised to keep him posted.

It was no use worrying, because we'd done all we could, and anyway I was sent off on a short assignment and that kept me occupied. It was nearly a month later that I received a letter from Waterhouse, through a private channel. The essential paragraphs read as follows:

We were all very intrigued by your sudden and unexpected departure, and one day I hope to hear the full story. The Russians, as usual, are taciturn. The first we heard of any development was a notification that Bolting had been removed to the hospital with pneumonia. The Embassy people have seen him and he is said to be getting on well. Speculation here about how you came to leave your luggage behind and take his is officially discouraged.

By the way, you'll be glad to hear that the waiter, Nikolai, has returned to the hotel. It was all done in the quietest way—nothing withdrawn or explained—and he won't talk, which is wise of him. He looks a little frailer, but he's very cheerful because his son has just been given a big appointment in the Lenin Hospital. He asked to be remembered to you. I know you always liked him. Clayton's bedworthy little blonde, Tanya, is back in circulation, too. At least, I don't quite mean that—she's actually been given a job in the English Language section at the University. She seems subdued, but otherwise she's much the same. I must say I hardly expected to see her again. Everyone here thinks you're keeping a great deal from us—it's a good thing you're not available for questioning!

I sent a wire to Jeff, and posted the letter off to him, and presently I got an ecstatic wire back. A few days later, my luggage was delivered at the office. It had come by Russian steamer, and was intact down to the last razor blade.

That's about the end of the story, except that one evening when I was traveling back to Fleet Street on a crowded bus my eye was caught by a large headline in the *Evening Gazette*. It said, M.P. SENSATION, and a smaller heading below announced, ROBSON BOLTING TAKES SOVIET CITIZENSHIP.

I thought of Arthur Gain. Whatever Bolting had done, he'd certainly paid the full penalty by becoming a Soviet citizen. There wasn't a worse fate than that.